Praise for Kevin Brockmeier's

THE VIEW FROM THE SEVENTH LAYER

"Brockmeier gives us whimsical, magical, quirky glimpses into a world we recognize and, at the same time, find weirdly unfamiliar. . . . A gifted storyteller and stylist. . . . Beautifully conceived and written." —*Rocky Mountain News*

"Extraordinary . . . entertaining . . . devastating." —*The Oregonian*

"One of the many things to like about Kevin Brockmeier's new collection of short stories is his appreciation of modest lives. . . . Such characters are not only elevated by Brockmeier's attention, they're often doused in a sort of grace." —*The Plain Dealer*

"Eminently pleasing. . . . Original and imaginative. . . . [Brockmeier] has certainly scored another winner." —*Associated Press*

"Reality and fantasy mingle inextricably and with apparent ease in these thirteen memorable stories. . . . There's an incandescent beauty to Brockmeier's prose." —Bookreporter

"Brockmeier's new collection of short stories ripples with wonder as he combines . . . lush language, quirky characters and thoughtful, provocative ideas to create his literary fables." —*Sacramento News & Review*

KEVIN BROCKMEIER

THE VIEW FROM THE SEVENTH LAYER

Kevin Brockmeier is the author of the novels *The Illumination*, *The Brief History of the Dead*, and *The Truth About Celia*; the children's novels *City of Names* and *Grooves: A Kind of Mystery*; the story collections *Things That Fall from the Sky* and *The View from the Seventh Layer*, and a memoir, *A Few Seconds of Radiant Filmstrip*. His work has been translated into fifteen languages, and he has published his stories in such venues as *The New Yorker*, *The Georgia Review*, *McSweeney's*, *Zoetrope*, *The Oxford American*, *The Best American Short Stories*, *The Year's Best Fantasy and Horror*, and *New Stories from the South*. He has received the Borders Original Voices Award, three O. Henry Awards (one, a first prize), the PEN USA Award, a Guggenheim Fellowship, and an NEA Grant. Recently he was named one of *Granta* magazine's Best Young American Novelists. He lives in Little Rock, Arkansas, where he was raised.

THE

VIEW

FROM

THE

SEVENTH

LAYER

THE

VIEW

FROM

THE

SEVENTH

LAYER

KEVIN BROCKMEIER

VINTAGE CONTEMPORARIES
VINTAGE BOOKS
A DIVISION OF RANDOM HOUSE, INC.
NEW YORK

FIRST VINTAGE CONTEMPORARIES EDITION, MARCH 2009

The following stories were previously published: "The Year of Silence" in
Ecotone; "The Lady with the Pet Tribble" in *Five Chapters*; "A Fable Containing
a Reflection the Size of a Match Head in Its Pupil" and "Home Videos" in *The
Georgia Review*; "A Fable Ending in the Sound of a Thousand Parakeets"
in *Granta*; "A Fable with Slips of White Paper Spilling from the Pockets,"
"Father John Melby and the Ghost of Amy Elizabeth," and "The View from
the Seventh Layer" in *Oxford American*; "The Lives of the Philosophers" in
StoryQuarterly; "The Human Soul as a Rube Goldberg Device: A Choose-
Your-Own-Adventure Story" in *Words and Images*; and "Andrea is Changing
Her Name" in *Zoetrope*. "A Fable with a Photograph of a Glass Mobile on the
Wall" appeared in *The Darfur Anthology* (Elgin Community College, 2007).

The Library of Congress has cataloged the Pantheon edition as follows:
Brockmeier, Kevin.
The view from the seventh layer /Kevin Brockmeier.
p. cm.
I. Title.
PS3602.R63V54 2008 813'.6—dc22 2007023404

Vintage ISBN: 978-0-307-38776-9

Book design by M. Kristen Bearse

www.vintagebooks.com

146119709

In memory of my grandfather,
William Sirico, and his last words:
"Well, I'm dying now. It was a pleasure to know you."

CONTENTS

THE

VIEW

FROM

THE

SEVENTH

LAYER

A FABLE ENDING IN THE SOUND
OF A THOUSAND PARAKEETS

Once there was a city where everyone had the gift of song. Gardeners sang as they clipped their flowers. Husbands and wives sang each other to sleep at night. Groups of children waiting for the school bell to ring raced through the verses of the latest pop songs to get to the pure spun sugar of the choruses. Old friends who had not seen one another in many years met at wakes and retirement parties to sing the melodies they remembered from the days when they believed there was nothing else in the world that would ever grip their spirits so and take them out of their bodies. Life was carried along on a thousand little currents of music, and it was not unusual to hear a tune drifting out from behind the closed door of an office as you passed, or even from the small back room of the art museum, which was almost but never quite empty. The people of the city did not always sing with great skill, but they sang clearly and with a simplicity of feeling that made their voices beautiful to hear. And because they loved what they sang, no matter how painful or melancholy, a note of indomitable happiness ran through their voices like a fine silver thread.

In this city there lived a mute, the only person who was unable to lend his voice to the great chorus of song that filled the air. The mute had spent his entire life in the city, and everyone from the members of the school board to the stock boys at the grocery store knew who he was. In some communities there is a man who sells whistles by the courthouse or paper kites down by the river. In others there is a woman who decorates her home with multicolored lights and streamers every holiday. Usually these people are no more than small figures at the periphery of everyone's attention, but when they die, it can be more surprising than the death of a prominent leader or a renowned artist, because no one has ever regarded them carefully enough to consider what their absence might mean.

The mute was of that age where his hair had turned white and his shoes no longer seemed to fit him properly. Some of his neighbors believed he was deaf—an understandable mistake. He was not deaf, though, only mute, and from time to time he liked to sit in a chair on his front porch and listen to the people around him chatting with one another as they took their afternoon walks. They would say things like "I'm telling you, buddy, the second my pension kicks in, it's off to the tropics for me." And "Peter asked me out for dinner tonight, dear thing. I think he's finally going to pop the question." And "That's the deaf man, Sarah. He can't hear you, but that's no reason you can't be friends with him. Why don't you go wave hello?" It comforted him to listen to these conversations. He had never married or fathered children, and behind the door of his house, there was only the quiet tapping of his footsteps and the endless chirping and fluttering of the parakeets.

The mute had gotten his first pair of birds when he was still a young man, purchasing them from a pet vendor he met in the city park. One morning he had seen them preening and tilting their heads in the sunlight, and that was all it took. The color of their feathers seemed to call out to him: the jewel-like greens and yellows of their wings, the shaded blue around their necks, but most of all the lovely soft purple above their beaks. It was not until he released the parakeets into his living room and watched them hop from the back of the chair onto the curtain rod, and from the curtain rod onto the shelf beside the mirror, that he felt something slipping loose inside him and realized how much he had needed their companionship. One of the parakeets turned out to be a male, and the other a female, and soon he had five birds to take care of. The next year he bought two more from the pet vendor and watched another three hatch from their eggs. It wasn't long before he had so many birds that he knew he had to do something. He hauled the good furniture out of the parlor and attached dozens of little swings, perches, ladders, and mirrors to the walls. He put a wooden gate in the doorway. He even installed a pair of recessed skylights in the ceiling so that the birds could watch the shadows of the clouds move across the floor. In the end he believed he had managed to create the kind of space a parakeet might enjoy.

He loved each and every one of his birds, and over the years, as the flock grew in size, he learned various tricks to distinguish them from one another. It was only from a distance, he realized, that their bodies seemed to blur together into a single shifting net of brightly colored wings and tails. When you looked more carefully, you noticed that one of the birds had a particular way of tucking her head under her wing while she ate. Another liked to stand by the window after the sun went down, pecking at her reflection in the glass. Another wore a set of markings on his back that looked like two-day-old snow, with dapples of wet grass beginning to show through. Every bird was unique.

He enjoyed watching their lives play out inside the walls of his house, and he took tremendous satisfaction in being able to feed and take care of them. It felt good to be needed by something with a working voice and a beating heart. He often wondered if the other people in the city knew how much happiness a creature so small could bring.

When did he first start giving the birds away as presents? No one could remember, least of all the mute. But a time came when he might be expected to turn up at any public celebration with a bamboo cage in his hands and a bag of fresh seed in his pocket, smiling and nodding in that richly communicative way of his. He became a fixture at birthday parties, baptisms, inaugurations, and weddings. There was always singing on such occasions, of course, a boundless wave of pop songs and old standards. As he listened to all the love and sorrow wrapped up inside the harmonies, he wished more than anything that he could join in, but the only thing he had to offer was his parakeets.

With every bird he gave away, he included a set of instructions that ended with the sentence "Parakeets are natural mimics, and if you treat your bird as you would a human being, it is likely that he or she will learn how to talk." Some of the people who accepted the birds from him were busy or practical-minded sorts who had little interest in keeping a pet, but were too polite to tell him so. They stowed the parakeets away in a dimly lit corner of their spare bedroom, or even set them loose in the woods at the edge of town. Others appreciated the birds as no more than a spectacle or a diversion, something to feed every morning and take out whenever they happened to grow bored. Only a few cherished them as much as the mute did. Still, most of the people who kept the birds were able to teach them such simple phrases as "Good morning," "What's your name?," and "I love you." A number of the birds were clever enough to learn a more complicated set of expressions: "It's a cruel, cruel world," for instance, and "How about this weather we're having?" One man successfully showed his parakeet how to say "I prefer the music of Brahms" whenever anyone turned on the radio. Another taught his bird to say "Hubba-hubba" every time a red-headed woman came into the room.

There was one particular bird who was able to reproduce almost any sound he heard, but when his owner coached him to repeat the phrase "I don't understand the words they're making me say," he refused to utter so much as a syllable.

For every parakeet the mute gave away, two more were born into his parlor. Some of the birds died of illness or old age, but there were always new birds to replace them, and the flock showed no sign of diminishing. It began to seem to the mute that the rules of time had been suspended inside the aviary—or if not suspended, then at least reshaped. When he brought his first pair of birds home from the city park, they had not been much older than children, he now realized—and neither, for that matter, had he. Then something changed, and he began to settle into the rhythm of his days and nights. His grandparents died, and later his parents. The long history of a lifetime fell into place behind him. And the birds, it seemed to him, were still not much older than children.

Sometimes he stood at the gate watching them flit about between their perches and allowed his mind to wander. He couldn't help thinking of his childhood, particularly those times when he would sit at the back of his classroom during choir practice. He remembered what it was like to listen to everybody singing, to feel the music scaling and building inside him, higher and higher, climbing toward the open air, until it became so powerful that he was almost sure it would not give way this time, though invariably it did. He used to shut his eyes and sway back and forth behind his desk. Anyone could see what was happening to him. The truth was that he, too, had the gift of song—it was just that he could not make use of it. One of his teachers had the idea of giving him a tambourine to shake, and that helped for a while, but the rattling sound it made was not quite what he was looking for. Later he thought about learning to play a real instrument—a flute, maybe, or a clarinet—but as it turned out, he did not have the talent for it.

The mute gazed at the birds until his memory faded away. Then he went to the front porch to wait for his neighbors to take their afternoon walks.

No one who has ever lived closely with a flock of birds and come to know their eccentricities could say that they are not intelligent. The parakeets were curious about this man who never spoke, who filled their seed dishes every morning and fed them sweet corn, grapes, and chopped carrots in the evening. Sometimes he stood behind the bars of their cage with a faraway look in his eyes and made a sound like the wind puffing through a long concrete pipe. Sometimes he fluttered his fingers at them, making a friendly *chook-chook-chook* noise with the tip of his tongue. What did these activities mean?

The birds studied the mute as though he were a puzzle. And because they had always understood the world best by participating in it, after a while they began to imitate him. They mimicked the clang that went echoing down the hall when he dropped a pot in the kitchen. They jingled like a pair of silver bells when his alarm clock went off in the morning. They duplicated the sound of his footsteps tapping across the wooden floor, the sigh that came from his chair when he sank into the upholstery, and even the small back-and-forth sawing noise of his breathing as he drifted off to sleep.

The mute noticed the various sounds the birds were making, and occasionally he said to himself, That was me popping my knuckles just now, or That was me slicing this apple in half, but generally speaking the thought did not occur to him. He had never listened as carefully to himself as he had to other people. He began to imagine that the reason the birds were raising such a commotion was because they were restless or unhappy, and eventually he decided to move the aviary's gate to the end of the hall so that they would have more room to spread their wings. A few weeks later he moved the gate again, this time into the entrance of the dining room, and a few weeks after that he installed it in the area between his study and the master bedroom. Finally, the only spaces he had left for himself were the kitchen, the bathroom, and the sitting room by the front door, where he managed to squeeze not only his lamp and his bed, but also the smallest of his dressers.

He never would have believed that a houseful of birds might be enough for him one day, and yet here he was, an old man, and though he had longed for many things over the years, and had some-times, like everyone else, felt an overwhelming sadness he could not explain, he had also experienced periods of great calm and radiant joy, and he did not believe that his life had been empty.

One morning he was cleaning the dishes when his heart gave out. There was no pain, just a sudden flooding sensation in his arms and legs that made him feel curiously light-headed. What was this? he wondered. What was happening to him? He sat down on the floor, lifted his hand for a moment, and then he closed his eyes.

Perhaps it was later that day, at the banquet in honor of the mayor's wedding anniversary, or perhaps it was the next afternoon, when the butcher's son finally graduated from law school, but it did not take long before the people of the city began to ask themselves where he had gone. They had grown accustomed to seeing him at one social occasion or another, making his way through the crowd with a handmade bamboo cage and the chattering little bundle of a parakeet. A few people thought to wonder if he was all right. They told a few others, who told a few more, and soon they all gathered together and set off down the road toward his house. They knocked on the door. When he did not answer, one of them said, "He proba-bly doesn't hear you, remember? The man's always been deaf as a post," and so they tested the knob and found it unlocked.

None of them had ever been inside the house before. How could they have guessed how many parakeets there would be, or how their voices, calling out in mourning or celebration, would fill the air? In a thousand different tones, a thousand different inflections, they reproduced all the sounds of the mute's daily life, from the steady beat of his footsteps to the whistle of his coffeepot to the slow, spreading note of his final breath. It sounded for all the world like a symphony.

The island was so small that Olivia could hear the ocean no matter where she went. She lived in a little red garden cottage with thin wooden walls, and sometimes, when her pills didn't work, she would wake in the middle of the night to the hissing of the waves and the washboardlike croaking of the herons. Her house was nestled behind a two-story villa with a high collar of hibiscus bushes. At least once a week a spider or a bumblebee would find its way into the villa, and the widow Lorenzen would summon Olivia to get rid of it for her. "Here, smash it with this," she would say, handing her a magazine or a scuba flipper. "Kill it! Kill it!" Her fingers were stiff with arthritis. Her hair was the color of water in a swimming pool. Olivia always tried to escort the insects outside without harming them. The rhythm of the waves raking the beach reminded her of a song whose lyrics she could never quite remember. She spent whole hours some days narrowly failing to bring it to mind. She felt as though she were standing at the most remote border of her consciousness, far away from the light and warmth of the fire, peering out into the darkness like an aboriginal priestess.

During tourist season, she worked as a map vendor at the marina, operating a stand that also carried umbrellas, candy, and prophylactics. She sold more prophylactics than she did maps, and more candy than she did prophylactics, and more umbrellas than she did either. The rain came every day, starting at 3:15. It was as though someone hovering behind the clouds had opened up a spill valve.

The water fell in coin-size drops that knocked against the masts of the boats with a sound like a bamboo wind ornament, and then, at exactly 3:45, it stopped. The sun was so clean and welcoming as it shone on the docks that it was easy for the tourists to imagine it would never rain again. They took their shirts off and put their sunglasses on, rolling their shoulders as though they had just woken up from a long nap. Dozens of half-closed umbrellas lay discarded over the glistening brown boards, their handles glowing in the flawless white light. The local children collected them like flowers.

There was a bug that arrived for a few weeks in May each year and chewed the wild roses to tatters. The bug was a thick cream color at first, but its wings burned red as soon as the summer settled in. The islanders called it the "tourist bug." At the end of the season, when the tourists left, the island's teenagers took their place, walking along the docks with their hands in each other's pockets. They bought ice-cream cones, T-shirts, and phone cards, but never maps. Sometimes Olivia thought that the rain which fell from 3:15 to 3:45 every summer afternoon was a message. She was convinced that she knew who had sent it.

Her father lived on the seaward tip of the island, in a colonial house with a wrought-iron balcony from which he could watch the gulls soaring out toward the open water. He owned the map-vending stand where Olivia worked in the summer, and the garden cottage where she lived when she was not working at all, and it was not unusual for her to find him sitting at her kitchen table when she got home. "You don't happen to have any gin here, I suppose?" he would ask, or "What do you say I hire somebody to give this place a good scrubbing down?" When she was a girl, some thirty years ago, he used to call her his little baby marshmallow puff. She had always liked the soft cap of foam that marshmallows formed in mugs of hot chocolate. She owned only two keys, to only two doors, and she never knew when she would find her father waiting for her behind one or the other. Her mother, on the other hand, lived in São Paulo, Brazil, with her second husband, Graciliano. She and Olivia spoke once a month on the telephone, and when the conversation died away, as it invariably did, her mother always asked her what book she was reading, and Olivia always named the last book she had actually been able to finish, *Paris Stories* by Mavis Gallant, and her mother always said, "Ooh, I've been wanting to read that one. Are you enjoying it?" It had been five years since the Entity had taken Olivia into the sky, whispering to her with a tremendous musical breathing sound that was like the striking of every key on a harmonium. She still felt the singe where it had touched the hollow of her neck.

There were days when Olivia could not ignore the tug of the sun as it crossed the sky. An overpowering dizziness took hold of her as the sun breached the horizon, subsided for a while as it climbed into the heights, and then seized her once again as it began to sink toward the mainland. It seemed to her as if every molecule in her body were tipping very slowly from the east to the west. The sensation reminded her of nothing so much as the feeling she used to get in her legs after she had finished a long day of roller-skating, when her sneakers were back on her feet but she could still feel her muscles swaying to the rhythm of the wheels. She used to love to roller-skate. Every year, beginning in the first grade, she had held her birthday party at the town skating rink—the Great Annual Birthday Bash, she called it. She invited all her friends from both the school and the neighborhood, and her parents reserved the party room for pizza and ice cream, until one day, during her freshman year of high school, Kim Olsen informed her that no one threw Birthday Bashes anymore and she was making a complete and total idiot of herself. Olivia had changed so much since then. She had changed in ways she would never have been able to anticipate. She had become the kind of person who was barely able to get out of bed in the morning without buckling beneath the tidal pull of the planets. If only she had known when she was growing up how hard the rest of her life was going to be, how diminished, she would have been so much more joyful, so much more daring. She would have done all the things she had failed to do. She would have hiked across Europe. She would have gone skating every day.

She had moved away from the Midwest at nineteen to go to college, and, after the suspicions came out and her parents divorced, there had been little reason for her to return. Her dad bought his beach house on the island, her mom left for San Diego and Boston and finally Brazil, and Olivia drifted around like a bottle tossed carelessly into the water until she ended up here at the garden cottage, where she could hear the ocean crashing even through the walls. Nothing was secure from one minute to the next. She did not remember her dreams when she woke in the morning. A wild rooster had made its nest in the palmetto barrens across the street. The only one of her classmates she had so much as laid eyes on since high school was Chad Hayden, the captain of the varsity soccer team, who had come to the island a few years ago on his honeymoon and stopped at her map stand to buy a package of condoms and a Milky Way bar. Though she used to trade notes with him almost every day in Mr. Picard's chemistry class, he had failed to recognize the girl she used to be in the face of the woman in the clean blue T-shirt offering him $1.50 in change and a package of Trojan Ultra Thins. She had been too embarrassed to say to him, "I'm Olivia, don't you remember? From East High? The one with the bangs?" Later that night, as she watched her dinner revolving in the microwave, it occurred to her that somewhere on the island he and his bride were moving against each other in the dark, making love with a condom that had passed through her fingers. She had read somewhere that the best way to reset your circadian clock was to illuminate the backs of your knees, and so every night, after she took her sleeping pills, she was careful to shield the lower half of her body from the light.

Her father once told her that the clapboards of her house were salvaged from an allotment of hardwood barrels. One of the island's earliest successful businesses was the Holt and Liverett Cooperage, he said, which specialized in making barrels to carry whole grains and seed corn. When the cooperage went bankrupt, the wood was sold off to the highest bidder. Many of the staves had already been bound together with metal hoops, which explained why some of the boards in her wall slewed outward when it rained. "You don't even know where you're living, do you?" her father asked her. "You need to wake up and open your eyes, baby girl." Olivia had read a story once about a house that was assembled from the boards of an old race track. She remembered that the man who lived there could hear hundreds of cars speeding by, one after the other, whenever he put his ear to the wall.

There was a time in her life—and not so long ago—when she read nearly every day. Back then her favorite books had been Joan Didion's *Slouching Towards Bethlehem,* Peter S. Beagle's *The Last Unicorn,* and everything by Jane Austen except *Northanger Abbey.* Then something went wrong, and she was no longer able to concentrate on the novels she brought home with her. Everything about them seemed imaginary, insubstantial, built on a tissue of fog and lies—and not just the settings and the characters, either, but the very words on the page. They might have been invented just that second by somebody who had never so much as set foot in the world. "This is a story about love and death in the golden land." "The unicorn lived in a lilac wood, and she lived all alone." "One half of the world cannot understand the pleasures of the other." What did it all mean? This was the truth: she could no longer hold a book in her hands without tasting the paper in the back of her throat and smelling the ink on her fingers. The whole experience made her feel unclean. And though she was better now than she had been in the beginning, she rarely picked up more than the occasional glossy magazine. She had lost the habit of reading for pleasure. She knew that this celebrity was dating that one, and that a third celebrity was divorcing a fourth one, and that a fifth celebrity was filming a movie in Nepal, and she did not like it.

The first few weeks of spring, when the butterflies arrived on the beach as if from another planet, had always been her favorite time of year on the island. The butterflies were the pale yellow color of primrose blossoms. They liked to rest on top of her map stand, exposing their wings to the sun. At certain times of the day she could see their shadows opening and closing on the underside of the awning—a phenomenon of nature. She had heard that you could balance a raw egg on its end during the spring equinox. She had heard, too, that tornadoes would not form along the equator because of the Coriolis effect. She could not remember which story was supposed to be true and which was supposed to be a myth. The widow Lorenzen had never asked her to kill one of the yellow butterflies, but she said that she considered them pests just the same. She liked to follow Olivia through her house as Olivia stalked the various beetles and wasps she had found. The widow ate pre-packaged chocolate-and-cream rolls she called Debbie cakes. Her face was always crimped with outrage over the insects. She never understood why Olivia would not kill them. "Why don't you just obliterate the damned things?" she asked. The portrait of her husband that hung in the parlor looked like Humphrey Bogart in *The Maltese Falcon*. Olivia guided each and every one of the insects carefully toward the villa's front door, closing cabinets and window shades as she passed from room to room to seal off the various pathways of the labyrinth. Often the bees and wasps made a creaky warning noise with their wings and then plunged as if to sting her. But they were frightened and disoriented, and she did not see how she could blame them. She had the same responsibility as everybody else did: to live as softly as she could in the world. It was one of the many things she had learned when the Entity took her into the sky and burned her with the soft touch of its fingers. It gave her water in a smooth silver cup, and it spoke to her without moving its lips, and the gentleness in its eyes nearly blew her heart out.

She still thought about Chad Hayden sometimes, though of all the people she had known before she grew out of her ease with the world, he was one of the least important to her. She wondered where he lived now, if he had any children, whether he worked in an office. She sat in the rattan chair on her little square porch and watched the palm leaves shivering in the wind. One time, when she was eight or nine, she threw a rock at her father while he was watering the lawn, and he sprayed her with the garden hose. Another time, on the last day of her senior year of high school, following an impulse she only barely understood, she wrote in Brian Plimpton's yearbook, *For what it's worth, I had a crush on you for most of the last three years, but I was too afraid to do anything about it.* She found the gesture so liberating that she decided to tell some tiny part of the truth in every yearbook she signed that day. In Chad Hayden's she wrote: *I will never forget the time the two of us hung the homecoming banner in the cafeteria and you lifted me straight up into the air by my ankles.* In Deborah Straw's she wrote: *I had a dream once that I was you, looking at me, and I said to myself, "I like Olivia, but I'm sure glad I'm not her."* In Kim Olsen's she wrote: *You were my best friend for so long that it slips my mind sometimes that you're not anymore.* It was the bravest thing she had ever done in her small, shy, carefully studied life.

———

Some of the maps Olivia sold were simple municipal street maps. Some were tourist maps, highlighting various houses and landmarks of historic and cultural significance to the area: the sculpture garden, the old town hall, the eyebrow house where the notable painter used to live. There were topographical maps and hiking maps and commercial maps emblazoned with the emblems of all the shops and restaurants on the island. If Olivia were to dive off the edge of any of the maps and travel southeast—through the sea, over the mountains, and into the jungle—she would eventually pass very close to her mother's house in São Paulo, Brazil. Once, when she called the house, her mother's husband Graciliano answered the phone and told her, "Your mother and I will be—how do you say?— *pleasing* each other this afternoon. Perhaps she will call you tomorrow?" Olivia had met Graciliano exactly three times, first at his wedding to her mother, then on vacation in New York City, and then at a short overlapping layover the two of them shared at the St. Louis International Airport. He had worn the same pair of shoes each time, a rich black leather with a needle-prick design like a spreading sunset on the toes. His shoes were objects of beauty. Olivia did not have a car, and when she was feeling healthy, she took a different route home from the marina at night. She liked the slapping sound her sandals made on the pavement. She knew the island well, but not as well as her father. She would never know anything as well as her father. The eyebrow house was called an eyebrow house because of the way the roof mantled the windows on the second floor, he told her when she finally asked, and not, as Olivia had thought, because of the eyebrows of the painter who used to live there, however thick and bearlike they might have been.

She worked as a maid for a house cleaning service one year. This was when she first arrived on the island, before her father bought the map stand, when she was young and wandering and still remembered her dreams when she woke in the morning. The cleaning

service called the houses on their roster "dwellings." Olivia was
expected to clean three large dwellings or five small dwellings a day.
After she had finished the floors and the carpets, she would always
take a break, drifting through the rooms like a specter. The heart of
every house was the kitchen, the soul of every house was the bedroom, and the mind of every house was displayed with hooks and
thumbtacks on the walls. But the conscience of every house—she
believed—the conscience of every house was the bookshelves. She
was demoralized by the number of houses whose shelves held only
clocks and geodes and a few back issues of *TV Guide*. She imagined
the consciences of the people who lived there hardening into a thousand immovable facets as they sat in their armchairs and watched
the minutes roll by. And many of the shelves that did contain books
carried only a few tattered romance novels or an oversize hardcover
tribute to some summer blockbuster or television series. It was the
rarest of houses that was actually equipped with books she would
have been excited to read. She knew that it was priggish, but she
came to rash conclusions about the people whose collections she
perused. She couldn't help herself. People who read Maeve Binchy
give their sympathy so indiscriminately that she wondered whether
it might not be self-pity simply masquerading as sympathy. People
who read Charles Bukowski believe that the only clear vision is a
disfiguring one. Olivia used Windex on the windows and Scrubbing
Bubbles on the bathtubs. She used Febreze on the carpets. People
who read Thomas Pynchon are smart but disdainful. People who
read D. H. Lawrence suspect that the forbidden is not necessarily
without its virtue, and so are easily persuaded that the forbidden
and the virtuous are one and the same. She stood on a stepladder to
wipe the dust off the blades of the ceiling fans. She took extra care
emptying the husks of insects from the light fixtures. The vacuum
cleaner moaned and howled like something that was wounded, but
she could hear the ocean again as soon as the motor died away.

Later, when she had stopped reading altogether, she filled her spare time listening to the radio and making pots of tea for herself. She captured insects for the widow Lorenzen. She allowed her mind to wander as she waited for the light to change. As soon as the sky went dark, she felt a tremendous loosening inside her body, as though some terrible knot had been teased apart and now all the threads that held her together were finally running straight again. She had no responsibilities once the sun set. Or rather she had only one responsibility—the responsibility to fall asleep—and for that she could use her tablets. A few nights a year, the island's main generator went out. The street lamps and illuminated signs were all extinguished, and on impulse everybody looked into the sky. The frogs and crickets fell quiet to the count of five before they began to sing again. The smaller stars were spread across the darkness in a fine white powder, and the brighter ones pierced the air like nail points. In Andrew Brady's yearbook she wrote: *The thing I will always remember about you is the time we were watching the film strip in Miss Applebome's class, and the lights were out, and you sat behind me scratching my back with your fingers.* Olivia had heard somewhere that the hour from midnight to one o'clock was called the witching hour because that was when the witches were supposed to be active, but she had heard somewhere else that the witching hour was simply that hour of the day when everything always went wrong. It was yet another instance when she could not remember which story was supposed to be true and which was supposed to be a myth. If the witching hour was the hour of hardship, the hour of lucklessness, then she had experienced witching hours that lasted for days on end, but if the witching hour began at midnight, then she usually slept right through it. Every night after she took her pill, she would watch TV for half an hour and then lie in bed staring at the wall of books that lined her cottage. She believed that her books were like the abandoned shell of a hermit crab—a historical record of the conscience of her house, rather than an actual living conscience. There was a Greek restaurant at the western edge of the marina where she liked to eat lunch. The restaurant served falafel platters, gyros, and glasses of Dr Pepper with wedges of lemon suspended inside them like tiny moons. Its rooftop dining area had a row of pay telescopes that were pointed toward the ocean. Patrons could purchase a minute of viewing time for a quarter, and each day at noon, when the crowd was at its thickest, a row of children stood there feeding quarters into the slots as though they were playing video games. The children, both boys and girls, wore baseball caps with pictures of Japanese cartoon characters on them. They had freckles and missing teeth. Olivia enjoyed looking through the telescopes herself, but only when the weather was right—bright and blue, with a few compact clouds riding the wind. The waiters at the restaurant knew her by sight, but not by name. "Miss?" they would say. "Oh, Miss? Why don't you step away from the machine for a while and give some of our smaller customers a turn?" Far out on the ocean, where the waves were slow and heavy, she could see the shadows of the clouds moving across the surface of the water. Once, a tourist who had just returned from an aquatic sightseeing trip told her that there were schools of fish that followed the shadows like newborn babies trying to keep their mother in reach. He said that the fish were the color of Dijon mustard. Olivia was more interested in the clouds than she was in the water, and she was more interested in the shadows than she was in the clouds. She did not know when she had become so unlike other people.

She took her pill every night at ten thirty. The television was in her bedroom, and she knew it was time to switch it off and slide beneath the covers when her vision began to blur—or not *blur* exactly, since no matter what happened, her eyesight remained sharp, but *separate*, splitting into two distinct images, one that stayed in place and a second that seemed to drift up and to the left without ever actually moving. There were times when she slept so heavily that she barely heard her alarm when it sounded in the morning. It was two hundred years ago, and she was living in a cabin on the frontier, and though she could see the fires smoking off in the distance, she knew that it would be days before the Indians were able to cross the prairie. Her trouble with the sun began not long after she started taking the pills. She could not help but wonder if there was a connection. *Warning: Side effects may include dry mouth, drowsiness, and an inability to tolerate the basic conditions of life on the planet.* One morning she woke up to find her father sitting on the edge of her mattress. Her sheets were awry, and his hand was resting on her leg. People who read Anne Rice believe that tragedy is romantic. People who read Salman Rushdie use their scruples like a blade: the humane ones use them for opening, the cruel ones use them for wounding. Her father had her copy of Ovid's *Metamorphoses* open in his free hand. He said to her, "Did you know that Cupid was the Roman god of love *and* the Roman god of revulsion? Here, listen: 'From his quiver, full of light, he drew two darts, with different properties. The one puts love to flight, the other kindles it. That which kindles love is golden and shining, sharp-tipped; but that which puts it to flight is blunt, its shaft tipped with lead.'" Then he put the book down on her nightstand, and outside, in the garden, a hundred birds stopped singing and took to their wings as the widow Lorenzen's old Cadillac backfired.

Olivia worked at the map stand in exchange for her rent at the cottage, her monthly utilities, and the small salary her father paid her. He called the salary her "bonus." He gave it to her in a plain white envelope each and every Friday afternoon, even during the months when the map stand was closed. She opened the stand each day at eight o'clock, unlocking the cash register and raising the awning. Sometimes, in the morning, when the wind was blowing just right, the sun caught only the tops of the waves, and it looked as though a thousand bars of light were following one another over the water into shore. There were days when she thought she could not bear to stand behind the counter another moment, but this was the truth: whenever she had some time off, she did not know what to do with herself. Toward the end of the tourist season, when the docks were busy only on the weekends, she liked to spread her maps open on the counter and trace the shoreline with her finger. The image of the island's loosely textured mesh of roads surrounded by the pale blue ring of the ocean always made her think of an old, torn fishing net. The net was ready to snap at any moment, and it caught only the slowest and least clever of fish these days. The fish were lifted from their avenues of water into the piercing blue air, where they thrashed their tails and struggled for breath. Every so often, after the 3:15 rainstorm, Olivia would close the stand early and walk home with her hands at her sides, weaving like a butterfly through the shining field of umbrellas.

She had been living on the island for eight and a half years. Every Tuesday afternoon the widow Lorenzen would rent the latest action movies from the new releases section of the video store, and every Tuesday evening Olivia would hear her yelling at her television through the window screens. "Fire! Fire!" she shouted, and "Kill the son of a bitch!" and "Right there! He's right behind you!" She liked Bruce Willis, Jet Li, and Harrison Ford, she said, but she hated Keanu Reeves and "all that supernatural stuff." The most formidable insects Olivia had ever had to coax outside for her were a pair of dragonflies. When Olivia asked the Entity where it came from, it explained that there were twelve layers of space, of which the average member of the human race was aware of only four, though mystics, small children, and mathematicians occasionally caught a glimpse of the fifth or the sixth. The Entity told her that it came from the seventh layer. In the seventh layer of space, it said, the past was indistinguishable from the present, so nothing was ever truly lost, and nothing was ever truly irreparable. The Entity fell quiet as it caught sight of her face. It cocked its head and asked her, "Do you need me to help you?" And Olivia realized she was crying. People who read Tolstoy find it difficult to be alive because they are reasonable, while people who read Dostoyevsky find it difficult to be alive because they are not. In Judy Cossey's yearbook she wrote: *When we were in the eighth grade, I found a love note from David Diehl to you on the floor of Miss Mount's room, and I kept it in my purse for more than a week before I slipped it back into your locker.*

Winter on the island was drowsy and temperate, a few short months of easy sleeping and cool wind gusts that carried the spindrift off the waves and sent it drizzling down over the beachfront shopping lanes. During the winter Olivia spent more time sitting outside on her patio, leaning back in her rattan chair and listening to the traffic on the street. The cars rolled by with a soft hiss of their tires. The bicycles gave off a barely detectable rattle of spokes. On the last page of the story Olivia recalled reading about the man who could hear the race cars in his walls, the protagonist discovered that the wood in his house was rotten with termites. She could never remember where she had originally read the story, or who it was that wrote it. Sometimes, when she was feeling well, she would set a winter evening aside to stroll through the island's Historic District and on out to the grassy rise of Norfolk pines. It was the kind of place where children chased one another through the trees and teenagers lay on picnic blankets with their hands inside each other's clothing. People smoked cigarettes, and picked flowers, and had conversations, and everything happened as though she weren't even there. She was like the ghost of the moon in that half hour before the sun fell, hanging imperceptibly in the branches of the pine trees.

She would not have been surprised to learn that she had become invisible.

She began walking home soon after the street lamps were lit. It was important to her that she have an hour of silence in the house before she took her pill and prepared for bed, a time when nobody would place any demands on her and she would place no demands on herself. There were lamps on the streets of the island that were still filled with the breath of the glassblowers who had originally created them, and as she made her way home, she thought of them suspended in neat rows above the cobblestones, perfect little bubbles of captive history. She always hoped that she would not find the lights on inside her cottage. And, if she did, she hoped that it was only because she had forgotten to shut them off—that and nothing else. Her fingers twitched as she unlocked the door, like grass blades springing upright behind the treads of a tire. This was what the Entity had told her when her tears were finally extinguished—that there were seven layers of space between itself and the foundation of the universe, just as there were seven layers of skin between the open air and the inside of the human body. Then it touched the hollow of her neck, and she gasped as she felt the heat scorching through her skin. The sky outside the portal was the most beautiful thing she had ever seen.

She had been on three first dates since she moved to the island. Two of the first dates had taken place in the very same week, when she was still working as a maid for the house cleaning service and had not yet broken the momentum she was sure would sweep her away to another place. Eventually, after some time had passed, she would form the habit that all shore dwellers had of hearing the ocean without noticing it, but in her first few months on the island she could never quite ignore the crashing of the surf. Night and day she felt as if she were lost at sea in a wooden raft, the waves lifting and releasing her again and again. The first of her first dates was named Richard Jackson. He spent their entire dinner telling her about the approaching age of digital consciousness, when the human mind would be subsumed inside a framework of superpowerful computers. He spoke in a thick chain of technological acronyms—CPU, MIS, LAN—and after a while, Olivia grew bored and bewildered and began interjecting various acronyms of her own into the conversation: "I'm worried about the MSG in this BLT," she said, and "I had a PYT who worked for KFC, but he turned out to have an STD." A long time ago there were people who used to tell her she was funny. The second of her first dates was also named Richard— Richard Pheby—and though he slipped his fingers under the table to make a spidering gesture on her knee, and she liked the way he smiled at her, he did not kiss her when the night came to an end, and he did not call her again.

The hurricane sirens went off every Wednesday at noon. She had weathered one major hurricane and three minor ones on the island. There were some things she would never get used to. She still flinched every time the horns began to wail. In the Midwest the sirens were called tornado sirens, and on the West Coast they were called air raid sirens. The one major hurricane that had swept through the island since she had been there—Carla, it was named— filled the streets with sand and tore a sheet of embossed tin off the roof of her house. For the next few weeks, until a good wind set it free, she watched it shining and swaying inside the coronet of the palm tree across the street. In Jared Serveert's yearbook she wrote: *I can see your backyard from the roof of my house. Once, when we were kids, Kim Olsen was spending the night with me, and we climbed up there and watched you doing leaps on your trampoline.* A few days after the sheet of tin came loose from on top of her house, a leak developed in her kitchen ceiling, passing a steady drip of coffee-colored water onto the linoleum. Her father sent his handyman over to repair the damage. The handyman wore a Harley-Davidson cap and a T-shirt that read NO JESUS, NO PEACE. KNOW JESUS, KNOW PEACE. He told her, "This primer works real good, boy, but let me tell you, you stand in those fumes too long and you're definitely killing off some brain cells. That's why so many painters are alcoholics. They walk around buzzed all day long." He made her open all the windows before he left. The widow Lorenzen cornered him in the driveway and asked him to help her kill a spider she had spotted crawling under her refrigerator—"a big fat, juicy one," she said. The next day, when Olivia's father came over to examine her kitchen ceiling, he stood on his tiptoes and prodded the plaster with his fingers. "The man may be an imbecile, but he does excellent work," he announced, and he paused to scratch his jaw. "Not a damp spot to be found."

The leak had left a puddle of brown water on the linoleum that Olivia had to soak up with a few dozen paper towels. She was lucky, her father told her, that the water had fallen over the open floor and that nothing important had been drenched. In the kitchen she had her microwave and her food processor. In the living room there was her couch and her aloe plant and her stereo. The bedroom was where she kept her books, her TV, and the sandalwood jewelry box she had bought for herself when she graduated from high school. The jewelry box was painted a bright jade green, and it exhibited an image of a white-breasted nuthatch on its lid. Inside, it held her earrings and her bracelets and the gold necklace she had not worn since the Entity brushed its fingers across the hollow of her neck and wounded her with the heat of its touch, which was what people did when they wanted to love you. Once, she was standing on top of the Greek restaurant looking through a pay telescope when the shadows of the clouds on the ocean began to flash with a range of colors that broke and swirled as she tracked them across the water. The effect lasted only a few seconds, and afterward, she could not be sure it had happened at all. When her time ran out, a black gate snicked shut inside the telescope, and the lens immediately went dark. The sound reminded her of the silver blade of the novelty guillotine her father used whenever he wanted to clip the ends off his cigars. Olivia had read somewhere that the brain sometimes remained conscious for several minutes after a person was decapitated, and that the head of Charlotte Corday had blushed and given an angry sneer when it was slapped by her executioner. She could picture the expression with no trouble at all.

Her third first date had taken place just last year. This one was not named Richard, but Cason—Cason Copeland—and she never would have gone out with him at all had it not been for her mother, who had made her promise that she would make an effort with the next man who showed some interest in her. "You keep trying to change yourself from the inside out, but it doesn't work that way, honey. People change themselves from the outside in. You have to *try*, Via." So she had met Cason Copeland for sushi and drinks at the little Polynesian restaurant by the sculpture garden, and she had listened to his stories about the commodities brokerage he owned, smiling when he seemed to be making a joke, and she had tried—or at least she had tried to try. After they ate, he suggested that the two of them go dancing, and though Olivia didn't really feel up for it, she remembered her mother telling her, "What you do is *pretend* that you're up for it, and if you pretend well enough, you'll find that you are." The club Cason took her to had a live DJ and a tequila bar. It was one of her spinning days, when she could hardly turn her head to the side or roll her shoulders forward without feeling that she was about to topple over. She knew she was in trouble when she found herself looking for the mirrored ball above the dance floor and realized that there wasn't one. The dance floor was covered with scuff marks that looked like the impressions that car tires leave in the sand: tiny tires with tiny treads. You could see them only when you were lying with your cheek pressed to the boards. People who read Anne Lamott, like people who read Anne Rice, believe that tragedy is romantic, but the people who read Anne Lamott believe it ironically. Olivia remembered the sound of Cason's voice apologizing to the other dancers as he lifted her up off the floor. "Sorry. I'm so sorry. I'm so sorry about this." He wrenched her out of the club and sent her home in a taxi. Later, when she looked in her bathroom mirror, she saw that the entire left side of her face was smeared with an oily black dust. She was too tired to wash herself clean. That night, as she slept, the dust came off in flakes against her pillow.

The map stand was built of cypress and heart pine, and was painted a salmon color that seemed to glow in the light of the marina. It looked flimsy, barely finished, and people imagined when they saw it that the first big storm would rip it away, scattering the pieces for hundreds of yards along the shore, but Olivia had watched it survive through all four hurricanes without so much as a cracked board. Once, she had come to work to find the lock hanging loose from the gate, and she was sure that thieves must have broken in and taken the cash register. But the only things missing were a box of thirty-six Mars bars and the LEAVE A PENNY, TAKE A PENNY cup. Four brass screws were standing in a row on the counter, their rounded ends pointing into the air like the noses of performing seals. When the locksmith arrived, he jiggled the lock and told her, "See, what you've got here is one of those crummy little Wal-Mart jobs. My guess is that whoever took your Mars bars there gave it a good tug and it just plain fell off. You folks need to get you a nice solid industrial lock, is what you need." Another time someone—Curtis Judkins, she presumed—spray-painted CURTIS JUDKINS DID THIS on the stand's back wall. The spray paint was a sickly fluorescent orange. Her father had the boards recoated by the end of the business day. As far as Olivia could tell, the structure had an unending capacity to withstand assault without suffering harm. It was as though it presented itself so modestly to the world that the world had decided it was not worth destroying. In the summer she liked to listen to the rain drumming against the awning as the latest batch of tourists scrambled for shelter under their jackets and umbrellas, in the shops along the beachfront, and beneath the tarry brown wood of the docks.

The only people Olivia spoke to regularly were her father, her mother, and the widow Lorenzen. She had overheard the occasional conversation, though, and spotted the occasional glance, and she knew that she was considered unusual by many of the islanders. She was aware of the things they said about her. They examined all her most shameful impulses—every fantasy, every fleeting thought— then passed them along to one another as if they had really happened. There were rumors that she stole from the grocery store, that she stabbed herself with pencils, that she urinated outdoors, that she slept with older men, that she had long conversations with herself when she thought no one was listening. She had never told anyone about the Entity. It had assured her that she would always be able to tell when it was nearby because of the variation in the color of the shadows the clouds cast on the water. It said that she should look for a pattern of iridescence there, like the designs she had sometimes noticed on the inner bindings of expensive books, except that the marblings of color would appear in every possible shade of blue, from the softest of azures to the darkest of indigos. This was what she saw when she looked out over the ocean: gulls diving into the waves, boats with their sails belling out in the wind, and, every so often, a Coast Guard vessel thundering out toward the open water. People who read Tom Clancy would not approve of Olivia—neither her weakness nor her sorrow.

One late-September Sunday, after the widow Lorenzen had

returned home from church, she found an infestation of reddish brown insects with clear triangular wings in her foyer. She called Olivia over to get rid of them. "There must be hundreds of them, crawling all over one another," she said. "Filthy things." Then she paused as she thought of a way to describe them: "It looks like a grasshopper and a mosquito got together and had babies." The insects were flowing over the small patch of tiled floor around the front door, spilling apart and then merging back together. They looked like the rain of static on a dead TV station. The widow wanted Olivia to kill them, but instead Olivia borrowed a broom and used it to sweep them out onto the porch, where they staggered around in a sunstruck daze. Half an hour later, they were back in the foyer. And half an hour after that, they were dead. Olivia was sure that it was her fault. The broom had broken their legs, or it had ruptured their hearts, and the injury had killed them. She was carrying the husks of the insects outside on a dustpan when a blast of wind sent them whirling off toward the palmetto barrens. People who read Tom Wolfe feel that they have never abandoned their ground, that it is the world around them that has snapped free of its foundations. The sheet of embossed tin that the hurricane had ripped from her house had sailed almost half a block after the wind lifted it out of the palm tree, landing finally in the pool behind the public kindergarten. Olivia paged through her copy of *Insects of the Greater United States* when she got home and discovered that the bugs were neither grasshoppers nor mosquitos, but mayflies. She felt sick to her stomach. Here was a group of insects that had been permitted only one day of adult life, and she had taken it away from them. If only she had known what she was seeing, she thought. If only she had been just a little bit smarter, just a little bit more careful. The kindergarteners liked to pretend that the sheet of tin roofing that had landed behind their school was a door to another world. They heard the splash when it fell from the sky. They called it "the moon portal." They dared one another to dive to the bottom of the pool and open it.

Most of Olivia's favorite people on the island were strangers to her: the woman who drove the car with the missing windshield, the old man who sold bird whistles he had carved into the shape of finger bones, the little girl she had seen burying Oreos on the beach and then watering them with a plastic bucket. Why was it that the people she liked best always seemed to be the ones who inspired odd looks from everybody else? They were like those deep-sea creatures with watery, transparent skin: you could see the soft little jerking beans of their hearts, you understood that the very thing that was supposed to protect them was the thing that made them vulnerable, and you knew that you couldn't help them, so you decided to love them instead. Sometimes, when Olivia was working, she filled entire days watching out for her favorite people: they were everywhere, the people she loved but could not help, like a linked chain stretching from the early morning into the late afternoon. There was the man who scraped the moss off the hulls of the boats when he thought no one was looking. There was the woman who sat on the same bench every day, flossing her teeth and staring out at the ocean. There were the twins who always stopped at her stand after school ended to buy two packages of Now and Laters—lemon for the girl with the pink backpack and cherry for the girl with the blue. Olivia could not remember whether she had read it in a book or seen it on a wildlife documentary or simply heard it in conversation somewhere, but one way or another she had picked up the idea that armadillos always give birth to identical twins. The story was almost certainly a myth, though. She traced the shore of the island on one of the maps. She watched the clouds making shapes against the sky. Her mother called her on the first Sunday of every month. The time difference was only two hours, but she could never recall whether the clocks ran earlier or later on the island, and she always seemed to think that she was rousing Olivia out of a sound sleep. "I'm not ringing too early, am I?" she asked, or "Am I calling you too late?" This was the truth: it was almost never too early. The pills Olivia took helped her to go under at night, but they did not necessarily allow her to sleep through till morning. Sometimes she would lie in bed for hours waiting until it was time to get up. She had become skilled at recognizing the first signs of morning. To begin with, the frogs and the night insects fell silent. The earliest of the cars went hushing down the street. The paperboy's bicycle rattled up the widow Lorenzen's driveway, and the paper landed on her porch with a flat little smack. The first few birds opened up their lungs as the farthest rim of the sky grew pale. But it was not until the great ball of the sun appeared that the curtains in her bedroom began to gather the light. Sometimes Olivia had already gotten out of bed to make her coffee before she remembered that she could hear the ocean. Her mother told her that there were times when the only sound she could detect from her window was the wind trickling through the orange trees like a cool, lazy stream. "Why don't you come down to São Paulo? Move in with Graciliano and me?" she asked when she called. And then, later, "What did you say, Via? *Paris Stories?* I've always wanted to read that book." And then, later still, "I can't believe you're still speaking to that son of a bitch." On the few occasions when Olivia managed to sleep through the night, she would wake to the sound of her alarm going off, or her father opening the door, or the wild rooster who nested across the street screaming bloody murder.

The town library stood next to the repertory theater, which stood next to a bed and breakfast, which stood next to the eyebrow house with the white picket fence and the ornate floral scrollwork around the porches. It had been a long time since she had read a book, but sometimes, in the evening, she still liked to sit in the New Acquisitions room behind the library's front counter and watch the people come and go. The leather chairs there were deep and comfortable, and the various readers were always poised and quiet. The wallpaper was decorated with seventy-eight hand-painted birds that the notable painter had brushed into place almost eighty years ago. If the bookshelves were the conscience of a house, Olivia thought, then surely the library was the conscience of the island. And the marina was the face, she supposed, and the shopping lanes were the appetite, and the grassy rise of Norfolk pines was that small peaceful place where it could forget what it was feeling for a while. Olivia approved wholeheartedly of people who read Carson McCullers— their open nerves and their beaten glances. She did not believe she would ever be capable of understanding people who read James Patterson. In Nathan Wilcox's yearbook she wrote: *I'm sorry I never got to know you very well.* In Indy Carmichael's she wrote: *I'm sure that things will be better for you someday.* The library had two sliding glass doors in front, one on either side of the lobby, and whenever both of them were opened at the same time, the air in the New Acquisitions room fell completely still for a few seconds. This happened once or twice an hour. There was something about that quickly passing perfect stillness that reminded her of the way she had felt in the presence of the Entity, the amazement and dazzled well-being that were so unlike anything she had known before.

In addition to the mayflies, spiders, beetles, wasps, silverfish, dragonflies, and bumblebees Olivia had helped the widow Lorenzen evict from her house, she had also been summoned to remove any number of mosquitoes and fireflies, as well as a pair of brown moths, a single green katydid, and a small mottled gecko that had suctioned itself to the glass front of her grandfather clock. Her husband had died almost ten years ago, the widow said, after a lingering emphysema that had confined him to the house for more than two years, and since that day the insects had never stopped coming. She told

Olivia that she used to imagine she had gotten over him and had finally moved on with her life, but lately, when she was not thinking about anything in particular, she would suddenly hear him whistling the old Sinatra songs he loved or catch the aroma of his Benson & Hedges Gold 100's, and she would wander into the other room fully expecting to see him sitting in his favorite chair with a crossword puzzle open on his lap. She was starting to worry about herself. On her coffee table was the video case for a movie starring Roddy McDowall and Paula Prentiss called *It Must Have Been a Nightmare*. When Olivia read the title out loud, the widow nodded her head and answered, "It still is." She had pale freckled skin that allowed a tracery of veins to show through the backs of her hands. Once, Olivia was trying to coax a wasp through the house and the widow was following along behind her with a Debbie cake when the wasp bobbed up toward the ceiling and the two of them had to wait for it to descend. They paused before the portrait in the parlor. Olivia told the widow, "Your husband was a striking man," and the widow gave her a look of squinting amusement and said, "That's not my husband." "Then who is it?" Olivia asked, and she answered, "It's Humphrey Bogart in *The Maltese Falcon*."

The island was shaped like a sneaker with a missing toe. The waves were strongest on the south side, where the sole would have been. There were so many undercurrents and slack areas in the water there, though, that the entire length of ocean had been restricted from recreational use. The waves on the north side were slower and heavier, and on any given day, Olivia could look past the boats in the marina and see them rolling deliberatively into shore. There were surfers who paddled their boards out to sea and tried to ride them back onto the beach, but they quickly discovered that it was no good. It was like trying to surf a supermarket conveyor belt, she had heard one of them say: you didn't feel invigorated, you just felt conspicuous. Sometimes, when she was in a particular sort of mood, she would purchase a few of the discarded umbrellas from the children who had collected them, paying half the original sale price. Some of the children spent the money on candy. Some of them used it to buy Black Cats and bottle rockets. Some of them saved it for the air hockey tables in the lobby of the movie theater. Olivia allowed the umbrellas to dry overnight, then restickered and sold them again. The perspiration on the Entity's skin (if that's what it was—perspiration) had drawn together in hundreds of quivering beads that looked to Olivia like the rain on a freshly waxed car. There were days when the sky was so spotlessly clear that the clouds never came to cast their shadows on the water at all. "We must be like insects to you," Olivia had said to the Entity, and it had smiled, closed its warm black eyes, and answered, "Yes, you are all like insects to me. But I am like an insect to myself."

The walls of the cottage were wood, and the palm trees at the edge of the yard were wood, and the summer cabin where her father used to take her camping when she was a girl was wood. Once, when she was thirteen, he had allowed her to invite her friend Katie Gremillion with them for the weekend. The three of them went motor-boating in the deep section of the lake, then hiking on the wilderness trail, then fishing in the lily pads beside the docks. The fish they caught worked their mouths open in astonished circles. Olivia knew what they must be wondering: How had the crickets they swallowed risen up like birds and wrenched them out of the water? She felt so sorry for them that she made her father release them back into the lily pads. On the evening of their second day in the cabin, he showed Olivia and Katie how to arrange a stack of cedar logs in the fireplace, building a teepee of kindling underneath so that the flame would catch and grow. The burning wood filled the cabin with its perfume. Eventually her father said, "It's getting late. You girls should go on back to your room and get some sleep now." The two of them brushed their teeth with the water from their canteens, and then they went to bed. It was just after midnight when the door to the room they were sharing came open, gliding around on its hinges as if by accident, making hardly a sound as it closed. It was surprising how empty a room could be with three people in it. The next morning Katie's eyes were shot through with red. She would not talk to Olivia. Later, in her yearbook, Olivia wrote: *You didn't see what you thought you saw.*

In the evening, just before the stars began to show in the sky, the western end of the island became like a painting. The sun grew larger and larger as it sank toward the horizon, laying an expanding cone of rippling red light across the water. The palm trees turned very slowly to silhouettes. Hundreds of tourists stood along the beach taking snapshots of themselves. Olivia had grown used to seeing them huddled together with their families, smiling and turning their faces to the lens. Their arms were always outstretched to hold their cameras at the proper distance, and it looked to Olivia as if they were trying to flatten something they did not really want to touch. She doubted that any of them would recognize her away from her station behind the counter of the map stand. Olivia had never operated a digital camera in her life. She had never carried a cell phone or owned a PDA. When she walked past a group of Girl Scouts selling cookies from a table in front of the Lutheran church, she closed her eyes for a moment and imagined she was roller-skating.

Her mother had told her many times about the days when she used to take her grocery shopping, how Olivia would sit in the cart scissoring her legs back and forth and strike up conversations with the people they passed in the aisles: *Hi, I'm Olivia. What's your name? I don't like vanilla wafers. Are you buying any Sunkist? Are you buying any root beer?* "You were quite the little charmer," her mother said. "Everybody used to love you," she insisted. It seemed clear to Olivia that the life she was looking at was one whose meaning lay entirely in the beginning. She had started out strong and beautiful, and she was not sure when she had changed. But surely anything that could change once, and change so dramatically, could swing back around and change again. This was what she told herself as she stalked another honeybee for the widow Lorenzen, or as she lay in bed waiting for the pills to take effect, or as she raised the awning of the map stand in the morning, or as she sat down to lunch in the restaurant at the end of the marina. Minute after minute, hour after hour, she turned her thoughts toward the day when the Entity would come back for her in its vessel. It would whisper to her with its tremendous musical breathing sound. It would burn her with the soft touch of its fingers. It would say her name, and it would carry her into the sky, and the two of them would set out from the island together, driven through the layers of space by a radiant dream of the way things could be.

THE LIVES OF THE PHILOSOPHERS

There must have been a window of seconds, after he was seized by his vision of the unknown but before he was awed into silence, when Thomas Aquinas would have been capable of describing what he had seen. He was working alone in his cell when it happened— drafting a sermon on the four cardinal virtues, maybe, or a commentary on the *Metaphysics* of Aristotle. A tallow candle was burning on his desk. The candles at the friary were not perfumed, so the odor of animal fat must have lingered in the air, but Aquinas would not have noticed that. He paused to blot the ink from his quill. Perhaps he heard the wind filtering through a crack in the shutters. Then he turned his head to follow the quivering motion of a cobweb and was filled with the white light of revelation.

Jacob can envision the scene down to the smallest detail. He can picture Aquinas hunched over in his wooden chair, his giant's body locked into its writing posture, his oxlike eyes absorbed in concentration. The sleeves of his robe were gathered at his elbows. A grain of sand, caught in the wick of the candle, gave off a tiny spark. He can see it all so clearly, but he cannot cross the threshold of the image and slip inside. He cannot guess what Aquinas was thinking. It is the one surpassing mystery of the great man's life, a mystery that has occupied the attention of the philosophical community for more than seven hundred years. What happened that night in his cell to make him lay aside his pen? What did he understand in that one brief moment before he lost the will or the ability to express himself?

Aquinas was not yet fifty at the time, though he would die just a few months later. When Friar Reginald asked him why he had abandoned his work, he answered, "I can write no more. I have seen things which make all my writings like straw."

I can write no more. I have seen things which make all my writings like straw.

Jacob has printed the words on the back of an envelope which he has tacked to the bulletin board above his desk. He shares his office, a converted classroom on the top level of the Humanities Building, with half a dozen other graduate students, but Bertram College is such a small institution, and the Philosophy Department so lackadaisical, that he often has the space entirely to himself. Sometimes, when he is trying to think through a rough spot in his thesis, he can stay at his desk staring at the words on the envelope until long after midnight, leaving only when he hears the custodian's cart rumbling down the hall, reverberating over the pebbled floor like an oncoming train. There is nothing waiting for him at home and no reason for him to hurry. His girlfriend, Audrey, works the late shift at the college health clinic. Even on her nights off the two of them no longer know what to say to each other.

It is a Thursday evening in early March when Jacob meets the woman he will later come to think of as the gypsy. He is supposed to be grading student midterms, but instead he has spent the last few hours bookmarking passages in Aquinas's *Summa Theologica*— searching for clues, as he thinks of it. He has become so engrossed in the project that when a knock comes at the door, he twists around in his chair as though someone has dropped an ice cube down the small of his back.

It takes a moment for his heart to settle. "The door's unlocked," he calls out.

The woman who comes edging into the room looks to be maybe nineteen or twenty. She is wearing a long, loose skirt, a sweater with a neck that reveals the collars of several smaller sweaters, and dreadlocks trussed up in a bright red scarf. "Sorry, man, you were the only light I could find on."

Jacob looks at the clock and sees that it is almost midnight. "That's okay. What can I do for you?"

"I'm having problems with the change machine."

She gives the words an unusual emphasis, hovering over them with her voice like a flyswatter before falling dramatically on the final syllable. The change machine? Jacob pictures something straight out of a science fiction novel, an immense apparatus of hatches, levers, and conveyor belts that allows you to step in as one human being and step out as another, in which atheists change into Christians, stock car drivers change into politicians, great beauties change into wallflowers.

"You know, the one over by the elevators," she says. "It ate my dollar."

"Oh—the *change* machine. Well, I'm not sure what I can do to help you out there. You'll have to talk to somebody in maintenance, I imagine."

"Yeah, I would, but that's the problem. I can't find anybody. And I need that money if I'm going to catch the bus. Is there some sort of refund button I can press, do you think?"

"I doubt it. But look, here—" He fishes a couple of dollars' worth of change out of his pocket, maneuvering his fingers past his keys, his handkerchief, and a tattered roll of breath mints. "Will this be enough?"

The woman's manner as she walks across the room, without hesitation, skimming the floor in her long brown skirt, reminds him of a tree in the late days of autumn. It is in the thinness of her limbs, he thinks, and the way that everything about her seems to rustle: her hair, her clothing, even her voice.

"That's *so* cool," she says as she takes the change. "Let me pay you back, man. Here. I know. Are you right-handed or left-handed?"

"Left-handed."

Thomas Aquinas was left-handed too. He had to hold his pen at a crook, writing from below the line to avoid smearing his letters across the page. The few surviving examples of his penmanship are barely legible.

The gypsy takes a chair out from under the desk next to Jacob's, sits down, and turns his hands palms up. "Okay, that means that your left hand is your active hand and your right hand is your passive one. Most people are right-handed, so for them it's the opposite. Basically how it works is that your passive hand shows you the character you were born with, and your active hand shows you the changes you make to yourself. The passive hand is heredity. The active hand is choice."

She leans in to peer at his hands like a jeweler examining a gem for flaws. Her lips are so close that he can feel her breath on his palms. For a moment he imagines that she is going to kiss him. The tips of his fingers give an involuntary twitch.

"Huh. That's weird. In your case, though, the lines are exactly the same."

"What do you mean?"

She traces each line slowly with the nail of her index finger. "Well, you've got your heart line here at the top. In your case it's got a sharp upward curve to it and a lot of little breaks, which means that you're affectionate but you're going to experience periods of sorrow in love. Then you've got your head line in the middle—

a good, sharp line, you see? That means you're intelligent. But there's this bit here at the beginning that shows me you're also kind of cautious. You're a teacher, right? That makes sense. And then this curved line at the bottom is your life line. There's a lot of space between the life line and the thumb in your case, which is good, but you've also got this strange gap here in the middle—not so good. At any rate, the line has a nice fluid curve to it, so all in all what I'm looking at is a pretty decent life. The weird thing, though, and this is what I was telling you, is that the lines on the passive hand and the lines on the active hand are absolutely, one hundred percent identical. I've never seen that before."

"Is it significant?"

She folds his hands together and gives them a motherly pat. "What it means is—no change. You were born to be a certain kind of person, and you're going to die a certain kind of person. Sorry, man." She is standing in the doorway again before he can decide what to say to her. "Thanks for the bus money, though. I hope your next life is a little more spiritually dynamic."

And with that, she is gone. He listens for the sound of her footsteps as she walks away, but there is only the crisp, irregular rustling of her skirt and then, from out of nowhere, the clatter of the custodian's cart.

Absurdly, Jacob finds that he is flustered. He can feel his palms gathering sweat. Everything the woman has told him about himself is true, he realizes. Every last detail. But then wouldn't most people describe themselves as affectionate and intelligent? And who doesn't experience periods of sorrow in love? It occurs to him that he ought to have asked her a test question, one with an answer he could either verify or falsify. Something about Audrey and the baby, maybe, or something about his dissertation. He rushes down the hall to see if he can catch her, but the elevator has already descended into the floor. He goes to the window that gazes down on the parking lot. The streetlights pick out a single abandoned car with an hourglass-shaped patch of rust on the hood.

He will continue to look for the woman over the next few weeks, searching for her face in the campus's flowing river of students, but he will never see her again.

Audrey is waiting for him at the kitchen counter when he gets home, using the ball of her index finger to cull the toast crumbs out of a tub of butter. There is a certain look she wears when she is too brittle or hopeless or beaten down by the demands of the world to sustain her disappointment in him any longer, a kind of bruised slackness concentrated mostly around her eyes and lips. He never knows whether it is his job at such times to put his hand on her arm and console her or to disappoint her so radically that the old passion takes spark in her again.

"Where have you been? I've been waiting for you," she says.

"I'm sorry. I thought you were on at the clinic tonight."

"I was. They sent me home early."

He has to be careful here and he knows it, so he flattens his voice, stripping it of even the slightest trace of emotion. "Is there something wrong with the baby?"

She shakes her head, concentrating on the butter again, and for a moment he is almost able to believe that he has gotten away with it. She says, "I had a touch of vertigo, that's all. But after the spotting last week, Dr. Phillips told me I should take the rest of the night off just to be on the safe side." Then she gives him a little poison dart of a smile. "Not the answer you were hoping for, is it, Jacob?"

"Now that's not true. You know it isn't. I want only the best for you."

She sniffs dismissively. "You know, maybe you really mean that. But listen to the way you say it. 'I want only the best for you.' For *you*, second person singular. Never *us*, first person plural."

He can tell that he is making a false step before the words have even left his mouth, but still he asks her, " 'Us' meaning you and me, or 'us' meaning you and the baby?"

He is not trying to lay the ground for a debate, only raising a question, but for the past five months, ever since Audrey felt the first intimations of the baby growing inside her, slowly spinning around on itself like a dandelion seed, it seems as though the two of them have been doomed to misunderstand each other. Her face tightens with indignation. She says, "*Us* meaning this family—all three of us." She wipes her finger clean on a paper towel and replaces the cap on the tub of butter, then thinks better of it, pries the cap back off, and flings it at him. It bounces ineffectually off his chest.

"Whatever you're waiting to figure out, you need to go ahead and figure it out, Jacob. Put the butter away for me," she says. And she storms off to the bedroom, slamming the door behind her.

Jacob has never wanted to raise a child. He has always thought of parenthood as something like those sand mandalas that Buddhist monks create grain by grain over a period of months, then sweep away in a matter of seconds—the sort of noble yet exhausting activity that, no matter how beautiful or enriching it might be, he can only imagine himself observing from a distance. Audrey used to tell him that she felt exactly the same way. It was one of the things that had bound them together through seven years and four apartments and all the changes life had brought them. But when she found out she was pregnant, a transformation took place inside her, as profound in its way as the transformation that turned all the accomplishments of Thomas Aquinas's life to straw in his eyes. She realized that she wanted to keep the baby and start a family. The fact that Jacob did not share this wish was at first a mystery to her, and later an annoyance, and finally, he had come to see, a humiliation, as though he were gazing through an open door at her deepest instincts, her most intimate desires, and refusing to step inside.

Which in a way, he supposed, he was.

It has become clear to both of them that if he does not experience a change of heart soon, they are going to split cleanly apart down the center, falling away from each other like the two halves of a plastic Easter egg.

He takes a bottle of water into the living room and sits down on the couch. Because of the hot spells Audrey has been having, she has left the apartment's windows cracked open an inch or two, and a small, soft wind flows through the air. He finds himself thinking of the mystery of Aquinas again—how the story of his final days was both like and unlike a fairy tale, since in the traditional fairy tale straw was transformed into gold, whereas in the case of Aquinas gold was transformed into straw.

He listens to Audrey washing her face on the other side of the bedroom door.

He does not know what he is going to do.

The light from the kitchen has turned the clock on the mantel into an expressionless white disk. Jacob glances at his wristwatch to check the time. But something is wrong. For some while now, he has been aware of a strange feeling of floatiness in his hand, the slight tingle of cool air on his skin, but not until this moment has he really given the sensations his proper attention.

He looks in his lap, on the carpet, and in the crevice behind the couch cushions. He gets up to check the inside of his satchel and the pockets of his coat. He even goes outside with a flashlight to search the sidewalk and the grass along the curb. It is no good, though. He must have lost his watch somewhere.

On the morning of January 3, 1889, Friedrich Nietzsche was walking through the Piazza Carlo Alberto in Turin when he experienced an insight that would cripple him for the rest of his days. It was a bright, brisk morning. The sun was spreading a glossy light over the pavements of black granite. Nietzsche must have been reasoning out some minor difficulty in his philosophy—the antagonism between the evolution of man and the persistence of the moral imagination, perhaps, or the problem of memory in the doctrine of the eternal recurrence. He was often incapacitated by headaches and nausea in those days, symptoms of his midstage syphilis, yet his boldest ideas always occurred to him while he was walking. He struggled against his illness for the sake of his work.

He was stepping into the lane when he saw a coachman thrashing his horse. The driver whipped the animal three, six, seven times. The horse locked its withers and lowered its head. It was the sort of sight one could witness on the streets of Turin every day, but something had been waiting for Nietzsche at the highest corner of his thinking, some desperate revelation, and at that moment, like a jumper perched on the edge of a building, it tilted forward and tumbled into space.

Nietzsche staggered into the square and flung his arms around the neck of the horse. He buried his head in the dark hair of its mane, and he wept. All around him people stood and stared.

"Someone should help that man," he heard one of them say.

When at last he lifted his face, the dust on his eyeglasses shone like a cluster of stars.

That night he wrote a few last letters, signing himself "Dionysus," "Nietzsche Caesar," and "The Crucified." After which, like Thomas Aquinas, Nietzsche, too, fell silent. He spent the final years of his life as a mental paralytic, barely aware of himself or his surroundings. He never explained—and Jacob imagines he was incapable of explaining—what it was that he understood that morning in the piazza.

It is late April now, six weeks since the gypsy stepped into Jacob's office and saw the contours of his life marked out on his hands, six weeks since Audrey told him he needed to figure out whatever it was he was waiting to figure out. The elms and the poplars have finished leafing out, and the students of Bertram College spend hours every day loafing around in the courtyard, tossing footballs and Frisbees to one another and spreading out in the sun and the clover. Jacob can see them from the window of his office. He has given himself until the end of the semester to come to a decision about Audrey and the baby. He loves Audrey, or at least he loves the Audrey he can still see glimpses of occasionally, the Audrey who has not yet lost the last of her faith in him. He cannot imagine the shape his life would take without her. But—and this is the problem—he cannot imagine the shape his life would take with a baby, either. Again and again he has tried to envision himself as a father, tending his child through thousands of late-night sicknesses and crying jags, but the picture will never come clear.

Maybe what he is really suffering from is a failure of the imagination. It certainly seems that way. But there is something inside him that resists thinking about it, and he is no closer to making up his mind now than he was before. He finds it easier just to prepare his lectures, grade his students' essays, and attempt to sort through the never-ending puzzle of his dissertation, which he has been putting together word by torturous word, a page or so every week, for almost two years now. He often feels as though he is making no real progress at all. It is not that he is unwilling to engage with the work or unable to tease out the implications of his ideas. It has simply become obvious to him that he is writing around the edges of his subject rather than directly into the center of it. He has all the right ingredients for a thesis—an interesting premise, a set of unusual propositions, an important question in need of an answer. And yet, somehow, no actual thesis.

Here is where he stands: the two figures at the center of his project, Thomas Aquinas and Friedrich Nietzsche, were polar opposites in their roles as icons and thinkers, one the father of Christian philosophy and the other the father of anti-Christian philosophy. Yet both of them underwent mysterious, deeply interior ordeals of thought that fundamentally reshaped their visions of the world. They were the two most articulate minds of their day, capable of expressing even the finest and most elusive distinctions, yet after they had their revelations—Aquinas in the darkness of the friary and Nietzsche in the cold morning light of the piazza—they ceased writing altogether.

The question Jacob has is why? What did they realize at the final stage of their lives? What was it that came apart or locked together inside them? And, more important, were the revelations they experienced one and the same? No matter how much consideration he gives the questions, he cannot seem to come to an answer.

The problem is never far from the center of his mind. He thinks about it while he is exercising and shopping for groceries, while he is walking across campus and preparing his notes for class. Sometimes, in the middle of a lecture, he will pause for a moment, pursuing the bright flash of an idea, but as soon as he goes to his desk to jot it down, he will find that it has been extinguished. Countless times he has fallen asleep thinking of Aquinas and Nietzsche, Nietzsche and Aquinas. He has even dreamed about them—dreamed that Aquinas was looking out over the Bay of Naples, watching the birds dive like white scythes into the ocean; dreamed that Nietzsche was dangling a pocket watch from his fingers and feeling its weight shift as it swayed back and forth; dreamed that Nietzsche was dining with Lou Salomé when he looked across the restaurant and saw Aquinas sitting alone beneath a yellow lamp, and he tore at his hair and held up his copy of Aquinas's *Summa Contra Gentiles*, and he dropped it in despair, saying, "He *knows* me, Audrey. He *contains* me." Jacob finds himself thinking about the men as if they are two old friends of his from whom he has been waiting to receive a letter: *Dear Jacob, I must offer my apologies for not writing sooner. I have been changed by the events of the last few weeks. Here is what happened* . . . Sometimes, when he and Audrey are alone in the house together, he will listen to her filing her nails with an emery board or watch her passing through the kitchen in her quilted blue robe, and though he is watching and listening to her, and it would seem that she should fill his senses, he will be unable to separate her from the great rolling mill wheel of his speculations. *Aquinas and Nietzsche and Audrey. Nietzsche and Audrey and Aquinas.* She no longer asks him what he is thinking about. She no longer wants to know.

One day, shortly after his morning office hours have ended, he goes to the cafeteria for a sandwich and some coffee and overhears a couple of his students talking about one of his classes. "I mean, you would think that a course like Introduction to Ethics would at least teach you something about the difference between right and wrong, wouldn't you? Isn't that like the whole point? But I don't understand anything more about the difference between right and wrong than I did back in January."

"The professors always cover their tails pretty well on that one. It's the standard first-day-of-class lecture: Philosophy Is About Asking Questions, Not Getting Answers."

"Yeah, but." It is a finished statement: *Yeah, but.* "Here's what I think: I think we should treat philosophers the same way we treat job applicants. Have them put down their name, their employment history, and their answer to every important philosophical dilemma of the last two thousand years. You can't get away with that kind of wishy-washy, the-questions-are-what-really-matters crap if you want somebody to hire you for their marketing team."

Jacob puts his hand to his mouth to cover his grin. The boy who is speaking is one of his least motivated students, someone who spends most of the class hour taking his baseball cap off, limbering up the brim, and replacing it on his head. Nevertheless, there is a part of him that can't help but agree with the kid.

Later that day, after he has finished teaching his Wednesday afternoon aesthetics seminar, he heads over to the humanities office to check his mailbox. He finds a note from the department chair:

J.—
Please stop by when you have a moment.
—H.

The fluorescent lamp at the end of the hall has burned out, which makes all of the offices there look deserted, as if that one small wing of the building has been abandoned for demolition. Jacob can see a thin rectangle of white light filtering out from around the edges of one of the doors, though, and he walks down the hall and gives a few raps on the scuffed blond wood beneath the nameplate: HART MOSER, PHILOSOPHY CHAIR.

He waits for an answer.

"Come on in."

Jacob opens the door. Hart Moser is sitting behind an electric typewriter, his hands poised over the keyboard, a blank sheet of paper curled around the roller. Friedrich Nietzsche owned a Malling-Hansen Writing Ball, a typewriter whose circular arrangement of keys prevented him from seeing his words as they struck the page. He was, like Jacob and Thomas Aquinas, left-handed.

"You wanted to see me?" Jacob asks.

"I did." Hart switches his typewriter off, and the humming noise of its machinery slowly dwindles away. He turns and sifts through the stack of material on his desk. "Ah, here it is," he says. He peers over his glasses at a sheet of paper, silently reading a few lines. "Yes, this is it," and he holds the paper out to Jacob. "Here you go, tell me what you think."

Jacob takes it from him. It contains a description of a summer course for upper-level undergraduates contrasting the religious philosophy of the medieval Scholastics with that of the existentialists—the kind of class he has been requesting from the department for years. "Are you asking me if I want to teach this?"

"Are you interested?"

"Definitely."

Hart takes a pencil from behind his ear. "I thought you would be. The class meets Tuesdays and Thursdays from three to five. It's a ten-weeker, beginning June the second. Should I put you down?"

"Yes, yes, absolutely."

"Good." He scrawls Jacob's name on a piece of correspondence paper, punctuating it with an emphatic period. "All right then. I'll have Theresa give this to Academic Affairs first thing in the morning. So how is your dissertation coming along, may I ask?"

Jacob can tell by the tightening in his cheeks that something is happening to his face. It must be something amusing, because Hart chuckles and says, "That bad, huh?"

"No, no, it's not so bad really. I just feel a bit overwhelmed by it all. For the amount of time I spend thinking about the damn thing, I should have a magnum opus by now."

Hart says, "It's like that for everybody. Do you want to hear how long it took me to finish my dissertation after my committee gave me the go-ahead? Eight years. You know that old chestnut about what ABD stands for, don't you? 'All But Dead.' " He punches the joke with a vaudevillian cock of his eyebrows. Then he swivels back around to his typewriter. "Well, listen, Jacob, I have to get some work done before I head home to the wife and kids. Oh, and by the way—your pen is busted."

"What's that?"

"Your pen." He motions toward Jacob's hand. "It's busted."

Sure enough, the ballpoint pen Jacob has been carrying has left a gummy black stain on his palm, so thick that it crackles when he flexes his fingers. He notices an ugly black streak at the belt-line of his pants, and another on his satchel, and, as he makes his way to the bathroom to clean himself off, another on the door of the mail room. He is like a character in a comic strip, he thinks, leaving a dotted line of filth behind him. With a little soap and water he is able to wash most of the ink off his skin, but a bruiselike trace of gray remains on his palm, thickening to black where it has collected inside the lines. It will be another full week before the mark fades away entirely.

Jacob takes the elevator up to his office and checks his voice mail. There are three messages waiting for him. The first is from Audrey: "Jacob, listen, I'm not feeling so well. If you get this message, I need you to come home and give me a ride to the clinic. The sooner the better. Please hurry."

The second, also from Audrey, says, "Jacob, where are you, Jacob? I'm not kidding, I need you to—" She lets out a gasp. "Jesus, it's like a soldering iron. All right, I'm going to try to make it to the clinic on my own. I want you to meet me there as soon as you get this message. Do you hear me? *As soon as you get this message.*"

The third message is from Dr. Phillips at the college health clinic: "Jacob, this is Nate Phillips—um—over at Health Services. Listen, we need you to come in right away. Don't worry, Audrey is going to be okay. But I'm afraid there's been an accident with the baby."

When did Jacob's baby first notice the heartbeat that enveloped him, the seawatery amniotic fluid in which he floated? Was there a moment when his consciousness began to stir and he knew he was alive? Sometime in the months following his conception, he must have undergone the transformation from a simple collection of cells and enzymes to an individual human being, from a process of assembly to the person being assembled. Jacob almost believes that he can imagine what it was like. His baby lay in the warmth and buoyancy of the darkness, immersed in a sound so engulfing that it seemed like just another kind of silence. He listened to the roar of his own blood and to the roar of the blood that surrounded him. There was the occasional tick of something settling into place. He noticed a mild gurgling sound that rose up from out of nowhere and he could not be sure whether the sound was something he heard or something he was.

Now and then the baby felt a soft elastic pressure against his skin—it was Audrey pushing down on her stomach with her hand, though he could not have known that—and he threw his head back and over to the side in order to roll. Audrey stacked three quick breaths on top of one another and sneezed. The baby dove and turned like a fish. He liked to move when Audrey was still, and to rest when she was moving. Her footsteps reverberated through his body like an incantation.

His thumb was tiny, the size of a cherry pit, and sometimes, without trying, he would find that he had fit it into his mouth. He could taste a salty, coppery flavor that seemed infinitely familiar to him. The gentleness of the sensation was everything he knew. And because he did not yet exist in synchronicity with time, with no memory of the past, and no expectation of the future, he was able to believe that it had been there forever.

Did he realize what was happening when his heart stopped beating and his muscles went limp?

What did he apprehend in that one brief instant before the light filled his head?

If the baby had lived, he would have been a boy named Nicholas.

Jacob repeats the name to himself as he goes sprinting across the campus. *Nicholas*, he thinks. *Nicholas and Audrey. Nicholas and*

Jacob and Audrey. Though he leaves his office as soon as the doctor's message finishes playing, taking a shortcut across the glass atrium of the Fine Arts Building, then cutting through the alley behind the cafeteria, he can tell by the dwindling number of cars in the parking lot that a large portion of the afternoon has passed.

The early-evening patient lag has commenced at the health clinic, and the waiting room is nearly empty. A man Jacob has never seen before is staffing the admissions desk where Audrey usually works. Nobody has to tell Jacob what has happened. He knows in his gut that Audrey has suffered a miscarriage. But there is still a part of him that has yet to accept the situation as fact, a part of him that is waiting for someone to utter the words out loud.

He gives the desk clerk a few seconds to finish slotting a patient file onto its shelf. Then he interrupts him with, "Excuse me, I got a call from Dr. Phillips a while ago. My girlfriend, Audrey, is—"

"Ah. Which would make you Jacob, right? Audrey's Jacob. Yes, the doctor called you, but that was two and a half hours ago. Don't you realize what time it is?"

Though Jacob has yet to replace his missing watch, he continues to check his wrist for the time once or twice every day. He feels like a fool whenever he catches himself doing it. To the average person, he supposes, it must look as though he is bowing his head in embarrassment—as though he is only barely managing to keep himself from covering his face with his hand. "I'm sorry, I'm afraid I don't."

"Well." It might be the first time he has ever actually heard a man tut. "Audrey was transferred to St. Vincent's at four o'clock this afternoon. I presume you're on foot. Would you like me to phone a cab to take you to the hospital?"

"Yes, I would appreciate that—" He pauses to let the clerk fill in his name.

"Monty."

"I would appreciate that, Monty. Listen, can you tell me what's wrong with Audrey?"

The clerk shakes his head. "No, I think you'd better wait for one of the doctors to give you that information. I'm not qualified."

By the time Jacob arrives at the hospital, the sun has fallen into the treetops, and the sky has taken on the motionless quality of a peaceful midspring evening—a pale blue, just beginning to darken to red, and stitched together by the condensation trails of half a dozen airplanes. Jacob pays the cabdriver and then finds his way to the reception area, where a nurse directs him to the obstetrics ward on the third floor. The waiting room is almost deserted, just like the one at the health clinic. The glowing panel of a vending machine flickers on and off with a barely audible ticking noise. An old man in hard-soled shoes and a fedora sits paging through a tattered magazine. A custodian walks by carrying a push broom over his shoulder.

It takes Jacob a few minutes to find a doctor who can tell him what has happened to Audrey. *Placental abruption:* those are the words the doctor uses, and he says that although most women go into delivery within fourteen days of termination, the hospital might need to induce labor "if it looks like your wife isn't cooperating. Look, I'm sorry for your loss," he tells Jacob, placing a meaty red hand on his shoulder. "But all the indications are that Audrey—it is Audrey?"

Jacob nods.

"That Audrey is going to come through this just fine. There's no reason why the two of you won't be able to try again."

A great tidal flood of relief spreads through Jacob: relief that he knows what has happened; relief that Audrey is out of danger; even, to his surprise, relief at the prospect that the two of them might still have a child together. It seems that, without his awareness, something has locked together inside him, tumbling to one side by the very slightest of degrees. He has figured out whatever it was he was waiting to figure out. He feels an overwhelming tenderness for Audrey, an irresistible desire to comfort her. "Can you show me which room she's in?" he asks the doctor.

"She's right down the hall—go past the swinging doors and it's the first room on your left."

"Thank you so much."

Jacob finds her lying down along the exact center of her bed, entirely hidden beneath the immaculate white sheets except for her head, which is propped up on two thick pillows. She reminds him of an overturned dressmaker's model he once saw: heavy with the weight of its body, fixed in its own curves. The skin of her face is colorless and slack. Her hair is damp, and she has tucked it behind her ears.

She tracks him with her eyes as he crosses the room, but does not say anything until he pulls a chair up to the bed and brushes her cheek with the backs of his fingers. "Oh, Jacob," she whispers, and before she can go on, her face crumples and she begins to cry.

His first instinct is to hush her and hold her close to him, to pat her back as a parent would a child, but Audrey has always hated being hushed, so he stops himself and continues brushing her cheek. "It's all right," he says. "Everything is going to be okay."

"It's not going to be okay. It's not. I lost the baby. Where have you been all day?"

"I was in class this afternoon, and then I had a meeting with Professor Moser. I didn't have my phone on me, Audrey. I'm sorry."

"Dr. Phillips had to drive me here from the clinic."

"I know." He watches her take a deep breath, then clench her jaw as though a fist has gripped her stomach. He says to her, "You're not still in pain, are you?"

"No. The doctors said that that part was over."

"Have they told you what's going to happen next?"

She nods and shuts her eyes. Then she brings her hands to her face to massage her forehead. The sheets rise up in a pair of slowly moving finlike ridges that subside back into place as soon as she has worked her elbows free. She is the only woman Jacob has ever loved. "Here, let me do that for you," he says.

She lets her hands fall to her chest, and he begins rubbing the soft notches of her temples with his fingers, tracing endless tiny circles over the stray wisps of brown hair.

After a while she asks, "Have you been in a fistfight with somebody?"

It is such an unusual question that he has to laugh. "Of course not. What do you mean?"

"Your hand," she asks. "What happened to your hand?"

"Oh, that. I broke a pen. I got ink all over myself."

She nods, satisfied. A patient walks down the hallway wheeling an infusion bottle on a tall metal stand, his loose clothing rustling in the draft from the overhead vents. Audrey lifts her head to watch him shuffle past the door. Then she falls back onto her pillow, giving a long exhalation through her nostrils. Jacob can feel it blowing against the side of his face. She begins to cry again. "I really wanted this baby," she says.

"I know you did."

"I'm so exhausted."

"Then you should let yourself rest. Don't worry. I talked to the doctor, and he says we can try again whenever we're ready."

He sees Audrey's shoulders go tense, hears the mattress creak as her body bears down against it. At first he imagines it must be some spontaneous expression of gratification, the final tightening of the spring before the watch begins to tick.

But then she grits her teeth and says, "We can try again?"

"That's what the doctor told me."

Her answer is slow and quiet. "It's been six months, and *finally*, after all this time, you tell me *we can try again*. *Now* you say that? I absolutely cannot believe you." She grips his hands, which are still reflexively massaging her temples, and sets them aside like a couple of broken toys. "Please leave, Jacob."

"No, you don't understand. I—"

"Get out," she tells him, and then she says it louder: "Get out!" And she must find it satisfying to repeat the words, because she keeps yelling them even as he stands up and backs away—"Get out! Get out! Get out!"—the venom rising in her voice as he passes through the door and out of sight.

As he stands in the hallway trying to decide what to do—should he leave Audrey to her grief and anger, or should he go back in and begin the long work of explaining himself?—the answer to his other dilemma, the one he has been considering for the past two years, comes to him in an instant. It is like the concussive burst of a camera flash. He knows, or believes he knows, what Thomas Aquinas comprehended that night in his cell, what Friedrich Nietzsche perceived as he watched the horse trembling beneath the blows of the whip. He knows why the two men laid aside their pens.

Both of them had spent their lives as thinkers and writers attempting to repair the material of the past. How could the past be salvaged? How could it be used to prepare the way for the future? Aquinas joined the philosophy of Aristotle with the teachings of the Church, showing how the mechanisms of logic might open up a pathway to God. Nietzsche concluded that the traditions of Christianity were a burden that must be cast aside so that the human race could achieve the nobility that was its true inheritance. They both had such hope for the dawning era, such confidence in mankind's ability to transform itself. And then, Jacob believes, they were given a glimpse of the future. They observed the brutality in whose service their ideas would be employed, the cruelty and the barbarism. They witnessed the centuries of suffering that lay ahead. They saw how the writings of Aquinas would lead directly to the horrors of the Inquisition and how those of Nietzsche would lead to the savagery of the Second World War.

Aquinas received his vision in a candle that burned like a stake. Nietzsche received his vision in a whip that fell like a thousand bombs.

And after their visions were disclosed to them, they folded their hands together and never wrote another word. They wished their ideas had never been set to paper.

Jacob waits in the stillness of the obstetrics ward, where the only sound he can hear is a hoarse voice telling him to get out, get out. There is no change machine, he thinks. The past is irreparable and so is the future. He presses his palms to the wall and listens to Audrey weeping for the child they have lost.

THE YEAR OF SILENCE

I.

Shortly after two in the afternoon, on Monday the sixth of April, a few seconds of silence overtook the city. The rattle of the jackhammers, the boom of the transformers, and the whir of the ventilation fans all came to a halt. Suddenly there were no car alarms cutting through the air, no trains scraping over their rails, no steam pipes exhaling their fumes, no peddlers shouting into the streets. Even the wind seemed to hesitate.

We waited for the incident to pass, and when it did, we went about our business. None of us foresaw the repercussions.

2.

That the city's whole immense carousel of sound should stop at one and the same moment was unusual, of course, but not exactly inexplicable. We had witnessed the same phenomenon on a lesser scale at various cocktail parties and interoffice minglers over the years, when the pauses in the conversations overlapped to produce an air pocket of total silence, making us all feel as if we'd been caught eavesdropping on one another. True, no one could remember such a thing happening to the entire city before. But it was not so hard to believe that it would.

3.

A handful of people were changed by the episode, their lives redirected in large ways or small ones. The editor of a gossip magazine, for instance, came out of the silence determined to substitute the next issue's lead article about a movie star for one about a fashion model, while her assistant realized that the time had come for her to resign her job and apply for her teaching license. A lifelong vegetarian who was dining in the restaurant outside the art museum decided to order a porterhouse steak, cooked medium rare. A would-be suicide had just finished filling his water glass from the faucet in his bathroom when everything around him seemed to stop moving and the silence passed through him like a wave, bringing with it a sense of peace and clarity he had forgotten he was capable of feeling. He put the pill bottle back in his medicine cabinet.

Such people were the exceptions, though. Most of us went on with our lives as though nothing of any importance had happened until the next incident occurred, some four days later.

4.

This time the silence lasted nearly six seconds. Ten million sounds broke off and recommenced like an old engine marking out a pause and catching spark again. Those of us who had forgotten the first episode now remembered it. Were the two occasions connected? we wondered. And if so, how? What was it, this force that could quell all the tumult and noise of the city—and not just the clicking of the subway turnstiles and the snap of the grocery-store awnings, but even the sound of the street traffic, that oceanic rumble that for more than a century had seemed as interminable to us as the motion

of the sun across the sky? Where had it come from? And why didn't
it feel more unnatural?

These questions nettled us. We could see them shining out of
one another's eyes. But a few days passed before we began to give
voice to them. The silence was unusual, and we were not entirely
sure how to talk about it—not because it was too grave and not
because it was too trivial, but because it seemed grave one moment
and trivial the next, and so no one was quite able to decide whether
it mattered enormously or not at all.

5.

A stand-up comedian performing on one of the late-night talk
shows was the first of us to broach the subject, albeit indirectly. He
waited for a moment in his act when the audience had fallen completely still and then halted in midsentence, raising one of his index
fingers in a listening gesture. A smile edged its way onto his lips. He
gave the pause perhaps one second too long, just enough time for a
trace of self-amusement to show on his face, then continued with
the joke he had been telling.

He could not have anticipated the size of the laugh he would
receive.

6.

The next morning's newspapers had already been put to bed by the
time the comedian's routine was broadcast. The morning after that,
though, the first few editorials about the silence appeared. Then the
radio hosts and TV commentators began to talk about it, and soon
enough it was the city's chief topic of conversation. Every family
dinner bent around to it sooner or later, every business lunch, every

pillow talk. The bars and health clubs all circulated with bets about the phenomenon: *ten dollars said the government had something to do with it, twenty said it would never happen again.*

When two full weeks went by without another incident, our interest in the matter threatened to shrivel away, and might actually have done so had the next episode not occurred the following Sunday, surprising us all in the middle of our church services.

There was another silence, more than ten seconds long, just a couple of days later, and a much shorter silence, like a hiccup, the day after that.

Every time one of the silences came to an end we felt as though we had passed through a long transparent passageway, a tunnel of sorts, one that made the world into which we had emerged appear brighter and cleaner than it had before, less troubled, more humane. The silence had been siphoned out of the city and into our ears, spilling from there into our dreams and beliefs, our memories and expectations. In the wake of each fresh episode a new feeling flowed through us, full of warmth and a lazy equanimity. It took us a while to recognize the feeling for what it was: contentment.

7.

The truth was that we enjoyed the silence, and more than that, we hungered for it. Sometimes we found ourselves poised in the doorways of our homes in the morning, or on the edges of our car seats as we drove to work, trying to hear something very faint beneath the clatter of sirens and engines. Slowly we realized that we were waiting for another incident to take place.

There were weeks when we experienced an episode of silence almost every day. One particular Wednesday saw three of them in the span of a single hour. But there were others when what the papers took to calling a "silence drought" descended upon the city, and all our hopes for a cessation went in vain. If more than a few days passed without some minor lull to interrupt the cacophony, we would become irritable and overtender, quick to gnash at one another and then to rebuke ourselves for our failures of sympathy. On the other hand, a single interlude of silence might generate an aura of fellow feeling that could last for the better part of a day. The police blotters were nearly empty in the hours following a silence. The drunks in the bars turned amiable and mild. The jails were unusually tranquil. The men who ran the cockfights in the warehouses down by the docks said that their birds lost much of their viciousness after the great roar of the city had stopped, becoming as useless as pigeons, virtually impossible to provoke to violence.

And there was another effect that was just as impressive: the doctors at several hospitals reported that their mortality rates showed a pronounced decline after each incident, and their recovery rates a marked increase. No, the lame did not walk, and the blind did not see, but patients who were on the verge of recuperating from an injury often seemed to turn the corner during an episode, as if the soundlessness had triggered a decision somewhere deep in the cells of their bodies.

Surely the most dramatic example was the woman at Mercy General who came out of a prolonged coma in the space of a five-second silence. First her hand moved, then her face opened up behind her eyes, and soon after the noise of the hospital reemerged, she moistened her lips and said that everything sounded exactly the same to her.

The doctors had a hard time convincing her that she was, in fact, awake.

8.

The silence proved so beneficial to us that we began to wish it would last forever. We envisioned a city where everyone was healthy and thoughtful, radiant with satisfaction, and the sound of so much as a leaf lighting down on the sidewalk was as rare and startling as a gunshot.

9.

Who was the first person to suggest that we try generating such a silence ourselves, one that would endure until we chose to end it? No one could remember. But the idea took hold with an astonishing tenacity.

Local magazines published laudatory cover stories on the Silence Movement. Leaflets with headings like PROMOTE SILENCE and SILENCE = LIFE appeared in our mailboxes. The politicians of both major parties began to champion the cause, and it wasn't long before a measure was passed decreeing that the city would take every possible effort "to muffle all sources of noise within its borders, so as to ensure a continuing silence for its citizens and their families."

The first step, and the most difficult, was the dampening of the street traffic. We were encouraged first of all to ride the subway trains, which were appointed with all the latest noise alleviation devices, including soft-fiber pressure pads and magnetic levitation rails. Most of the cars that were left on the road were equipped with silently running electric engines, while the others had their motors fitted with mineral wool shells that allowed them to operate below the threshold of hearing. The roads themselves were surfaced with a reinforced open-cell foam that absorbed all but the lowest-frequency sounds, a material that we also adapted for use on our sidewalks and in our parking garages.

Once the street traffic was taken care of, we turned our attention to the city's other sources of noise. We sealed the electrical generators behind thick layers of concrete. We placed the air-conditioning equipment in nonresonant chambers. We redesigned the elevators and cargo lifts, replacing their metal components with a clear durable plastic originally developed by zoos as a display barrier to prevent the roars of the lions from reaching the exhibits of the prey animals. Certain noises that weren't essential to either the basic operations or the general aesthetic texture of the city were simply banned outright: canned music, church bells, fireworks, ring tones.

IO.

We were exultant when the roads fell silent and pleased when the elevators stopped crying out on their cables, but by the time the cell phones and the pagers ceased to chirp, we were faced with a problem of diminishing returns. The greater the number of sounds we extinguished, the more we noticed the ones that remained, until even the slightest tap or ripple began to seem like an assault against the silence.

A clock ticking inside a plastic casing.

Water replenishing itself in a toilet tank.

A rope slapping languidly against a flagpole.

A garbage disposal chopping at a stream of running water.

The flat buzzing of a fluorescent light.

A modem squealing its broken tune.

A deodorizer releasing its vapor into the air.

An ice maker's slow cascade of thumps.

One by one, perhaps, these sounds were of little account, but added together they grew into a single vast sonority, and no matter how many of them we were able to root out, we kept discovering others. Now and then, while we were working to eliminate the noise of a match taking light or a soda can popping open, another episode of true silence would occur, a bubble of total peace and calm enwrapping the city in its invisible walls, and we would be reminded of the magnitude of what we were striving for.

How inexcusably flimsy, we realized, was the quiet we had managed to create.

We redoubled our efforts.

I I.

We were more resourceful than we had imagined. It seemed that for every noise that cropped up, there was at least one person in the city who was prepared to counteract it. An engineer bothered by the medical helicopter that beat by his office a dozen times a day drew up plans for a special kind of rotor blade, one that would slice through the air as smoothly as a pin sliding into a pincushion. He handed the plans over to the hospital, and within a few weeks the helicopter drifted so quietly past his window that he was surprised each time he saw it there.

A single mother raising an autistic son who was provoked to fits of punching by the tone of her doorbell devised an instrument that replaced the sound with a pulsing light. She said that her son liked to sit on the floor watching now as she pressed the button again and again, a wobbly grin spreading over his face like a pool of molasses.

A carpenter designed a nail gun that would soak up the noise of its own thud. A schoolteacher created a frictionless pencil sharpener. An antiques dealer who liked to dabble in acoustic engineering invented a sonic filter that could comb the air of all its sounds before releasing it into a room.

Eventually every noise but the muffled sigh of our breathing and the ticking of our teeth in our mouths had been removed from inside our buildings. The wind continued to blow, and the rain continued to fall, and no one had yet proposed a method to keep the birds from singing, but as long as we did not venture outside, we remained sealed in a cocoon of silence.

12.

There were times when the silence was close to perfect. Whole minutes went by after the early morning light breached the sky when the surging, twisting world of sound left us completely alone and we could lie there in our beds simply following our ruminations. We came to know ourselves better than we had before—or, if not better, then at least in greater stillness. It was easier for us to see the shapes we wished our lives to take. People changed their jobs, took up chess or poker, began new courses of exercise. A great many couples made their marriage vows, and not a few others filed for divorce.

One boy, an eight-year-old who attended the Holy Souls Parochial Academy, left school as the rest of his class was walking to the lunchroom, rode the subway to the natural history museum, and found his way to the dinosaur exhibit. He waited until the room had emptied out and then stole beneath the tyrannosaurus, using the giant ribs of the skeleton to climb up to the skull. He was found there late that evening by a security guard, sitting hungry but uninjured on the smoothly curving floor of the jaw. The boy had left a note in his teacher's paper tray explaining himself. He had dreamed that the dinosaur was still roaring, the note said, but so weakly that the sound could be heard only from directly inside its head. He wanted to find out if it was true.

13.

The boy who climbed the tyrannosaurus was not the first of us to feel that his dreams were blending together with his reality. There was something about the luxuriousness of our situation that made it tempting to imagine that the space outside our heads was conforming to the space inside. Yet we did not really believe that this was so. It was just that we were seeing everything with a greater clarity now, both our minds and our surroundings, and the clarity had become more important to us than the division.

14.

The silence was plain and rich and deep. It seemed infinitely delicate, yet strangely irresistible, as though any one of us could have broken it with a single word if we had not been so enraptured. Every so often another natural episode would take place, and for a few seconds the character of the silence would change slightly, the way the brightness of a room might alter as some distant roller in the current surged through a lightbulb. But the quiet we had generated was so encompassing by now that only the most sensitive among us could be sure that something had truly happened.

15.

In the abundant silence we proceeded into ourselves. We fell asleep each night, woke each morning, and went about our routines each day, doing the shopping and preparing our tax returns, making love and cooking dinner, filing papers and cupping our palms to our mouths to check the smell of our breaths, all in the beautiful hush of the city. Everywhere we could see the signs of lives in fluctuation.

A librarian who had worked in the periodicals room for almost three decades began displaying her oil paintings at an art gallery— hundreds of them, all on lending slips she had scavenged from the library's in/out tray, each tiny piece of paper flexed with the weight of the paint that had hardened onto it. The flyers at the gallery door proclaimed that the woman had never had the nerve to show her work before the silence was established.

The bursar at the university was caught skimming money from the school's pension fund. In her letter of resignation, she said she was ashamed only that she had been found out. If there was one thing the silence had taught her, she wrote, it was that any grief that befell a professor emeritus could never be more than a fraction of what he deserved.

A visiting gymnast giving an exhibition on the pommel horse at the midtown sports club fractured his wrist while he was doing a routine scissor movement. But up until the moment of the accident, he reported, the audience in the city was the most respectful he had ever seen, barely a cough or a rustle among them.

16.

Gradually, as we grew used to the stillness, the episodes of spontaneous and absolute silence came less frequently. There might be a three-second burst one week, followed by a one-second flicker a few weeks later, and then, if the episodes were running exceptionally heavy, another one-second echo a week or two after that.

One of the physicists at the city's Lakes and Streams Commission came up with what he called a "skipping-rock model" to describe the pattern. The distribution of the silences, he suggested, was like that of a rock skipping over the water and then, if one could imagine such a thing, doubling back and returning to shore. At first such a rock would land only rarely, but as it continued along its path, it would strike down more and more rapidly, until eventually the water would seize it and it would sink. But then, according to the paradigm, the rock would be ejected spontaneously through the surface to repeat its journey in reverse, hitting the water with increasing rarity until it landed back in the hand of the man who had thrown it.

The physicist could not explain why the silence had adopted this behavior, he said—or who, if anyone, had thrown it—he could only observe that it had.

17.

A time came some eight months after the first incident took place when it had been so long since anyone had noticed one of the episodes that it seemed safe to presume they were finished.

The city was facing an early winter. Every afternoon a snow of soft fat flakes would drift gently down from the sky, covering the trees and the pavilions, the mailboxes and the parking meters. Recalling the way the snow used to soften the noise of the traffic made us experience a flutter of helpless nostalgia. Everything was different now. The sound of our footsteps creaking over the fresh accumulation was like a horde of crickets scraping their wings together in an empty room.

Not until we walked through the snow did we really discover how accustomed we had grown to the silence.

18.

We might have been content to go on as we were forever, whole generations of us being born into the noiseless world, learning to crawl and stand and tie our shoes, growing up and then apart, setting our pasts aside, and then our futures, and finally dying and becoming as quiet in our minds as we had been in our bodies, had it not been for another event that came to pass.

It was shortly after nine a.m., on Tuesday, January the twenty-sixth, when a few seconds of sound overtook the city. There was a short circuit in the system of sonic filters we had installed in the buildings, and for a moment the walls were transparent to every noise. The engine of a garbage truck suddeny I backfired. A cat began to yowl. A rotten limb dropped from a tree and shattered the veneer of ice that lay over a pond. Ten thousand people struck their knees on the corner of a desk or remembered a loss they had forgotten or slid into an orgasm beneath the bodies of their lovers and cried out in pain or grief or sexual ecstasy.

The period of noise was abrupt and explosive, cleanly defined at both its borders. Instinctively we found ourselves twisting around to look for its source. Then the situation corrected itself, and just like that we were reabsorbed in the silence.

It seemed that the city had been opened like a tin can. So much time had gone by since we had heard our lives in their full commotion that we barely recognized the sound for what it was. The ground might have fallen in. The world might have ended.

19.

Four days later another such incident occurred, this one almost eight seconds long. It was followed the next week by a considerably shorter episode, as brief as a coal popping in a fire, which was itself followed a few days later by a fourth episode, and immediately after by a fifth and a sixth, and early the next afternoon by a seventh.

We were at a loss to account for the phenomenon.

A cryptographer employed by the police force announced his belief that both the episodes of silence and the episodes of clamor resembled communications taking the form of Morse code, though from whom or what he could not say. A higher intelligence? The city itself? Any answer he might give would be no more than specula-tion. His hunch was that the sender, whoever it was, had resorted to using noise because we had ceased to take note of the silence. He said that he was keeping a record of the dots and dashes and hoped to be able to decipher the message very soon.

20.

The cryptographer's theory bore all the earmarks of lunacy, and few of us pretended to accept it, but it was, at least, a theory. Every so often another event would transpire, interrupting the stillness with a burst of shouts and rumbles, and we would stop whatever we were doing, our arms and shoulders braced as if against some invisible blow, and wonder what was going on. Many of us began to look for-ward to these eruptions of sound. We dreamed about them at night, awaiting them with a feeling of great thirst. The head of the city's Notary Public Department, for instance, missed the noise of the Newton's Cradle he kept in his office, the hanging metal balls click-ing *tac-tac-tac* against one another as they swayed back and forth. The cabdriver who began his circuit outside the central subway ter-minal every morning wished that he was still able to punch his horn at the couriers who skimmed so close to his bumper on their bicy-cles. The woman who ran the Christian gift store in the shopping mall designed a greeting card with an illustration of a trio of kittens playing cymbals, bagpipes, and a tuba on the front. The interior caption read MAKE A JOYFUL NOISE UNTO THE LORD. She printed out a hundred copies to stock by the cash register, along with twenty-three more to mail to the members of her Sunday school class.

21.

It turned out that in spite of everything the silence had brought us, there was a hidden longing for sound in the city. So many of us shared in this desire that a noise club began operating, tucked away in the depths of an abandoned recording studio. The people who went to the club did so for the pure excitement of it, for the way the din set their hearts to beating. Who needed serenity? they wanted to know. Who had ever asked for it? They stood in groups listening to the club's switchboard operator laying sound upon sound in the small enclosed space of the room. The slanting note of a violin. The pulse of an ambulance siren. A few thousand football fans cheering at a stadium. Gallons of water geysering from an open hydrant.

Afterward, when the club's patrons arrived home, they lay on their pillows unable to fall asleep, their minds spinning with joy and exhilaration.

22.

The episodes continued into the spring, falling over the city at intervals none of us could predict. Whenever we became most used to the silence, it seemed, the fundamental turmoil of the world would break through the tranquillity and present itself to us again. More and more people began to prefer these times of disruption. They made us feel like athletes facing a game, like soldiers who had finished their training, capable of accomplishing great things in battle.

A consensus slowly gathered among us. We had given up something important, we believed: the fire, the vigor, that came with a lack of ease. We had lost some of the difficulty of our lives, and we wanted it back.

23.

The city council drafted a measure to abolish the silence initiative. After a preliminary period of debate and consideration, it was adopted by common consent. The work of breaking the city's silence was not nearly as painstaking as the work of establishing it had been. With the flip of a few switches and the snip of a few wires, the sonic filters that had sheltered our buildings were disabled, opening our walls up to every birdcall and thunderclap. Scrapers and bulldozers tore up the roads, and spreading machines laid down fresh black asphalt. The cloth was unwound from the clappers of the church bells. The old city buses were rolled out of the warehouses. A fireworks stand was erected by the docks, and a gun club opened behind the outlet mall. A man in a black suit carried an orange crate into the park one evening to preach about the dangers of premarital sex. A man with a tattoo of a teardrop on his cheek set three crisply folded playing cards on a table and began shuffling them in intersecting circles, calling out to the people who walked by that he would offer two dollars, two clean new, green new, George Washington dollar bills, to anyone who could find that lovely lady, that lady in red, the beautiful queen of hearts.

24.

In a matter of weeks, we could hear cell phones ringing in restaurants again, basketballs slapping the pavement, car stereos pouring their music into the air. Everywhere we went we felt a pleasurable sense of agitation. And if our interactions with one another no longer seemed like the still depths of secluded pools, where enormous fish stared up at the light sifting down through the water—well, the noise offered other compensations.

We became more headstrong, more passionate. Our sentiments were closer to the surface. Our lives seemed no less purposeful than they had during the silence, but it was as if that purpose were waiting several corners away from us now, rather than hovering in front of our eyes.

For a while the outbreaks of sound continued to make themselves heard over the noise of the city, just as the outbreaks of silence had, but soon it became hard to distinguish them from the ongoing rumble of the traffic. There were a few quick flashes of noise during the last week of May, but if they carried on into the summer, we failed to notice them. In their place were dogs tipping over garbage cans, flatbed trucks beeping as they backed out of alleys, and fountains spilling into themselves again and again.

The quiet that sometimes fell over us in movie theaters began to seem as deep as any we had ever known. We had a vague inkling that we had once experienced our minds with a greater intimacy, but we could not quite recover the way it had felt.

25.

Every day the silence that had engulfed the city receded further into the past. It was plain that in time we would forget it had ever happened. The year that had gone by would leave only a few scattered signs behind, like the imprints of vanished shells in the crust of a dried lake bed: the exemplary hush of our elevators, the tangles of useless wire in our walls, and the advanced design of our subway lines, fading slowly into antiquation. That and a short item published in the Thursday, July the eighth, edition of the morning newspaper, a letter detailing the results of the log the police department's cryptographer had been keeping, a repeating series of dots and dashes whose meaning was explicit, he said, but whose import he could not fathom. Dot, dot. Dot, dot, dot. Dash. Dot. Dash, dot. Dot, dash, dash. Dot. Dot, dash, dot, dot. Dot, dash, dot, dot. Dot, dash, dot, dot.

A FABLE WITH A PHOTOGRAPH
OF A GLASS MOBILE ON THE WALL

Once there was a cabinetmaker who had lived all his life in the same small town. There was a workshop along the western wall of his house, and in the afternoon, when the sun came pouring through the windows, he could be found there planing and turning and sanding pieces of walnut or cherry wood, coaxing himself along with phrases like "Take care it doesn't split along the grain" and "A little bit narrower at the base, I think." Eventually the light would become peculiar, its edges softening into shadow, and he would step back from his bench and survey the work he had done: a half-finished wardrobe or a dresser waiting to be stained. The bands of pale and dark wood seemed to pulse like waves in the fading light. When he heard the clink of silverware in the kitchen, he would give his equipment a quick wipe down, wash the sawdust from his hands, and sit down to dinner with his wife and boy.

The cabinetmaker enjoyed his trade so much that he rarely gave himself a day off. Sometimes, though, when the sky was gray and he could not make out the contours of the sun, he would put his boots on and take a long afternoon walk. There was a high school with a football field and a set of metal bleachers, a courthouse with a galvanized tin cupola, and a dance hall that stood empty in the middle of the week, haloed by gnats and moths, but that filled with music every weekend. Birds passed in and out of the hardwood forest on the far side of the meadow, and the stream that ran past the little stone church smelled like the snow from the fold of the mountains, a wonderful fresh smell of nothing living and nothing dying. The cabinetmaker's wife might come with him if the bank was closed, and his boy, too, if the schools were on holiday. A tremendous feeling of pride and satisfaction would wash over him whenever the three of them walked through the town together. It was the one place in the world where he truly felt familiar to himself.

The cabinetmaker had never considered himself an artist, only a craftsman, but as he approached middle age, he developed a richer intuitive sense of the woods he used: which knots would weaken a board and which would lend it distinction, how dark a particular piece would become after he applied the stain, how much a joint would expand and along which plane when the humidity rose. His reputation spread, and he began to take orders from other nearby communities and occasionally even from the big cities on the coast. He was a rarity, apparently—a joiner who did all his own work, using only local timber.

Then someone wrote a profile of his cabinetry for a magazine called *Fine Furniture*, and suddenly everything changed.

It started with the letters, which began arriving a few days after the article was published, forwarded to him in bundles of twenty or thirty by the magazine's managing editor.

I recently read the feature story about you entitled "Artisan of the Sticks," and I was wondering, do you also do sofas?

Do you have a web address? You really ought to have a web address.

We at Design Expressions wish to distribute your furniture directly to discriminating consumers from each of our more than one hundred stores nationwide.

Then came the second wave. Every afternoon, from the shelter of his workshop, the cabinetmaker was interrupted by dozens of phone calls from journalists and retailers, carpentry societies and parents looking for wedding gifts. It became harder and harder for him to find the time and the silence he needed to understand the wood he was trying to shape, the secrets it held in its rings and fibers. It would not be long, he thought, before cars and minivans started nosing up to his yard, coughing blue smoke into the air as they disgorged round after round of passengers.

One evening at dinner, listening to him complain about how little work he had gotten done that day, his wife said, "You know, you don't have to answer every single phone call that comes in."

But he *did* have to answer every single phone call: there was a conscientiousness about him that could not stand to ignore them.

"Well, then maybe you should think about taking a little break," she said as he sat stirring his peas together with his mashed potatoes. And although he had never before considered such a thing, the idea must have appealed to him, for a few days later, when he received a call from a small Northeastern college asking him if he would like to serve as a visiting professor in their woodworking program that fall, he surprised himself by accepting.

He had grown so accustomed to his town that it was hard for him to imagine living anywhere else, even for only a few months. What would he do without his wife and son? he wondered. What would he do without his workshop, with its fine clear sunlight and its smell of walnut and cherry? And then there were the little things: the sight of the radio tower winking above the hills at night, the sound of the trees rattling after an ice storm, the rhythm of the automatic doors at the grocery store, the grasshoppers that sprang up from the fields like sparks from a bonfire—what would he do without those?

Yet he had agreed to take the job, and the day soon came when he had to say good-bye to his family, squeezing the back of his son's neck and tucking a lock of hair behind his wife's ear, and climb aboard the plane that would carry him to a city he had never seen before, a city of asphalt and washed yellow brick, so that he could move into the house he had arranged to sublet for the semester.

There is something innately sad about other people's homes. The rooms are crowded with the thousand-odd belongings that mark the presence of someone else's daily life: lamps and rugs, books and dishes, all of them gathered together in a process as slow and unthinking as the one by which a stream carves its way into the earth and dries up. You can walk along the bed of such a stream, you can trace the tooling lines left by the current, but you will never taste so much as a single drop of water. Other people's homes present you with the same ornate sense of emptiness. This is never so obvious as when the people who live there have gone away.

The couple who owned the house where the cabinetmaker was staying were spending the fall in Italy, and their son had just left for his freshman year of college. The cabinetmaker felt as though he drifted over the floors of their home almost weightlessly, sleeping in their bed and drinking from their glasses without leaving the slightest trace of himself. He was always surprised when he found one of his fingerprints on the bathroom faucet or one of his stray hairs on the pillow. The Atlantic was only a few blocks away, and he could smell the salt in the air whenever he cracked open a window. Much of the furniture the couple owned was brushed steel and glass, though he was pleased to see that their two or three wood pieces—a dresser in the guest room, a sideboard in the dining room—were neatly constructed of Norway maple. The classes he taught were all in the morning, and on those afternoons when he would ordinarily have been shut away in his workshop with his thicknesser and his trying plane, he wandered around the house reflecting upon the various possessions he found. An oven timer in the shape of a pear. A hanging display of herb sachets. A Ping-Pong table with a loose net.

Most of all there were the photographs that decorated the walls, small clusters of them in every room, capturing the child of the family at every phase of his life. Here he stood propped in the fork of a willow, tilting his head to look at the camera. There he occupied the stage in front of his high-school orchestra, grimacing slightly as he drew a bow across his cello. And over there he sat in a terry-cloth shirt with a frog and a bee stitched onto the front, dreamily poking his finger into his belly button.

Anyone could see how much his parents loved the boy, and as the cabinetmaker looked at the pictures, he thought with some small pensiveness of his own son, wondering how he was getting along with his new teacher and whether his wife had been able to convince him to give his bicycle another try.

The photos the cabinetmaker found the most puzzling were massed together in the front hallway: eighteen of them, of any subject or none at all, including a blurred image of somebody's sneaker, a closeup of a pretty girl in a woollen hat, a picture of what appeared to be the band of light along the bottom of a closed door, and a shot of a stained-glass mobile made up of five red, blue, and yellow fish, taken from directly underneath. It looked as if someone had fired off the pictures without even bothering to glance through the eyepiece.

There was no way the cabinetmaker could have known that this was exactly what had happened, that the images had all been captured by the same boy he could see perching in the willow tree and playing his cello, one on each of his eighteen birthdays, a tradition that began the day his parents left the camera in his crib and he accidentally released the shutter, taking the picture of the glass mobile.

Nor could he have known that while he was lying awake in bed at night, unable to fall asleep without the slowly swaying whisper of his wife's breathing beside him, the boy in the pictures was lying awake, too, staring at his dorm-room ceiling and wishing he were back home.

Nor, finally, could he have known that as he passed from one end of the house to the other, listening to his footsteps and gazing at the photographs on the walls, the photographs were gazing back at him. It is no easy thing to wrest yourself away from a place where you have grown into your habits, and no matter how hard you try, some part of you is bound to remain behind. There was a fragment of the boy that had never left the house at all, just as there was a fragment of the cabinetmaker that was still tending the machines in his workshop and sitting down to dinner with sawdust all over his clothes. This fragment of the boy watched the cabinetmaker from out of the flat blue eyes of the photographs, following his movements with great curiosity. Why did he sleep so long in the morning? What did it mean when he laced his hands together and sighed through his nose? What did it mean when he started laughing, suddenly, out of a dead quiet?

The boy in the pictures did not always understand the man, but the more he watched him, the more he grew to like him. Every day, for instance, in plain view of the photo magnets on the refrigerator, the cabinetmaker made a sandwich for himself out of luncheon meat and Swiss cheese, and every day his face gave a pucker of revulsion as he ate it. The boy in the superhero pajamas thought this expression of distaste was the funniest sight he had ever seen, the boy in the Cub Scout uniform showed a curling little smile as he looked on, and even the boy in the graduation gown found the phenomenon strange but somehow endearing: What was the story here? Was it the only sandwich the man knew how to make?

The boy in the framed portrait that stood on the desk in the study learned that he could listen to the cabinetmaker as he spoke on the phone at night. He said things like "No, the classes are going fairly well, actually. I don't know how I'm doing it, but they really seem to be learning something," and "That makes only the second call this week, doesn't it? It looks like all the fuss is finally dying down," and "I'm just so exhausted by the end of the day," and "I miss you, too, honey," and "Give him a kiss from his dad, will you? And tell him he'd better not forget me." Afterward, when the cabinetmaker hunched over to rest his forehead on the desk, the boy wished he could reach out of the picture frame and pat him on the back, as his parents had always done for him whenever he had a bad day at school.

The boys on the wall of the family room, their faces dimmed by more than a decade of sunlight, watched the cabinetmaker from their swing sets and their bumper cars, eavesdropping as he practiced his lectures. They did not always follow the meaning of his words, but they liked the way he paced back and forth between the stereo and the television, flinging his hands around like someone conducting a symphony. "You can't just fit a few boards together and expect to have a lasting piece of furniture," he said. "You have to pay attention to the direction of the grain and the features of the particular wood you're using. Personally, I've always felt that it's best to choose a wood that's native to the landscape where you're working. Wood isn't like steel or plastic, after all. It comes from life, and even after you cut the roots and drain the sap, it continues to live in some way. It shrinks and expands with the seasons. It weighs more on a rainy day than it does on a dry one—did you know that? My point is that when you remove a piece of wood from the environment in which it has grown, it's much more likely to warp or break on you."

The cascade of words came to a stop every so often as the cabinetmaker stood before the wall of photographs thinking through some idea that had occurred to him. Once, he reached out and brushed the cheek of the boy sitting behind the wheel of a tractor.

The boy felt the touch as a soft wind blowing from the direction of the stables.

The cabinetmaker lived in the house for four months. The individual days seemed long and slow to pass, but the weeks went by more quickly than he would have imagined possible. The leaves turned colors, and the frost took the vines, and soon he was folding his clothes and finishing off the food he had bought and filling the giant filing cabinet in his head with the last time for this and the last time for that. It was the last time he would wash this glass. It was the last time he would empty this drawer. It was the last time he would open a window and breathe in the ocean air, with its great bold pinching smell of everything living and everything dying. The cabinetmaker had spent so many hours in the presence of the boy in the pictures that he barely noticed him anymore, but he could have seen him walking down the street at any stage of his life, and instantly he would have recognized him.

When he finally locked the door and slid the key under the mat, the boy was sorry to see him go. The house seemed bare and lifeless without him. A silence soaked into the rooms. The furniture stood peacefully in the shadows. The only sign of motion was inside the photographs on the walls, where the bow swept across the cello, the leaves of the willow shivered in the breeze, and the glass fish swam in leisurely circles through the air.

FATHER JOHN MELBY AND
THE GHOST OF AMY ELIZABETH

On Sunday the tenth of September, as Father John Melby stood groping his way through yet another sermon, he was taken aback by the sensation that one of his parishioners was listening to him—and not only listening, but listening with total absorption. Father Melby had never been a very good preacher. No matter how carefully he prepared his sermons, when it came time for him to take the pulpit, his words would go loose at the joints and scatter into the air like a thousand blackbirds dispersing at the crack of a gunshot. And yet suddenly, for no reason he could imagine, he had managed to excite someone's attention.

Was it Mrs. Kiesig, sitting with her three children by the offertory, her lips pursed energetically around a cough drop? Or Mr. Passarello, whose oldest son Father Melby had visited just last Wednesday in the Recovery Center? Or was it Katie Becker, all brushed and straightened in the second row, who he was fairly certain had taken to flirting with him at the church's monthly service meetings? It was impossible to tell.

The scrutiny he felt seemed infinitely charitable, and it caused his entire manner to change. His shoulders lifted, his voice took on vigor, and his thoughts began to come clear and strong. He looked out over the pews of St. Andrew's and saw the faces of his congregation slowly lifting free of their ordinary polite expressionlessness, a hundred little candles taking flame in the dark. The original spark of attention was still hanging in the air somewhere, but it was soon joined by so many others that it was nearly imperceptible, and try as he might, he could not trace it back to its source. Even so, it gave him a feeling of balance, of composure, and it was that feeling more than anything else that propelled him to the end of his sermon.

He knew as he finished that every single person in the sanctuary was aware of the change that had come over him. For once the air was empty of that rainlike rustling sound that a thousand restless fingers made creasing programs and paging through hymnals. After the benediction, when he took his place by the front door, he could hear the shock of sincerity in his parishioners' voices as they offered him their compliments.

That was something else this morning, Father.

My husband sends his regrets. I think he'll really be sorry to hear what he missed this time.

A pleasure that was . . . as always, of course, Father, as always.

Father Melby pressed their hands and smiled, saying his thank-yous in a voice no louder than a whisper. He was as baffled as they were.

Over the next few days he found himself wondering whether he had only imagined that initial flicker of interest coming from some undefined pair of eyes in the congregation. It had always embarrassed him that he was such a feeble speaker. Years ago, he had handed himself over to the priesthood with all his heart. His weaknesses were not hidden from him, but he had never stopped believing that God would provide him with the strength to overcome them. So maybe he had truly turned a corner, he thought. Maybe God had reached down and given him his voice. Maybe, and at long last, he had settled into the pulpit.

But the next Sunday, when it came time for him to deliver his sermon, he discovered that he was the same preacher he had always been, stumbling for purchase up a rickety staircase of words. He could hear the hesitancy in his voice, the awful timidity. He watched as young Jeffrey Rohrenbeck, nestled between his parents in the second row, began drawing on a leaflet with one of the church's little yellow half pencils. A trickle of cold sweat rolled down his side, soaking through his T-shirt and into his vestments. Then, suddenly, he felt it again, that pure white focal point of concentration arising from somewhere in the pews, and once more he began to speak with confidence.

A week later the same thing happened—at the very second he imagined despondency was going to strip him of his voice altogether, he sensed that someone was listening to him, and he became caught up in the current of his sermon. And the week after that, it happened yet again. By then the news of his transformation had spread, and the sanctuary was nearly full. Was it wrong to feel elated by the sight of so many people leaning forward in their seats to hear what he was going to say? Even the children, it seemed, were stretched tight with curiosity.

Later that day, in the silence of his office, he came to a realization. It was God, God and no one else, who kept fixing His attention upon him. God was watching over him—as He watched over everybody, of course—but with one essential difference: in Father Melby's time of need, in the moment of his despair, God had allowed him to sense the warmth of His gaze. That was why the scrutiny Father Melby felt was so exalting and yet so difficult to pinpoint: it was coming from everywhere at once.

For the next few days Father Melby seemed to view the world through a curtain of bright and rippling water. Entire hours might pass when he would forget that God had taken on a deeper presence in his church, and then, without warning, something would catch in the back of his mind and he would remember, like a new bride remembering she was married, and he would smile at the thought of the strange and lovely turn his life had taken.

He slept in the vicarage on the second floor of the building. One night, as he was lying in bed thinking over the latest manifestation of God beneath the oak rafters and hanging brass lamps of the sanctuary, he became aware of an unusual sound, a tiny arrhythmic clicking noise, like marbles falling one by one through the inside of the wall. As he listened, he realized he had heard the sound before—had heard it several nights in a row, in fact—but always just as he was dropping off to sleep, when it was easy to allow it to fade into his fantasies.

Tonight, though, he was wide awake. He decided to get out of bed and investigate.

He put on his slippers and tightened the belt on his robe. The sound seemed to be emanating from a spot directly above his mahogany dresser, midway between the mirror and the crucifix. As soon as he put his ear to the wall, though, it went away. Despite several minutes of careful listening, he wasn't able to make it out again.

He was just about to return to bed when it started up in another place, this time coming from the darkness of the hallway. He followed it through the door and across the carpet. Once again, though, when he bent in for a closer listen, the sound vanished and reappeared somewhere else, almost ten yards away, at the landing by the bend of the staircase.

Father John Melby began to feel as though he were falling for some sort of elaborate trick, reaching for a dollar bill that someone kept yanking away with a fishing line, but just the same he decided to pursue the sound downstairs. He followed it past the altar and through the chapel, threading his way between one set of pews and another, until finally he came to a stop in the alcove that held the statue of the Virgin Mary. One last noise passed through the wall, a sudden cluster of surprisingly insistent knocks that reminded him of the odd metallic percussions of the radiator in the basement, before the sound fell flat to the floor.

A votive candle was still burning on the pricket, which was unusual. The only candles the church provided had thirty-minute wicks, and, since he locked the doors every night at precisely ten o'clock, they ought to have burned out already. On any number of occasions, in fact, Father Melby had sat on the bench until ten thirty to watch the last few wicks send scribbles of black smoke into the air.

He was debating whether to extinguish the candle himself when a little breeze came sailing in from somewhere, snuffed the flame out between its finger pads, and immediately fell still.

Father Melby must have been cold, because the hairs on the back of his neck stood on end.

The sound in the walls did not return, and the next morning, when he woke up, he had great trouble convincing himself he had heard anything at all.

The Sunday that followed was his most successful yet. The pews were so full that he had to send the altar boys to erect a row of folding chairs in the back of the sanctuary. Even then, the size of the crowd required that a number of parishioners volunteer to spend the service standing on their feet. Every time the front door opened, Father Melby allowed his gaze to pass out over the lawn to the sea of cars glimmering in the parking lot, more cars than he had ever seen at the church before. It was as though a second Easter had taken hold of the congregation.

He began his sermon with the same terrible nervousness as always, that watery sensation in his knees and in his stomach, but God was much quicker to come to his aid this time. He found his self-assurance within seconds. All of a sudden it was as if his voice were traveling through him from somewhere else, a cool and pleasantly sunlit place where the wind sent ripples through the soft, high grass. His mind was luminous. His words perfectly filled their own shapes. He could see what the Pentecostalists meant when they talked about the Spirit flowing through their bodies.

After the service, the receiving line came together in the central aisle like a river taking form from a hundred different streams. Father Melby stood at the door to greet his parishioners as they left, his face tingling with the kind of blood-heat he imagined long distance runners must experience after winning a race.

That was one heck of a Mass today, Father, Simon McCallister said, smacking his shoulder. One *heck* of a Mass. My dad would have been here, but he's laid up in the hospital with a bout of the sepsis.

Father Melby shook his head. I'll say a prayer for him. And let me know his room number. I'll make time to visit later this week.

Next in line was Paul Pulido, who attended church every Sunday. Usually he sat as lightly as a sparrow at the far end of the back pew, fluttering faithfully out the side door as soon as Father Melby had delivered the benediction, but not, for some reason, today. Today he left by the front door, and though Father Melby could not imagine why, he sounded obscurely embarrassed as he quoted from the morning's sermon. *The action of God in our own hearts and spirits.* You've really given me something to ponder there, Father.

Well, I'm glad to hear it, Paul. He watched the man open his mouth as if to say something else, then shake his head and blink a few times before slouching away. There was no one alive who did not contribute his share of mystery to the world.

Madeline Quinn covered her mouth as she spoke. Gene Barrett gave him a military salute. One of the Davidson boys accidentally stepped on his shoe. Katie Becker rubbed her finger along the inside of his wrist as she took his hand. He stiffened his arm and let his face go blank, trying his best not to allow her to think he was yielding to the gesture.

Soon the last few members of the congregation were gone, and Father Melby was standing alone in the doorway. Sometimes, after the church emptied out, he could swear that he was still able to hear the din of the crowd lingering around him, as if the whole immense bubble of voices and footfalls had been absorbed into the walls and was gradually leaching back into the air. He walked through the dull cascade, knowing it would be hours before the full silence of the building was restored.

Later that week he was in the confessional, offering absolution to the day's penitents, when there was a brief pause in the procession and he gave himself a few seconds to rest his eyes. Father Melby was used to dropping off easily when he went to bed at night, but ever since he had followed the noise of marbles downstairs to find the votive candle burning, his sleeping patterns had become erratic, and by midafternoon every day his energy began to flag. Perhaps that was why he failed to notice the sound of footsteps approaching before the curtain on the other side of the booth opened. The sanctuary light came scissoring through the darkness, and he opened his eyes, preparing himself to enact the familiar ritual.

Immediately he could sense that whoever had entered the booth was sad and solemn, strangely willful, with a presence that was somehow plainly feminine.

The usual "Forgive me, Father" was slow to arrive.

After some time had passed and no one had spoken, Father Melby asked, Do you wish to begin, my child?

There was no answer. The wooden grate that separated the two chambers of the confessional was composed of a dense pattern of St. Andrew's crosses and fleurs-de-lis, and the gaps were so slender that he could never see more than the vague conformation of a face through them, along with an occasional flash of muted color, but at the moment he failed to spy even so much as a single curve of skin. All he could detect was a soft rhythm of breathing, like water lapping gently over a shoal of small, rounded pebbles, and that peculiar aura of sadness and femininity.

How long has it been since your last confession? Father Melby asked.

Then he said, Can you hear me?

Then he said, Hello?

And maybe it was simply his exhaustion, but he had a sudden blossoming sensation in his head that made him feel as though he had become unfastened from the forward motion of time. How many minutes went by? He wasn't sure. But a voice finally answered, faintly but carefully, offering each word up to him like a berry picked delicately off a stalk. I'm afraid that I wasted my life.

Why do you say that? Father Melby asked.

I am here. I can feel that it's true.

Father Melby responded in his gentlest tone. The Church teaches us that a wasted life is a mark of idleness. Idleness is indeed a grave sin. But in the eyes of God, no life is truly a waste until it's over. You still have time to change yourself, my child.

The woman on the other side of the confessional gave a one-note sigh. No, she said.

You do. You have time. You can't give up on yourself.

It's not myself I've given up on, she said. It's time, and he heard the faint sound of her fingers brushing over the grate. Can you help me?

How? How would you like me to help you?

But before she could answer, the curtain opened again. The gaps between the fleurs-de-lis were filled with a white light, and the next thing he saw was the hunched outline of an old man taking the bench. The nimbus of barely restrained grief had disappeared. A throaty voice announced, Forgive me, Father, for I have sinned.

Where did she go? Father Melby asked.

What was that? Hold on a minute. The old man's hearing aid gave a ventilating whistle. Okay, now, what was that?

The woman who was just in the confessional. Where did she go?

Mrs. Bruno, do you mean? She was lingering over by the holy water when I came in. Do you want me to go out and fetch her?

Mrs. Bruno was a retired hairdresser whose skin bore an indomitable odor of rose oil and baking flour—definitely not the woman who had been speaking to him. Father Melby felt something twitching in his lap and saw that his hands were sifting instinctively through his rosary beads.

No. No, I'm sorry. Tell me, how long has it been since your last confession?

Over the next few days he continued to think about the woman in the confessional. He wondered who she was and how he might have helped her. Where had she gone when the curtain opened? Why couldn't he pick her out from among the members of his congregation? He would be sitting at his desk trying to fit together the puzzle pieces of a sermon when all at once he would find himself reflecting on the timbre of her voice, fragile and whispery, so very unlike that of the other voices he knew. Or he might be organizing the pamphlets on the literature stand when he would glimpse the tail of one of the banners twisting against the wall and for just a moment he would suppose that it was her, leaning over to straighten a loose stocking. He was sleeping well again, deeply and without interruption, but often, just before he woke in the morning, he would sense that atmosphere of gentle sorrow he had noticed in the confessional, and in the last few crumbling seconds of his dreams he would imagine she had been sharing his bed.

Sunday by Sunday, the audience for his sermons kept growing. The altar boys added row after row of folding chairs to the back of the sanctuary, and when the back of the sanctuary was full, along the side aisles. It seemed that no matter what subject Father Melby chose to address—the parable of the vine and the branches, the visions of St. Lucy, the story of Jacob and Potiphar's wife—the ideas that came to him were shapely and true. It was as if his words were being incised into the air as he spoke. He could feel the members of the church becoming more involved with every syllable.

He recognized the phenomenon for what it was, a miracle of God's grace, but he knew better than to tell anybody about it. He had always been afraid that his voice would desert him at the pulpit, but now he found himself nursing the opposite fear: that he would become too sure of his skill, losing his modesty before the Lord. It was the smallest of distances between pride and vanity, after all, and he was oddly relieved now by that moment of disquiet that unfailingly greeted him whenever the congregation closed their prayer books and he found himself fumbling for the opening thread of his sermon.

Soon it was mid-October, and an unexpected cold snap had brought the first hard frost of the season to St. Andrew's. The dogwoods at the border of the courtyard began shedding their leaves in great bunches, and one day Father Melby decided to take care of them with a rake. Ever since he was a child, he had enjoyed combing carefully through the grass to gather all the leaves into a neat pile, which he would flip with the rake tines into a black plastic trash bag. The pleasure it brought him was mild but dependable, and he associated it with the satisfaction some people took in completing a crossword puzzle or wiping the rain spots off a window: yet one more symptom of the human desire for ideal arrangement. It was the same desire that had eventually carried him into the priesthood, after half a dozen meaningless retail jobs and an aborted semester as an accounting major.

The trees were remnants of the town's original landscape, left standing when the church was constructed some forty years before. They fell pell-mell along the margin of the yard—a cluster of three here, another two over there, and four or five lonely strays in between. It took him half an hour of work to rake the leaves into a single pile beneath the center-most dogwood. He was just about to scoop them into the trash bag when a gust of wind blew past, plucking one glossy red leaf from the top of the pile and sending it rolling across the grass. He dropped the rake and gave chase. The leaf somersaulted up the concrete walk, showing first its bright side and then its pale side, and he ran after it. It veered away from the front of the building, slipping past the azalea bushes and circling the corner. The wind changed direction again and yet again. The leaf swerved past the vestry and the meter box, the memorial stone and the fire exit. It seemed that no matter how quickly he went, it remained always a few steps out of his reach, and yet the longer he ran, the more ridiculous it began to seem that he might give up before he actually caught it.

Finally, as he rounded the final corner of the church and came back to the front yard, the wind gave one more rallying gust, and the leaf was returned to the same pile from which it had started. Father Melby stumbled the last few paces to the dogwood tree and stood there doubled over, clutching his knees.

Are you okay, Father?

He looked up to see Carol McDonnell peering out at him from beneath a hat the color of pumpkin-pie filling. Yes, he laughed. Just a little winded. I think someone is having a bit of fun with me.

Excuse me?

Never mind, never mind. What can I help you with, Ms. McDonnell? Some more leftover SASC business? Ms. McDonnell was the president of the St. Andrew's Service Committee, though Father Melby often found himself shouldering the responsibilities of the position.

Well, yes, in fact, she said. I came to see you about the next meeting. It's supposed to be on Thursday the second. But I found out my nephew is having his wisdom teeth out on Thursday the second.

I see. Well, that won't be a problem. We can certainly postpone the meeting until your nephew is on the mend.

Actually, what I was going to ask was if you could take over the chair for me? It would only be this one time, you understand. I don't want to be a burden on you.

Not a bit, not a bit. He was still breathing hard. Just give me a copy of the agenda, and I'll be happy to take care of it. And now, if you'll excuse me . . .

He took up the lawn rake, flipping the first batch of leaves into the trash with a twist of his shoulders. By the time he reached for the second, Ms. McDonnell was gone, stabbing across the parking lot in her high-heeled shoes.

It was late Monday afternoon when the woman with the delicately fearless voice returned to the confessional. Father Melby was lost in thought when she entered the chamber and once again failed to get a proper look at her. There was something inside him that desperately wanted to see her face, even though—and he realized this—he was disappointing his office by trying.

She was not so slow to speak this time. I'm afraid that I wasted my life.

What is your name, my child?

My name . . . There was a slip of paper sealed in a metal canister, and the canister was buried in a nameless field behind an old wooden house, and the house was slumping gradually back into the earth. Father Melby waited as she went there to retrieve the information. My name is Amy Elizabeth.

Amy Elizabeth, do you wish to make a confession? he asked.

She did not respond.

What is it that's troubling you, Amy Elizabeth?

I'm afraid that I wasted my life.

It was as though he had wandered into the presence of a doe or a fox, some infinitely sensitive wild creature that would take to its heels the second he made an unexpected move. Then you need to change your life. If you feel that you're wasting your life, you need to change it, he said. The Church can help you do that.

It's too late for me to change my life.

It was an argument he would not allow himself to get drawn into. Tell me, then, why do you feel that your life has been wasted?

Instead of answering him, she said, When you die, the energy that kept you alive filters into the people you loved. Did you know that? It's like a fire you've tended all your life, and the sparks are all scattered into the wind.

I don't understand, he said.

That's why we survive as long as we do, because the people who loved us keep us going. Our parents. Our spouses. But what if you failed to love anyone? Have you thought of that? Then the energy that kept you alive is wasted. It has nowhere to go. What happens to it?

It occurred to him that she might be contemplating suicide. As cautiously as he could, he said to her, I think what you're talking about is the soul, my child. That part of us which is eternal. God tells us that after we die, if we've died in Jesus, the soul is translated into Heaven.

Quietly, giving off the air of someone speaking not so much to be heard as to amend her own interior record of the conversation, she said, Not the soul, the spirit.

Was he even necessary to the process? he wondered. Was she talking to him at all? Then she asked, Can you really help me? and he chastised himself.

I'll do anything I can, of course. I've been worried about you, Amy Elizabeth. Why is it that I never see you at Mass?

I'm there every Sunday.

Where do you sit?

I've been watching you, she said.

He was startled by a knock on the wall of the chamber.

Just a moment, he said.

It was Ms. Baskind, the church receptionist, who told him through the curtain that she didn't mean to interrupt, but she had only now received a phone call from the bishop and she'd ventured to place him on hold. Would you like me to take a message? she asked.

Father Melby was going to urge her to do exactly that, but then he noticed the silence from the other side of the grate. He understood that the woman—that Amy Elizabeth—had stolen away again. Are you still there? he whispered. His voice met the empty air.

The shadows were dark, and the curtain was still. In the sanctuary he saw not the slightest suggestion that she had ever been in the confessional at all.

The bishop, as it happened, was calling to tell the Father that he had heard about the blossoming attendance at St. Andrew's and was planning to pay the church a visit on Sunday the fifth of November. This gave Father Melby almost two weeks to plan his sermon. He had spoken before the bishop only once since he had taken his vows, but he would never forget the feeling of shame he experienced that day as everything he had intended to say came apart and went side-sailing away from him, leaving him little to do but mumble his way toward the benediction as swiftly as he possibly could. Nor would he forget the look on the bishop's face as he said good-bye to him at the door, a look not of disappointment but of fulfilled expectation, as if to say, Well, you're a good man, at least. You care for the souls of your flock, and by the grace of God maybe that will be enough.

Father Melby was determined to redeem himself this time. He had already prepared his sermon for the coming Sunday, and he set his revisions aside to concentrate on the next one. He began scouring the Bible for ideas before he went to bed, leafing through the Gospels and the Epistles, the Major and Minor Prophets, until finally his fingers buzzed with tiredness and his vision started to swim. And it was curious: even when he was certain that he had replaced the Bible on his bedside table, in the morning he would invariably find it splayed apart and resting on the carpet, the pages fallen open somewhere in the middle of the Song of Solomon.

He continued to wonder about Amy Elizabeth. How had she fled so quickly? What did she want from him? She had said that she attended Mass every Sunday. In between researching his sermon and counseling his parishioners, he combed through the church's photo directory for her, but the only Amys he could find were Amy Glassman, Amy Bright, and Amy Chase, whose voices in the confessional he was sure he would have recognized. Nor were there any unfamiliar Amys on any of the recent attendance slips. He even glanced at the local phone book on the thin chance that Elizabeth was her last name and not her middle one, but there were no Elizabeths at all listed in the white pages, much less any Amy Elizabeths, just a seamless conversion from William Elias to Benjamin J. Elkins.

———

That Sunday he was only a few syllables into the sermon when he felt the eyes of God settling upon him again. His skin began to tingle. He heard the shift in his voice. He saw the numerous tiny signs of interest breaking open in the faces of the congregation: tilted chins, clearer gazes, slightly parted lips. He was filled with an ascendant confidence. But for the first time he noticed another sensation riding along behind it, like a scrap of paper caught in the slipstream of a train: that aura of finely measured, intimate regret he always felt in the company of Amy Elizabeth. He was on the verge of understanding something. Deep in his head he heard a voice, and that voice was whispering to him.

I've been watching you, it said.

And, It's not myself I've given up on. It's time.

But it wasn't until his sermon ended that the suspicion he had been courting actually took shape.

It had never been God who was watching him. It had never been God at all. From the very beginning it had only been Amy Elizabeth—Amy Elizabeth and no one else. As the congregants stood and opened their prayer books, he scanned the pews for her. A thousand familiar faces were reciting the prayer of St. Sebastian in the soft yellow light of the hanging brass lamps, but no matter how diligently he looked, he couldn't find her there.

He was certain he was right, though. He had to be.

One by one, his thoughts were tumbling into place, each shiny wheel locking teeth with the next. The way she had vanished so suddenly from the confessional. The empty air he had glimpsed through the openings in the grate. The clicking noise that had summoned him out of his bed at night. The votive candle pinched out by a pair of sourceless fingers.

She had said, The energy that keeps you alive is wasted.

She had said, I'm afraid that I wasted my life.

There came a moment when his intuition carried him out in

front of himself the way the wind carries a kite and all at once he guessed what she was, then another moment when he told himself that it could not be, that God in His mercy laid every spirit to rest, and then at last a moment when he knew for certain that he was right. He spent the rest of the service sailing through his own head on alternating currents of doubt and belief, returning again and again to the thought of Amy Elizabeth. Why had she appeared to him? Why had it taken him so long to catch hold of the truth?

If he let them, it seemed, his hands and his voice would complete the routines of worship for him. He followed absently along in his missal until one of the altar boys gave an inquisitory little cough to get his attention, and he realized that it was time to say the final prayer. In the name of the Father who has created you, the Son who has redeemed you, and the Holy Ghost who has sanctified you. Amen.

It took all his concentration to greet his parishioners as they filed out of the sanctuary. He had fulfilled his duties, apparently, for no one betrayed the smallest awareness that anything had gone wrong.

Your best yet, Father Melby.

The Lord was truly in the room with us this morning.

I tell you, Father, I'm going to have to get here early next week. Those folding chairs do a real number on the old lower back.

When the last of the congregants had departed, Father Melby allowed the front doors to swing closed on their hinges, their bottom edges brushing perfect quadrants of circles into the carpet. He took a deep breath and set to work. He went through the rooms of the church one by one, dowsing for Amy Elizabeth, calling out her name. It was a struggle to prevent his voice from trembling. I know you're here somewhere, he said. I'm ready to talk to you. Why don't you show yourself to me?

But she never answered. He resigned himself to the fact that he would have to let her come to him on her own terms.

He did not have long to wait. The next day he was in the confessional when suddenly he became aware that she had appeared on the other side of the fleurs-de-lis. He heard the gentle, whisked sound of her breathing, felt the unmistakable quality of her presence in the air—so very sad, so very determined—and said, It's you, isn't it, Amy Elizabeth?

She did not respond.

After a moment he continued. I have a question for you. If you are what I believe you are, why is it I can hear you breathing?

A watch—his own—gave a dozen loud ticks.

Slowly she answered, Because it pleases me to remember.

It pleases you?

Yes. Some things are hard to remember. Like talking. I remember words, but remembering how to talk is like remembering yourself as a child, so very small. All those times you saw your hands moving without understanding who they belonged to. Breathing is easier.

You're the one who's been listening to me on Sundays, aren't you?

Yes.

I used to think you were someone else.

He heard the curtain rustle and settle back into place. He had the distinct impression that she had swayed forward off the bench for a moment.

Why are you here, Amy Elizabeth?

It's not so hard to talk in here. So much . . . remorse in the air.

Not here in the confessional. Here in the church. Here in this world.

It seemed that he had triggered the switch again. I'm afraid that I wasted my life.

In his impatience he wanted to smack the wall of the booth, but instead he brought his hand to the cross he wore around his neck.

He tried to remind himself of the duty toward compassion. I understand, he said.

You told me you could help me. Did you mean that?

You're in pain, Amy Elizabeth. I'll help you any way I can.

There's only one way.

Tell me.

I have to hand myself over to somebody, somebody who will accept me willingly. I failed to love enough. The energy has nowhere to go.

What do you mean, *hand yourself over?*

Stay right there, she said, and she gathered herself into a hollow whistling wind, blowing through the holes in the confessional grate. In an instant, he felt her wrapping herself around him, a warm-blooded buzzing sensation that seemed tighter against his skin than his own clothing. His nerves pricked in a hundred different places. His breathing came quick and shallow. His penis grew rigid, and he felt as though he were on the brink of handing himself over to something, some disturbance preparing to branch its way up through his body from the compressed center of the earth.

He wrenched away from her, scrambling for the curtain. The next thing he knew he was standing in the broad-backed space of the sanctuary, his face beaded with sweat. His legs felt simultaneously as heavy as stone and as buoyant as froth.

I'm a priest, he said after he had gained his balance. I took vows. I can help you, Amy Elizabeth, but not that way.

There's only one way, she said again from inside the empty confessional, a wrought-iron sorrow stiffening her voice. And then she was gone and Father Melby was alone.

The days that followed were a cataract of doubts and waking fantasies. He kept expecting her to reappear. He could hardly open a door or lie down to sleep at night without anticipating the whisper of her breathing. Every time a breeze touched the back of his neck, he felt his stomach drawing tight inside him. Every time he noticed a strange sound in the church, a tick in the walls, or a creak in the rafters, he stopped whatever he was doing to investigate, listening like a madman for signs of intention. He was still coming to terms with the realization that Amy Elizabeth was the one who had been scrutinizing him with such care. It would not be fair to say that he had been abandoned by God, he supposed, since his place within God's gaze had never been more than an illusion, a whimsy born of his yearning for some sign of divine patronage. But the gap he was left with felt nonetheless real to him: the absence of God where before he had imagined His presence.

He tried his best not to think about it. There was still the matter of the bishop's visit to worry about, after all. Every day, to the best of his ability, he marshaled his concentration to sit down and work on his sermon. But he seemed to carry the thought of Amy Elizabeth along with him wherever he went, like a rattling silver shopping cart filled with dozens of boxes and cans. It was moving through the church now, past the altar, the pricket, the stairs. It was right in front of his eyes. He could never completely ignore it, and the effort to pretend he could was distorting his behavior. Surely the members of his congregation had noticed his recent callousness. On Tuesday he snapped at the choirmaster, hanging up the phone when she called to tell him the dry cleaner had lost a bundle of the chorister's robes. On Thursday, at the SASC meeting, he took a seat in the chair by the window, directly next to Katie Becker, and when she pressed her knee against his under the cover of the table, he told her, brusquely, I would appreciate it very much if you would refrain from touching me like that, thank you, Ms. Becker. A look of humiliation spread over her face like a dark stain. He hardly noticed when she got up to leave.

By Saturday night, after two weeks of preparation, he had finally managed to complete his sermon, a lesson taken from the thirteenth chapter of St. Paul's Letter to the Hebrews. He was running a slight fever, and before he went to bed he swallowed a couple of Tylenol.

It was some five minutes later, while he was lying in the dark waiting for the medicine to dissolve through its casing, that Amy Elizabeth returned. She didn't say anything, but he knew right away that it was her. A spark of cold blue static leapt off his blanket. A powerful hopelessness soaked into the air. He felt he was being watched by the same pair of eyes that had watched him at the pulpit, heard by the same pair of ears. It was the first time she had come to him outside the confessional. She seemed to be waiting at the very edge of his room.

I thought you would be back again, he said. He was speaking quietly, but in the darkness his words fell like stones into still water, each one bold and insistent. I'm sorry if I upset you last time. I didn't mean to. But you surprised me.

She gave no response, but he could tell what she was thinking just the same. Her grief and her longing reached out to him from across the room.

Are you going to be all right? he wanted to know.

Again she refused to speak. He listened to the melting sound as she drifted away from the wall, wondering when she was going to answer him, what she was going to say.

Within seconds, she was standing at the foot of his bed, she was floating in midair, she was lingering at his pillow. And then she was under the blankets, and inside his clothing, and covering him like a sheet of thick, flowing oil. And it felt so nice, and he was so nearly asleep, that it would have been easy to accept it all like a dream, a dream of rising slowly toward the sun, its yellow glow and cells of fire, simply giving himself over to it until he woke in the innocence of the morning and wondered whether anything had happened at all. But he had made a promise before God and the Church, and he would not allow himself to abandon it.

He screwed his eyes shut and twisted out from under the covers, falling onto the floor. He backed away on his elbows. I can't help you, he said to her. Get away from me.

Amy Elizabeth billowed toward him like a wave, and he repeated it: I can't help you, Amy Elizabeth. Go away. Go away now and leave me alone.

And that was where he was, propped on his back on the carpet, as the determination that held her together weakened and came apart in a mist of confusion and sorrow. He listened to the rustling noise as she disappeared from there to everywhere.

He had almost forgotten how empty a building could feel.

He failed to sleep that night—or if he did sleep, he failed to recognize it—and by the time he took the pulpit the next day the church shone in his eyes with a brilliant insomniac clarity. The columns at the end of the aisles were like spotlights aimed straight at the floor. The cross was like a stencil placed over a lantern. His parishioners filled every seat and their faces seemed to burn from the inside.

After the announcement of the Gospel, he cleared his throat and spoke. My children, St. Paul had this to say of strangers.

They were the first words of his sermon, and behind them lay all the others, but no one was listening to him with any special attention, and he could not remember what he was meant to say next.

My children, he began again. My children, St. Paul had *this* to say of strangers.

He felt a fluttering sensation inside him—the feeling of every word he had ever been given being taken away like a stack of loose paper caught by the wind. In the back of the church a baby began to gurgle. Someone tried to stifle a cough and sneezed instead. The bishop stared up at Father Melby from the corner of the first row, his eyes glowing with that look of fulfilled expectation. Though the pews were full, the sanctuary was empty, the ghost of Amy Elizabeth was nowhere to be found, and as Father John Melby stood before his congregation, waiting without hope for his mind to yield up the rest of his sermon, he knew that he had been damned by the purity of his devotion.

THE HUMAN SOUL AS A RUBE GOLDBERG DEVICE: A CHOOSE-YOUR-OWN-ADVENTURE STORY

You are returning the milk to the refrigerator when your head begins to swim. Red shapes like semitransparent scarves flare open in your vision, brimming over with light before they dwindle away. For a moment you think you are going to collapse. You put your hand on the counter to steady yourself. Your heart ticks down the seconds like a bomb. Then the sensation passes, and it is an ordinary day again.

It is the sort of thing that used to happen to you all the time: you would stand up too quickly from a chair, and the whole room would pitch to one side as the blood rushed to your head. The first time you heard this expression you were seven years old. You stumbled getting up to take your turn at the chalkboard, and your teacher asked, "What's wrong? Is the blood rushing to your head?"

The phrase was confusing to you. You imagined your face turning an exotic, beetlike red, like the picture on the cover of *The Very Hungry Caterpillar*.

Mrs. Pritchard—that was your teacher's name.

You remember how surprised you were when she moved away with her husband over the summer, the first of who knows how many people you never imagined you would never see again.

It is a clear Saturday in late September, with insects stitching patterns over the grass and an invisible jet etching a narrow trail in the sky. For once you have no work to catch up on, no chores to finish, no errands to run. You head upstairs to the bathroom, where you brush your teeth and comb your hair. There is a tree outside your window swaying slightly as the air filters through its branches, like a dancer who can't keep still no matter how hard she tries. You think about the cool silence of a concert hall before the first note falls over the audience.

You think about a woman you once saw lifting her skirt up to her knees as she waded into the green water of a river.

If you decide to put your shoes on and go out for a walk,

turn to page 120.

If you would rather spend a quiet morning at home,

turn to page 154.

The bricks covering the plaza are a deep chocolate brown. They seem to absorb every trace of sunlight, magnify every trace of sound, and you play the same game you have played a hundred times before, walking so that your footsteps fall parallel with them. You make it almost as far as the coffeehouse before you begin to feel a restlessness in your joints and have to quit. You veer off toward the public library. Chestnut saplings have been planted in gaps in the paving, and you approach one of them from between a pair of benches, ducking beneath a little elastic suspension of its leaves. An ambulance starts racing its siren. You step out from under the branches just in time to watch it tear away, a big white box that takes the corner with improbable speed.

A cluster of blackbirds goes beating into the air as you approach, scattering across the roofs of the buildings and reconverging in the arms of a willow. A bicyclist pumps his way slowly up the hill that runs past the Methodist church, his legs moving in a kind of exultant midair parade march.

Your left shoe is beginning to float free of your heel, so you prop your foot on the ledge of a low window to tighten the laces. You look up to see a girl stepping into the bead store. She is wearing a shirt the color of Dijon mustard. You are just close enough to read the message printed across the back: LIFE IS A BEDTIME STORY.

If life is a bedtime story, then what kind of story is death, you want to ask her? A horror story? A fairy tale? Or simply a mystery?

There is a loud crack, and you jerk your head around. A kid whose skateboard has come out from under him stands up from the bricks. It looks as if he fell trying to skim along the top of a bike rack, but he does not appear to be hurt. He levers the board up with his foot and backs up to try again.

You, on the other hand, have suddenly become dizzy. You lean against the window and wait for your vision to stop spinning. When did you became so fragile that merely twisting your head around could make you feel as if you were about to collapse? you wonder.

A man walks by with his son, a boy no older than seven, who says, "I would be awesome at that. I want a skateboard. Can I have a skateboard?"

"You can have a soccer ball, or you can have an Xbox game, but you can't have a skateboard."

The boy gives the pavement a scuff of his sneaker. "Soccer is *boring*. Xbox is *boring*. I never get to do *anything* awesome."

And his father answers, "When you're older, you can buy yourself all the skateboards you want."

Is your adult life anything like you thought it would be?

If so, turn to page 118.

If not, turn to page 152.

Susannah answers her phone on the third ring. As always, for the first few steps of the conversation, her voice sounds flat and exhausted. It begins to take on vigor, though, as the two of you settle into your familiar rhythm of jokes and questions, trial anecdotes, split-second pauses. She tells you about her computer, which has been, as she puts it, *backsliding.* "It's been—what? Three months? And already I've got another virus. This time what happens is the screen will lock up for a minute, and when it comes back on, the cursor will just stick there. Motionless. Like a lump. Of gum. When I try to move it, it only *selects* everything. I was just getting ready to unplug it and take it into the computer place when the phone rang. Speaking of which, what's up with you?"

"Well, I had an unusual conversation this morning," you say, and you tell her about the wrong-number call and how the man's voice seemed to weaken and grow ragged the moment you told him who you were. "Or told him who I wasn't, I guess I should say. To be honest, I felt kind of bad for him. Guilty, if you can believe it."

"It sounds to me like he was having a hard day, and the pressure of it finally got to him. Maybe you should feel bad for him. That doesn't mean you did anything wrong."

"I know, I know. But still—"

She has known you for so long that you don't even have to finish the thought. A muffled noise of understanding escapes from her throat, just loud enough for you to hear. Outside a pair of boys are tossing a soccer ball back and forth as they walk down the street. One of them hunkers down over the ball, dribbling it off to the curb in a diagonal, then swivels around and backboards it off the side of the other's head, giving the sign for two points. The second boy throws his arm out and says, "You're an asshole, Morganbarron."

You think about the poster of Michael Jordan you used to see in the window of every shoe store.

You think about the fragrance of freshly mown grass, a smell of shock and abundance.

Susannah allows the silence to fill its own time. "So I'm wondering if I should replace the lamp in my bedroom. It's got this straight-angled, the-future-is-now look I'm not so sure I like anymore."

"Does it still give off light? Is it still standing upright? If so, you shouldn't replace it. See, I hate this idea that everything needs to be traded in for something else. I can't imagine a better way to waste a life."

It is a declaration, not a question, what she says next. You can hear a hint of half-amused peevishness in her voice. "So you'd say that you're *not* wasting your life."

Would you say that you're not wasting your life?
If so, turn to page 126.

Would you say that you are?
If so, turn to page 164.

You have organized your books by genre, with all the science fiction in one area and all the mysteries in another, all the contemporary fiction over here and all the classics over there, with special recesses set aside for poetry and plays, criticism and nature writing, memoirs and graphic novels. Here is the problem, though: you are not sure whether *The Baron in the Trees* should be shelved with the literary fiction or the fantasies—or even with the slender pocket of historical fiction you haven't quite gotten around to reading yet.

You let your eyes pass over the titles. Maybe you are tired, because for a few seconds all you see is a peacock smear of colors blurring out to either side of you. Then your vision clears and all the pieces fit back together again.

You are staring at an old Alfred Bester novel. Recently you have been toying with a certain thought about science fiction, a thought you find yourself rehearsing again. It seems to you that all the classic science fiction writers—or at least the best and most stirring ones: Ray Bradbury, Theodore Sturgeon, Arthur C. Clarke—practice literature as a form of nostalgia. With all their alien vessels and technological wonders, what they're really doing is running their stories through the gears of a consciousness that no longer quite belongs to them, casting their minds back to their own childhood, a time when the future seemed limitless and there were a million possible stories to be told. This is why their books contain such a strong current of melancholy tangled together with such a strong current of enthusiasm: they are gazing into the future as a way of recapturing the past.

You decide to sandwich the Calvino novel between Bohumil Hrabal's *I Served the King of England* and Walter Tevis's *Mockingbird*, on the border separating the literary fiction from the fantasy, so that anybody who looks at your bookshelves will be able to make up his own mind which side of the divide it is meant to lie on. You square the books' edges. You see a speck of dust on the wood and press it away with the pad of your finger.

You think again, with a quality of sudden disclosure, about the wrong-number call you received, the way the man's words came pouring into your ear, the fierce emotion in his voice as he said, "Oh God, I didn't mean to trouble you." At first, when the ember flares open in your chest, you imagine it is your conscience bothering you. But what, you wonder, did you do wrong?

You stagger and throw your arm against the bookcase, taking just enough care to keep the books from overturning as your legs buckle beneath you.

Go on to page 146.

Maybe the boy has nothing more to say to his father, or maybe he is just salting his counterargument away for another time. Whatever the case, the two of them fall silent as they pass in front of you. You wait by the window until there is no danger that you will stumble into them, then take a couple of swaying steps to the bench by the chestnut sapling and sit down. You lay your head in your lap, letting the dizziness roll straight through you, a giant wave that makes your ears ring and your skin grow warm.

The fog clears from your mind in a sudden rush of white noise. You look up to see the skateboarder crouching over the deck of his board, the chestnut leaves forming patterns of shadow lace on the bricks, a yellow jacket orbiting a trash barrel. The old Greek man who runs the secondhand clothing store is staring at you from his window, an expression of concern etched on his face. "I'm all right," you mouth to him. He makes a gesture you do not understand, tapping the glass a few times with the beak shape of his fingers, then shakes his head and turns back into his store.

You gain your feet again and begin walking. These episodes of light-headedness have been happening a lot to you lately, and you worry sometimes that your health is on the verge of abandoning you, but then you reflect that it has been this way your whole life. For as long as you can remember, every toothache and stomach cramp has presented itself to you as the usher of some irreversible decline. You have always gotten better, though, and you are sure you will again. You will wake up one morning flush with health and energy. Your mind will be sharp, your muscles strong, and you will be able to live as though you have never known the slightest trouble.

You catch sight of your image in a window, straighten your gig line, smooth a cowlick back from your temple. You swat at an insect hovering by your ear.

You have ordered a table lamp from the furniture shop a few doors down, and you stop inside to see if it has arrived. The sales assistant taps a couple of keys on his computer. "It's set to ship from our warehouse on the first of October," he tells you. "We've already got your phone number in the system. You have my word, we'll call you the moment it comes over the transom."

Is he using the word *transom* correctly? You're not sure. You repeat the word to yourself so that you won't forget to look it up in the dictionary when you get home. *Transom. Transom. Transom.* It is at that moment, on the last closed *m* of the third repetition, that you lose your balance. You feel something inside you becoming infinitely fine and subtle. Your heart seems to drift right through you, and it diffuses into the open air.

Turn to page 146.

The day is beautiful, with only a few horsetails of cloud brushing the sky at the horizon. Two sparrows are singing to each other from the gutters of the house across the street, a squirrel crawling over the brickwork in fitful little snatches of motion. Your phone begins to ring as you lock the door, but you decide to let the answering machine take the call.

Your neighbor is washing his car, his ears cushioned behind an old pair of headphones, and as you pass him, you catch a few beats of the same music you occasionally hear pouring like a river through the walls of his house: REO Speedwagon's "Take It on the Run."

Instinctively, you begin walking toward the shopping plaza two blocks down from you and one block over. At the corner, a couple of boys are playing soccer in their front yard—or rather, you realize as you get closer, pretending to play soccer, one of them narrating an imaginary game as the other boots the hard white ball over the grass. "Morganbarron takes it to the goal. He fakes to the left, he fakes to the right. He fakes up. He fakes down. He fakes in a circle. He fakes in a square." When the ball comes bouncing into the street, you block it with your shin and kick it back to them. The boy doing the play-by-play bows to you and says, "You have done us an act of great kindness, and we thank you."

All this nervy kidding around, half-sophisticated and half-naïve—it makes you happy just to see it. You remember having friends who used to lampoon the world so effortlessly, crouching at the verge of every joke and waiting to pounce on it, and you remember how they changed as they grew older and the joy of questioning everything slowly became transformed into the pain of questioning everything, like a star consuming its own core.

Who was it who said that every virtue contains its corresponding vice? C. S. Lewis? Virginia Woolf? You forget. But it has always worried you that what the virtue of wit contained was the vice of scorn.

You should get more exercise than you do—you know that—but you didn't anticipate how winded a simple walk would make you. By the time you reach the shopping plaza, you are gulping at the air like a fish. You feel as if you could sit down and drink for a solid hour. Your favorite coffeehouse, Sufficient Grounds, is just on the other side of the wrought-iron benches. The waiters there know you well, but there are days when you enjoy being recognized and days when you don't, when you want nothing more than the simple curt reactiveness of a stranger.

*If you decide to stop for a while at the coffeehouse,
go on to page 132.*

*If you head for the McDonald's across the street,
turn to page 166.*

The drawing you did has left an ink contusion on your little finger, and before you leave, you go upstairs to wash it off. Some bird or frog is in the tree outside your bedroom, croaking with a noise like ball bearings rattling in a tin can. You listen to the fan spinning and the lightbulb humming, to the hot water tank replenishing itself. You open your mouth as wide as you can to see if the sounds will become any clearer, but they are already as loud as thunder in your ears. Nothing you do makes any difference.

The sun has passed from the window above the stairwell. On your way back down you watch a squirrel graze up against the opening, perching its front paws on the sill and fastidiously lowering its head to the glass. You could swear that it is looking inside, but by the time you reach the porch and have a straight view of the roof, it has gone, leaping onto a tree branch or a telephone wire. You see a crow wheeling in the sky. You smell the match scent of a wood-burning grill. When did the breeze begin to blow? Just an hour ago the weather seemed almost perfectly still, and now the grass by the fence, so long and slender, is whipsawing around with every breath of air.

A creek runs behind the houses on the other side of the street, a freshet of colorless water no wider than an arm unless it has been raining, and you decide to take a walk along the bank. It is not unusual to find minnows swimming in the current. Today there are nearly a dozen of them, quivering in and out of the shade of a rock in tight silver curves.

A green leaf floats by, its stem ranging out in front of it like a bowsprit. A car honks its horn, and a door slams somewhere. It is a sad, beautiful, ordinary day.

Every September you resolve to schedule a vacation for this time of year, a whole month or two so that you can just sit back and appreciate the change of the seasons, but you are always too busy. Next year, you tell yourself. Next year maybe you'll actually do it.

You sit down on the grass and dangle your legs over the bank, allowing your shoes to brush the water. You close your eyes for a few seconds and listen to the trickling sound, and when you open them again, you are staring directly into the stream. The sun is scrambled into a mass of loops and wires. It seems as if the light is fabricating the water, rather than merely uncovering it. The sight is mesmerizing. You would barely notice you were there at all if not for the pain that suddenly overcomes you, a million steel spokes radiating out from your heart.

Continue to page 146.

For as long as you can remember, you have been fascinated by Rube Goldberg devices. When you were little, you had a neighbor who owned the board game Mouse Trap, and you used to lie on your stomach as she pieced the game together and set it into operation, watching the shining silver marble roll through its system of slides, buckets, and cages with all the screwy accuracy of a circus performance. Sometimes, when you have trouble falling asleep, you like to pretend that you are designing such a device for yourself. You have to crack an egg, so you pull a cord, which lifts a curtain from around a carrot, which causes a rabbit to start racing around inside a wheel. The friction from the wheel lights a match, and the match lights a candle, and the candle burns through a string, which causes a weight to drop from the ceiling and land on a teeter-totter. At the other end of the teeter-totter is a ball. The ball bounces across the floor onto a table, where it knocks over a box of pins, and one of the pins pops a balloon. The noise of the balloon causes a dog to start barking and straining forward on its leash, which is tied to a door, on top of which is a ball-peen hammer knotted to a small silk parachute. When the door swings open, the hammer topples off and parachutes slowly to the kitchen counter, where it taps against the egg, and, finally, cracks it into a bowl—though by this time, if you are lucky, you will have floated out of your own awareness and will no longer be there to see it.

You have a pet theory, one you have been turning over for years, that life itself is a kind of Rube Goldberg device, an extremely complicated machine designed to carry out the extremely simple task of constructing your soul. You imagine yourself tumbling into the world like a marble, rolling with an easy momentum over the chutes and ramps of your childhood, falling through traps here and there, sailing over various hills and loop-the-loops, then flying like a shot from the cannon of your adolescence and landing with an ungoverned bounce on the other side, where you progress through all the vacuum tubes and trampolines and merry-go-rounds of your adulthood—your job and your family, your hobbies and your lovers, the withering of certain friendships, the blossoming of others, the birth of your children and the death of your parents, the softening of your body and the hardening of your habits—plummeting sometimes into the sinkholes of accident and disease and at other times thinly escaping them, and all the while changing, changing at every moment, because of the decisions you make and those that fate makes for you, until finally, with your dying breath, you emerge from the mouth of the machine and roll to a stop, as motionless as you were before you began, but scarred and colored and burnished now with the markings you will carry with you through an eternity.

Continue to page 146.

"I don't know. I hope I'm not. What I would really say is that the two of us have very different lamp philosophies. I'm pro-same, and you're pro-different. Or I'm pro-old, and you're pro-new."

"And pro-new is wrong?" she asks.

What is it about her voice that tells you she is irritated? There is a tightness to it, an edge of eager muscularity, so that in truth it almost sounds as if she is smiling. You try to make a joke out of the argument, pretending to confuse *pro-new* with *pro-gnu,* pronouncing the hard *g* in a deliberate effort to ruin the pun. It is the kind of vapid absurdity she would ordinarily play along with, but instead she just says, "Listen, I really need to take care of this computer thing now, so . . ."

"So."

"So I'll talk to you soon, okay?" And to make certain you know her bad humor is only temporary, she adds, "And you have no reason to feel guilty about that phone call you got. None. I mean it."

"I'll try not to."

There are people who hurt themselves by saying too little and people who hurt themselves by saying too much. You have always thought of yourself as falling squarely in the former camp—the people who hurt themselves by saying too little—but it could be that you are mistaken. Usually, when you find yourself making some fiery statement or another, it is only because you are playing a role, or, if not playing a role, because you are skimming the thinnest layer of what you actually believe off the top of all your doubts and contradictory hunches. You presume that people will understand your intentions, but when they don't, you rarely bother to explain yourself. So is that saying too much or saying too little?

After you hang up, you take some time to straighten the magazines on your coffee table. You hear a fire engine starting its siren up a few blocks away. Who was it who said that fire engines always sound as if they're running away from a fire rather than toward one, like enormous beasts fleeing through the city in a panic?

Laurie Anderson?

Andrei Codrescu?

You can't remember. But whenever the trucks go howling down the streets of your neighborhood, the thought passes reliably through your mind.

Your last trip to the grocery store was just an early-morning dash to buy some milk, so there isn't much to eat in your kitchen, but you find a box of granola bars and unwrap one. When you have finished the last bite, you pour yourself a glass of water. You upend it, then put the glass in the sink. Suddenly, and to your wonder, you feel the need to make something out of your day.

If you decide to do a little grocery shopping,
turn to page 156.

If you decide to clean the bathroom mirror,
turn to page 170.

You look through the cabinets and the refrigerator, but find only a few boxes of snack food, a tomato, and half a package of bagels—nothing you feel like eating. Obviously it is time for you to do some grocery shopping. For now, though, you decide to phone the Chinese restaurant around the corner, New Fun Ree, and place your usual takeout order.

"I'd like item number twenty-four, the mixed vegetables with snow peas, and a side of egg drop soup."

"Okay. Ten minutes. Bye."

This might be what you like best about such inexpensive little pigeonhole restaurants, the way all notions of hospitality are thrown over in favor of a simple curt proficiency. The cooks and counter clerks are like the mechanics you have sometimes met at the gas stations between small towns: craftsmen who would rather finish their work as efficiently as possible than shanghai you into liking them.

You put your shoes on, then head for the restaurant. The sun is shining down from the middle of the sky. The reflectors in the street pop on and off like lightbulbs as you walk past them. New Fun Ree is nearly empty, just the same limp-haired boy who's always standing at the cash register, sketching on a place mat with a blue ballpoint pen.

You sit down at one of the tables, running your fingers over the bamboo surface and waiting for him to call your order. After a minute or two, he shouts out, "Mix vegetable snow pea? Egg drop soup?" Your wallet is open by the time you reach the counter.

The boy bags your food and hands it to you. "Five-seven-three," he says.

"How much?"

"Five-seven-three," he repeats, "five-seven-three," proclaiming the numbers with a strange insistency, like a quarterback announcing a change in play.

As you walk home, your neighbor passes you in his freshly polished car, giving a friendly double tap of his horn. A dog scampers over to you from across the street, nudging your wrist with his nose. He stares up at you as though waiting for you to do something extraordinary, then scampers away at the sound of his owner's whistle. Your left arm has begun to tingle. You give it a shake to restore the blood flow. All at once you lose sensation in your fingers.

You drop the bag of Chinese food. One of the containers splits open, and a long flare of steamed rice spills out—hundreds of white grains against the yellow-green grass. You ought to clean it up, you think; you really shouldn't leave it there. But before you can bend over, you are lying on the ground beside it.

Go on to page 146.

The air is beginning to warm up. You decide to take the oblique route home, making a loop through the plant nursery at the west end of the plaza. Many of the trees there are only a little taller than you are, and you feel like a giant lumbering through their ranks, paddling your hands through their spires as easily as if you were smacking a row of parking meters. By the time you reach the end of the lane, one of your palms is coated with the scent of magnolia, the other with the scent of pine. Your lungs are full, your hairline slick with sweat. You watch a pair of robins land on the lip of a stone basin, offering faint subliminal muttering noises to each other. You watch a little boy throwing pebbles at the trunk of an ash sapling.

A song has broken out on your tongue. It takes you a moment to recognize it as "Somewhere Over the Rainbow"—not the standard Judy Garland version, but the Israel Kamakawiwo'ole rendition, with the soft, drawn-out *oohs* at the beginning and the melody that floats effortlessly out over the strum of the ukelele. It is a song you love, so simple and pretty that it is hard for you to imagine the person who would dislike it, but why are you singing it now? Did David say something to you about rainbows, or dreams, or bluebirds? Did you overhear one of the customers in the coffeehouse laying a stress on the word *somewhere*?

You are puzzling it over when you realize: the meter of the song matches the pace at which you have been walking. Undoubtedly that's where it came from.

This has happened to you before: you will find yourself rehearsing a particular run of lyrics for days on end, with no idea why, until eventually you will discover that the tempo of the steps you are taking between, say, the couch and the refrigerator exactly duplicates the cadence of the song in your head. Everything has a rhythm, you sometimes think. Everything, given the possibility, would choose to be a song.

The gate of the nursery, swinging gently about on its hinges, would be a dance hall waltz.

The squirrel sprinting across the grass would be a ragtime tune played on an upright piano.

The sprinkler dousing the flowers would be an old gospel hymn.

You are walking past the dogwoods when a thrill of pain in your chest makes you drop to your knees. Your heart, too, has a rhythm, one that catches, stutters, and comes to a halt. It would be the slowest song in the world if it were a song at all.

Continue to page 146.

Though the coffeehouse is busy, you find an empty armchair in the well beneath the staircase. The seat gives you a good view of the plaza, a low table of chocolate-brick paving interrupted by trash barrels and brackets of wrought-iron benches. You order a large chai tea, drinking a glass of water as you wait for it to arrive and crunching the ice between your teeth as your father used to do. A teenage girl sweeps past the window, angling her body forward as if she is trying to pierce a heavy gale. A man in a business suit walks by wheeling a ten-speed bicycle, a leather briefcase jammed into its basket. At the far end of the plaza, a father swings his son around by the arms, tracing low-dipping circles in the air. Sometimes, watching people through the flat silence of a window, you feel that you are on the verge of understanding a human mystery that has managed to evade you your whole life, but that is where you always remain: on the verge.

You spot the barista coming with your order. She must be a new hire, because you don't recognize her. On the wall beside your chair is an M. C. Escher illustration of a grid of triangles evolving gradually into a flock of black and white birds. As you sip your chai, you catch yourself staring right through it, slipping into a mindless reverie of shapes and colors. You think about a black leaf you once saw pasted to a window during a rainstorm. You think about the shifting brown tones of a southern creek.

"See, first you've got your triangles and then you've got your birds," a voice says. You look up to see David, your favorite waiter at Sufficient Grounds, his eyes hooded in a mystic burnout routine. "What it is is a map of the development of being, man. If you keep following the pattern, you'll find airplanes, then spaceships, then angels, then God, and then triangles again. Triangles are always at the top. No one knows why."

You give his arm an amiable nudge, and he abandons the performance. "How are you doing, David?"

"Not bad, not bad." He strokes his mustache. "Rhonda ditched me, though. Moved out and everything."

"I'm sorry to hear that."

"Yeah, well, me too. But I think we both saw it coming. I'm just relieved I've got the whole thing in the rearview now. Waiting for it was worse than living through it."

"Then you're happy with the way things turned out?"

"Happy?" he says. "Well—no."

He shrugs and laughs, lets off a wilting smile.

"But who's ever really been happy?"

If you have ever really been happy,
turn to page 158.

If you haven't,
turn to page 174.

You head toward the redbrick warehouse that used to house the brewery. Only a few years ago the bottling carousel operated seven days a week, even on major holidays, like a hospital or a fire station, but now the only human activity at the building is a small Toyota running in cautious circles through the parking lot, halting every so often and then starting back up again.

You can still smell the wheat soap in the air as you pass the loading dock.

A paper bag drifts down the alley. The wind steals through the windows in a low sigh.

It has been a while since you took this particular side street, and a homeless encampment has taken hold beneath the bridge: a gas-powered generator, some shopping carts, and a dozen pup tents strung together out of bedsheets and fishing wire. You see a group of men sitting together on a sprung mattress, engrossed in conversation.

Is it possible, you wonder, to expend the last of your luck? Once, you were driving along a narrow stretch of highway when you got trapped behind a string of trailers. You tacked into the facing lane to pass them, but the line was longer than you had expected it to be, and before you were able to clear it, you saw a pickup truck barreling toward you. You did the only thing you could think to do— swerved onto the shoulder, threading the needle between the truck and the curb at sixty miles an hour and hoping the other driver would stay in his lane. The rumble strips made your car vibrate with a terrific chattering noise. Your legs turned to liquid. You drifted to a stop and watched the trailers disappear.

You can still see the image in your windshield: a single lane of sun-beaten concrete curving past white frame houses and billboards with pictures of Jesus on them. The sky was bruised with rain in the distance. The driveways of the houses looked like black pudding poured directly onto the grass. And you remember thinking that whatever luck had been allotted to you at your birth was now used up, spent, and that the rest of your life would pass in misfortune.

It did not turn out that way for you, but maybe it did for the men beneath the bridge. Maybe they made one foolish mistake and had just enough fortune to carry them through to the other side, but not enough to take them any further. Maybe some truck nicked them at the corner and sent them spinning off the edge of the road. Lives fall apart in all sorts of ways.

You duck between the legs of a street sign. There is a convenience store standing on the corner, the light above its door flickering on and off. You taste the tang of gasoline in your mouth from the leaking pump out front. Something seems to grip your chest. You lose your breath and fall to your knees. There are times in your life when, despite the steel weight of your memories and the sadness that seems to lie at your feet like a shadow, you suddenly and strangely feel perfectly okay.

Turn to page 146.

You select a mix CD a friend sent you and put it into the stereo, listening as the first song strikes up with an artificial needle hiss. Sometimes, during the slow-lit, lingering afternoons of high school, you would sit down and close your eyes for an entire album, just letting the music wash through you. Every so often back then you might catch yourself swaying your neck or whisking the air with your hands during one of the more expressive passages, but mostly you would lose track of your body altogether, until the last note of the last track faded away and you returned to the four walls of your bedroom as if awakening from a dream.

These days you need something to occupy your other senses while you listen. As the CD plays, you let your eyes travel over your bookcase, following a stepladder of colors from the top shelf to the bottom. This is the test: to see if you can make the entire climb using solely the books with red bindings, say, or solely the books with blue. It is a pointless exercise, but you are secretly pleased when the only color that gives you any trouble is brown.

Midway through the disc is a scratchy recording of Hoagy Carmichael singing "Stardust." Every time you hear the piece, it makes you think of your grandparents dancing to songs like "How Much Is That Doggie in the Window?," holding each other close to songs like "The Little White Cloud That Cried," falling in love to songs like "Ah, Sweet Mystery of Life." How such simple tunes could have stirred such emotion in them will forever bewilder you, though no doubt your own grandchildren will someday think of you dipping your shoulders to "This Charming Man" or feeling your heart screw tight to "Hallelujah" with the same feeling of affectionate mystification.

Outside a siren goes racing toward somebody's tragedy. There is a ten-second gap in the music as the noise drowns the instruments out. Then the drums knock through the blare, making room for the guitars, and gradually the song reclaims the room.

The CD ends with Van Morrison singing "Sweet Thing," a track you never tire of listening to. You love the way it loops and rises and loops around on itself, again and again and again, like a hundred circles stacked one on top of another, and the way Van Morrison's voice seems to carry so much sorrow and so much exultation at one and the same time. It is as if he were calling out to himself from the cusp of some precipitous decline, just young enough and just wise enough to celebrate in the face of all his suffering.

"And I will walk and talk in gardens all wet with rain," he sings, "and I will never, ever, ever grow so old again."

There is a part of you that would like to adopt those words as your manifesto.

If you feel a bit hungry,
turn to page 128.

If you feel a headache coming on,
turn to page 140.

"Damn, someone's thirsty today," the boy working the cash register says when you ask him for another refill. He winces as if a fire-cracker has exploded, lets a glance fly past his shoulder. "Lucky my manager didn't overhear that. He said one more time cursing in front of a customer and he'll serve my ass to me on a silver platter. Look, don't say anything to anybody, all right? Here, I'll let you have this one for free."

"You don't have to do that."

"Please. The syrup costs us, like, nine cents. Come on, hand it over." He fills your cup and fastens a new lid on top. Outside a fire engine is working its siren. The sound spreads open in three distinct phases, dipping slightly, pausing, and then increasing, as if some giant mechanical beast were struggling to release a yawn. You listen as it vanishes down the road.

"We cool?" the boy asks as he gives you back your Coke.

"We're cool."

You carry the drink outside and across the street into the plaza. A breeze makes the leaves chatter. The sun presses against the crown of your head. One of your shoelaces has come loose, and you prop your foot on a bench to tighten it.

A street performer parades past you, a pair of yo-yos spinning from each of his hands. He sends them looping around the world in matched sets, the symmetry so perfect you might almost imagine you were viewing the scene through a kaleidoscope.

A girl strides out of the bead store on the other side of the square in a T-shirt the color of spicy mustard. There is a message printed across her back in white block letters, but she is too far away for you to make out the words.

It takes you another five minutes to finish your Coke. By the time you have thrown the cup away, you can feel the pressure beginning to mount in your bladder. Maybe three cups was too much. You were so thirsty, though, and you found it next to impossible to stop yourself. Clearly the soda has gone pouring right through you. You duck into a restroom and relieve yourself, then wash up at the sink and step back into the sunlight. You have a touch of heartburn, and you press your hand to your chest, digging the hinge of your knuckles into your ribs and massaging the spot in a tiny circle. It is an old remedy you picked up from some casual gesture you saw a character make on a television commercial. You are not sure whether it really works or whether you simply like the illusion of control it offers.

You intend to start for home, but then you spot the movie rental store on the corner. It might be nice, you think, to pick up a DVD for the afternoon.

If you go inside to rent a movie,
turn to page 150.

If you continue walking home,
turn to page 160.

Your medicine cabinet is choked to the corners with expired prescriptions and over-the-counter pain relievers: aspirin, Tylenol, Advil, Bufferin, Motrin, Aleve. It looks like how the inside of a sewing box might look after tumbling down a flight of stairs—a chaos of spools and thimbles.

You take two Advil gelcaps, downing them with a glass of tap water. There is a hair clinging to the wall of the sink, and you turn the faucet on and watch it give a tremor as the outer current splashes against it, then lift free and snake into the drain.

You lie back on your bed and spend a few minutes staring into space. The fan has been adjusted to the lowest possible setting, and the motion of the blades is nearly hypnotic—an endless procession of shadows drifting languidly over the ceiling.

You think about the phone call you received this morning, how quickly the man spoke, then how soft his voice became when he understood that you weren't the person he thought you were. "Oh God, I'm so embarrassed," he said. It sounded as if he didn't even realize you were listening anymore, as if he were merely talking to himself in some seizure of private humiliation.

You know the feeling well. You can't count the number of times you have remembered one long-gone mortifying act or another and begun firing off a quiet rebuke to yourself, saying it over and over again like a penitent thrashing his back with a switch: *so embarrassing, so embarrassing, so embarrassing, so embarrassing.*

There was the time you hopped up to sit on someone's counter at a dinner party and cracked the picture frame that had been left lying there.

The time your mother caught you rewrapping the presents you had opened the week before Christmas.

The time you phoned a friend one night as you were getting ready to go to bed and instead of leaving the message you had intended to leave said what you were actually thinking, which was, "I'm in love with you."

You have learned that it's best not to get yourself started.

You stretch out your limbs and stand up. The blood rushes to your head for a moment. The carpet seems as hard as a board. You are walking down the stairs when your heart clenches tight inside you.

A fist. That's what it feels like—a fist.

There is just enough time for you to think of something you once read in a popular science book before the pain overwhelms you: that if you form your hand into a fist, you'll have an object roughly the size of your heart, and if you wrap your other hand around it, you'll have an object roughly the size of your brain.

Turn to page 146.

You make a small lunch for yourself, toasting a bagel and topping it with cream cheese and a slice of tomato. As you return the unused portion of the tomato to the produce drawer, you wonder for what must be the thousandth time whether a tomato is properly considered a fruit or a vegetable. When you were growing up, you were taught that it was a vegetable—or was it a fruit?—but later you learned that it was actually a fruit—or was it a vegetable? You can never remember.

After you have finished eating, you go to the computer to check your e-mail. Susannah has not written back yet, and you find only one message waiting for you: a shipping confirmation for a DVD you ordered. It is buttoned together with a list of other movies you are told you might enjoy but which you know from experience you probably won't.

You spend a few minutes reading the headlines, then a few more minutes fiddling around with a search engine, using it as you so often do to hunt for various people you let slip out of your life when you were too young to understand how much they would one day mean to you. You wonder what it says about you that you never go probing after your own name online, or the names of people you see all the time, but only those people who have disappeared into the world as thoroughly as a drop of water into a lake. To make matters worse, most of the names you find yourself looking for are relatively common—Ann Williams, Tim Carter, John Young. Is the John

Young you knew when you were in high school the same John Young who placed seventeenth in the Hospital Hill Half Marathon? He could be. But then he could also be the John Young who produces handmade knives out of sheep's horn and snake wood, or the John Young who sells real estate in Palm Springs, or the John Young whose grandfather passed away last year at the age of eighty-four. You have no way of knowing.

Ordinarily, you might find it saddening, the fact that so many of the figures from your past have been covered over by the anonymity of their lives, but *The Baron in the Trees* has left you with a lingering feeling of contentment. You can hardly imagine what it would take to discourage you right now.

You log off the Internet, then go to the door and open it to look at the breeze combing through the grass. You hear a ticking coming from somewhere—either the cistern in the closet warming up, you think, or a tree limb tapping against a drainage pipe.

It is a perfect early-fall day, with a wonderful parched quality to the air. It is almost as if it had never rained at all, not once in the entire history of the world. It is only a small pain, at first, the pinch you feel in the hollow of your chest.

Turn to page 146.

It is curious: the sounds of the neighborhood seem heavy on the air now, but really they are no more distinct than they were before, since the whole aura of ambient noises has become louder right along with them.

Birds and wind currents.

Clocks and ventilation systems.

You hear a helicopter beating at the air, or maybe it is a lawnmower. You hear a set of tires pressing the asphalt. Perhaps the mail truck has come with its morning delivery, you think, but when you look outside, you see only your neighbor backing out of his driveway, his window melting down into its carriage like a sheet of ice. He pulls into the street in a nimbus of hard rock. You recognize the song just as it fades away—Boston's "More Than a Feeling."

It is a song you will forever associate with rec-room basements thick with speaker fuzz and cigarette smoke, just as "Bad Moon Rising" is your brother's car parked with its wheels on the curb, and "Crazy" is a nightclub with a black marble counter and one small mirror on the wall, and "Come On Eileen" is the arcade room of the state fair when you were still young enough to find the crowds and the din there exciting. Your memory is so packed with the last few decades' worth of pop music that there is barely a phrase in common conversation that can't summon a lyric to your mind. There are times when you think you could fill an entire day simply following their traces from one tune to another.

The sunlight is coming in through the window at a high slant, picking out the ribs of the end table, and you notice they are fleeced with dust. Your housekeeping can be haphazard sometimes. You take a paper towel and wipe the wood clean, catching the spillover in your palm, then dumping it in the trash. Before you have finished, you begin to sneeze.

It is probably the dust, you think, but it could also be your seasonal allergies setting in. You have never understood why your sinuses would cause you such trouble at this time of year. In the spring, when everything is blossoming and drifts of pollen ride the breeze, chalking all the windshields with a fine yellow powder—yes, okay, in the spring it makes sense to you. But why now, in the fall, when everything is drying up and dying?

You sneeze two more times, then a third in quick succession. You decide it would be best to close the window. The sash tends to stick in temperate weather, so you brace your palms against the lip and lean into it. When it doesn't move, you lower your full weight onto your hands.

A noise of strain escapes from you, surprisingly high and mouselike. You feel a sudden flush of heat. The window is just beginning to fall when something in your heart goes still, wringing the breath out of your body.

Go on to page 146.

There you are, lying flat on your back, staring into the air as if through a sheet of glass. The pain is not the worst you have ever endured, but it is intense and steady enough that you quickly cease to recognize it as pain at all. It becomes just another background component of your awareness, like the scratching of the insects in the trees, like the gradual churning of sensations on your skin, a simple field upon which to observe your reactions to the world.

You are having trouble sitting up. You feel a pressure against the back of your head. You close your eyes, then open them, and by the time you do, you have lost track of how long you have been lying there. From some infinite distance, ten thousand twists of light are suddenly projected into your eyes. You watch as they shimmer and tighten together like the hooks of metal in a tangle of barbed wire. More and more of them appear, filling the gaps one by one, and soon you are conscious of nothing else.

What would the sky be like if there was nothing to see but stars?

You know that you will never experience anything so beautiful again.

It will be several thousand years before the human race develops a procedure to retrieve the memories of the dead from their bodies. By then the age in which you lived will be recollected as a time of barbarism and brute physical destruction, of interest only to historians of cultural degradation. But in the name of scientific research, a few sample bodies from your century will be exhumed for memory reclamation, and among those selected will be your own.

The technicians will lift you carefully into the sunlight, unwinding your memories like a long, thin thread. The process will not be perfect. Because you died so long ago, only the last few hours of your life will be recoverable—from the moment you returned the milk to the refrigerator to the moment the barbs of light finally flickered from your eyes.

As usual, after the technicians have examined and recorded your memories, they will provide them to the museums for public display. To the surprise of everyone involved, you will prove to be a very popular exhibit. People will wait for hours to get a glimpse of you, some of them returning many times. You will come to be regarded as a sort of cult phenomenon. There are days when the line to your gallery will reach all the way through the entrance hall and across the courtyard, fading like a plume of smoke into the broken red skies of the city.

THE END

Your computer is running slow this morning, and you have to switch it off and allow it to reboot a few times before it begins working properly. Why this should have any effect at all, you couldn't say—after all, no matter how many times you put a bent fork back in a drawer, it won't be any straighter when you take it out again—but it does work, somehow, and you log on to your Internet account and read the day's headlines before tapping out a message to Susannah.

Well, as usual, strange things are happening here on the island, you begin, and you end with,

So what do you think? Should I have said something other than what I said? Done something other than what I did? Please send help or I will perish when the waters rise.

This is a long-standing joke between the two of you—treating every letter as though you were marooned on a desert island tossing a message out in a bottle. You suppose the joke has endured for so long because you find it satisfying to imagine yourselves as castaways, sitting by the ocean with knotted hair and tattered shorts, enduring the isolation of your own lives as you would a little hump of sand with a coconut tree standing in the middle.

You wait a few minutes for Susannah to respond, but she must be away from the computer, and you log off and slide your chair back under the desk. You hear something outside. When you go to the window, you see a couple of boys bouncing a soccer ball off the asphalt to each other as they stroll down the middle of the street.

The noise echoes off the broad side of the house with a hammerlike crack that seems to break open as soon as it hits the air.

In a shoe box in your bureau, there is a photograph of you at the age of eleven or twelve—the same age these boys appear to be—trying to throw a boomerang with your brother. Your tongue is in the corner of your lips. Your brother is visoring his eyes against the sun. You have an impulse to go upstairs and look at the picture. By the time you reach the bedroom, though, you have forgotten what you came there for. You stand in the doorway staring at your walls, your bed, your ceiling fan. You think about the entertainer who used to perform in the shopping plaza down the street, juggling knives with long, flat blades. You think about a wilderness of red sand, soft winds blowing across it in thousands of overlapping ripples.

You walk back downstairs and hear the boys with their soccer ball again. For some reason that triggers the memory of the photograph you wanted to find, but by then the impulse to look at it has abandoned you. You pause there in the hallway for a moment with your hand resting on the wall.

If you decide to put some music on,
turn to page 136.

If you would rather sit down with a book,
turn to page 172.

You circle the perimeter of the room inspecting the new releases: frat-boy comedies and superhero blockbusters that surge across the shelves in wave after swollen wave, with a slender thread of foreign and independent films cutting through the center. Nothing looks very promising to you, and eventually you end up at the staff recommendations rack, always the most intriguing display in the store, with its perfect capsule versions of all the employees' personalities. You have the film purist, the deliberate eccentric, the baggy sentimentalist. You have the child at heart. You have the stranger so far from home.

"Have you seen this one?" a clerk hovering nearby asks you. He taps his finger against a movie called *Ponette*, with a little girl lost in pensive rumination on the cover. "It's the best movie in here. Most of the characters are just children. The lead is a four-year-old girl whose mother dies in a car accident. She spends the movie trying to figure out what that means, whether her mother can come back to life, whether God will listen to her if she prays to Him—that sort of thing."

"It sounds sad."

"Well, it is. But it's charming and funny, too. And beautifully shot. And filled with life and color. And just kind of miraculously authentic all around. The only question is whether your heart is strong enough to take it."

The clerk at the front register calls out, "You should rent *Breaking the Waves* instead."

The first clerk indulges a sigh, which leaves you with the impression that you have blundered into the middle of a long-standing feud. "*Breaking the Waves* is a good movie—no doubt about it. Courageous. Harrowing, even. But you get the sense that Emily Watson is suffering because the director is a sadist, whereas Ponette is suffering because life is painful. Look," he continues, "it depends on what you want from a movie. If you want art, rent *Ponette*. If you want sophomoric nonsense masquerading as art"—he scans the shelf marked ETHAN'S PICKS and selects a movie called *Dogma*— "rent this."

The other clerk, the one behind the counter, gives an indignant "Hey!"

What you truly want from a movie, though you almost never get it, is to have your life changed by it. You want the story to become a part of you, folding itself into your skin and growing like a shoot grafted onto an orange tree. "All right, I'll give it a try," you say.

"Excellent. You'll have to let me know what you think."

You are following the clerk to the register when you feel a sharp pain in your chest. Your breath surges out of you. Your legs grow weak. And it turns out that your heart was not so strong after all— a pane of glass that shatters when the window opens, a walnut that crumbles when the shell is cracked.

Turn to page 146.

Your vertigo expends itself in a surge of incandescence. You hear the blood beating in your ears—an oceanic rumble with a strange electricity behind it. Everything around you seems to go crooked and tilt to one side. You brace your hands against the window and wait for the sensation to go away. By the time you can see straight again, the boy and his father have passed out of sight, though the skateboarder is still making runs at the bike rack, his arms outstretched in a posture of flying.

Someone knocks against the inside of the window. You turn around to see the old Greek immigrant upon whose storefront you have been leaning upon gesturing at the glass. Loudly enough for you to hear, he says, "You're leaving smears, you. Go be tired somewhere else," and makes a shooing motion with his hands.

You mouth the word *sorry*, wave an apology, and set off across the plaza. The Greek's business is a secondhand clothing store called—charmingly, you have always thought—The Tired Old Man. The sign above the door depicts a tattered coat draped over the back of a chair. You have always meant to set an hour aside someday to look through his merchandise. Now, though, he is destined to remember you as yet another inconsiderate American, a sort of bush-league window vandal, and you will probably be too embarrassed to walk through the door.

How often, you wonder, has the direction of your life been shaped by such misunderstandings? How many opportunities have you been denied—or, for that matter, awarded—because someone failed to see you properly? How many friends have you lost, how many have you gained, because they glimpsed some element of your personality that shone through for only an instant, and in circumstances you could never reproduce? An illusion of water shimmering at the far bend of a highway.

Sometimes you imagine that everything could have been different for you, that if only you had gone right one day when you chose to go left, you would be living a life you could never have anticipated. But at other times you think there was no other way forward—that you were always bound to end up exactly where you have.

It is as if some invisible giant has taken control of your existence, setting his hands down like walls on either side of you. He has changed your course with each bend of his fingers. He has urged you along with gusts of his breath. He has stripped you of each of your choices until there is only one path for you to take, one turn for you to follow. And at that moment, as you swing past a mailbox, he tips your head back and fills your heart with lead. The weight is like an anchor inside you. It pulls you to the ground.

Turn to page 146.

At this hour, and at this time of year, the window in the roof above your stairwell is directly illuminated by the sun, and as you walk downstairs, it hovers over you like the opening to some other, brighter world, a dazzling square of white. On your way through the kitchen, you hear the refrigerator humming. You nudge it with your shoulder to stifle the noise. Something about the action reminds you of a bull bringing its mass to bear on a wooden gate, though as far as you can remember you have never seen such a thing in your life. Where would the image have come from, you wonder, if not your own experience?

The house seems too still now without the hum of the refrigerator filling the air. You open the living room window to let in the sounds of the street. Your neighbor is cleaning his car, dunking his washcloth into a plastic bucket and slowly wringing it out. The big drops fall into the water like silver coins. A pair of birds are exchanging notes with each other in gorgeous flurries.

You are just about to sit down on the couch when the phone rings. You do not recognize the number on the display, but you decide to take the call anyway. The voice on the other end of the line is quiet and obliging, plainly masculine, and it asks for you by name. "Speaking," you answer.

"Thank God you didn't go anywhere."

The man lunges ahead without stopping to say who he is. There follows a short, fogbound conversation in which he tells you with great emotion about someone named David. David has made it through the surgery. David is in recovery. There was a complication having to do with the anesthesia, but you don't need to worry, because everything is just fine now, and David is going to be all right. You have an uncle David, and you knew a David Summers when you were in high school; one of the waiters at the coffeehouse down the street is named David, and there are a number of other Davids in the middle pages of your address book. But it is not until the man says, "Is Frances there? Put Frances on the phone" that the truth finally dawns on you: he believes he is speaking to a different person altogether, one who just happens to share your name.

This is too much for the man. You hear a sound like puffs of steam sputtering from a teapot, a sound of heat and pressure, and you realize he is weeping.

"I'm sorry," he says. "This is embarrassing. Oh God, I didn't mean to trouble you."

He makes a thready little noise of wounded feeling and hangs up.

You sit there thinking over the conversation. You barely said a word, so how could you have said something wrong? But irrationally you feel a pang of guilt. It is the kind of story you usually share with your friend Susannah. You wonder whether she is home.

Do you call Susannah on the phone?
If so, turn to page 114.

Do you send her an e-mail instead?
If so, turn to page 148.

The grocery store is swarming with young parents and college students, nightshift workers and middle-aged businessmen, all trying to get their shopping done on a sunlit autumn Saturday. You make your way slowly down each of the aisles, stopping to wait for a little girl to root through the coloring books and for an elderly man to pick out his birdseed. You are hanging back from a tangle of carts by the baked goods counter when an image comes to you of Susannah thinking of you with exasperation. A flush of embarrassment makes you tingle from head to toe. You can feel your fingers buzzing and prickling against the handle of the shopping cart. Even when you shake them, drawing a look from the stock boy unloading the crouton boxes, the sensation does not go away.

You work your way through the grocery list you keep posted on your refrigerator, scratching your purchases off one by one.

Broccoli—check.

Sweet potatoes—check.

English muffins, ginger ale, milk, eggs, laundry detergent—check, check, check, check, and check.

Your shopping cart has a trick wheel that keeps popping around on its axle, causing the frame to lurch to the left with an indignant rattling noise. The store's intercom system is malfunctioning, but no one has bothered to turn off the music. You recognize a poor translation of the Five Stairsteps' "O-O-H Child" in the rasps and hisses trickling down from the ceiling.

You stop at the greeting card rack to find a card for your brother's birthday. When you were ten or eleven, too young to have much of your own spending money, you saw a particular birthday card at a gift store in the shopping mall. It featured a lineup of animals on the front, standing side by side as if posing for a school picture: "Hippo birdie two ewe. Hippo birdie two ewe. Hippo birdie deer ewe. Hippo birdie two ewe." You have been searching for another copy ever since. It is unfailingly strange to you, the way some random object that went sailing through your childhood for no more than two minutes can still mean something to you so many years later.

You do not find the card, of course, so you pick out a different one and take it to the register. You pay for your groceries and wheel your cart into the parking lot. The sun is shining down on the asphalt. The prickle in your fingers has spread like a rash through the rest of your body. You feel a grasping sensation in your chest. You're finding it hard to keep walking. You think perhaps you should take a nap.

Turn to page 146.

"*I* have," you say. "And I think you have, too. In fact, I'm sure you have. Don't you remember that time with the kid and his stun glove?"

You are talking about the night a high school boy came into the coffeehouse with his science fair project—a glove he had wired to a model airplane battery so that it would deliver a mild electric shock through the index finger. "Now, this is just a prototype," he kept saying as he fiddled with the current. "The real version will have a lot more juice to it." But a few minutes later, when he reached for the calzone he had ordered, the battery discharged itself all at once, and the calzone popped open in a geyser of ricotta and marinara sauce.

"Don't tell me you weren't happy then. I was here when the smoke cleared. I saw the look on your face."

David nods, laughs, nods again. "Good times."

An ambulance is coasting to a stop at the corner when suddenly its lights begin to flash and it pulls away in a burst of noise. "I've always wondered—do you think they just drive around the streets waiting for something to go wrong?" he asks. "Seems like a waste of gasoline to me."

The manager gives him a two-fingered whistle, and he says, "Uh-oh, that's me. Catch you later," rushing off to the counter with a tray of empty plates in his hands.

You have already finished your chai, but you upend the mug and tap the last few drops into your mouth. The maneuver does something strange to your inner ear, and you become light-headed. You close your eyes and rest your forehead in your hands. The room is crowded. The conversations around you seem to rise to a moment of crystalline poise and then dash against the wall, again and again, like waves breaking over one another as they come into shore. You feel as if you could wade into the sound and float out to sea. It takes a minute for the sensation to fade away and by the time it does, someone has collected your mug and your water glass and left the check for you to pay.

You watch as the morning sunlight, so bright inside the room when you first came in, travels a few last inches across the polished cedar and passes through the window. A coffee grinder screams out with a guttural wail. A piece of silverware drops to the floor, springing end over end. You would like to say good-bye to David, but he has either disappeared into the kitchen or gone upstairs, and it looks as if you will have to catch him the next time. You leave a five-dollar bill on the table and stand up.

If you head out into the plaza again,
turn to page 130.

If you stop off at the bathroom to wash your hands,
go on to page 168.

It takes you only a few minutes to walk from the plaza to your front door. As you stride down the street, your neighbor passes you in his car. He waves and taps his horn, the guitar strains of Boston's "More Than a Feeling" trailing in the wind behind him. A dog feints toward you on the sidewalk, but swings back around when her owner shouts, "Zelda! Hyah!" as if he were urging on a horse.

The air carries a slight scent of burned matches, a smell you have always associated with the first days of fall: how the leaves will soon turn crisp and come loose from the trees, how the evenings will begin to bite into the afternoons. Something about the smell makes you lighthearted. On your way to the door, you flick the stiff red flag of your mailbox, and it springs back into place with a birchy *thwack*.

You go to your kitchen and pour yourself a glass of water. There is a long message waiting for you on your answering machine. It commences with a sigh: "I can't believe you're not home. Listen, call me back as soon as you get this message. David is in recovery. There was a complication, but you don't need to worry about that, everything is going to be fine, it's just . . ." The man on the machine takes a ragged breath. You wonder if he is crying. "Never mind. It doesn't matter. The important thing is that David is going to be okay. I'll fill you in on the details when you *call me back*. Oh, and tell Frances that he was asking about the two of you before they put him under. All right. I guess that's it. All right."

It is not until the last few sentences that you realize the man must have dialed the wrong number. You do in fact know several Davids—there is your uncle David, the David who rode the bus with you in high school, the David who waits tables at Sufficient Grounds—but as far as you can remember, you have never known a Frances in your life. You play the message once more, listening for a callback number, but you fail to hear one. The caller ID display on your phone shows only an "out of area" notice, and since the man did not even leave his name, there is no way for you to track him down and explain his mistake.

You wander into the living room, where you absentmindedly scan the titles on your bookcase. You lean back against the arm of your couch. You are still nurturing an inexplicable cheer, and you wonder if you ought to feel worse for the man than you do.

There is something wrong with your equilibrium suddenly, something wrong with your legs. You forget the question you were asking yourself. You do not even realize you have fallen until you feel the carpet scratching the back of your neck.

Turn to page 146.

You head toward the church at the open edge of the plaza. It was built nearly fifty years ago, long before the local church boom, and its family of parishioners is small but dedicated. The building is a modest structure of oak and limestone, only a single square steeple rising above the trees to impale a corner of the sky. Because it is Saturday, the parking lot is essentially deserted, with only a pair of empty white church vans waiting in the drive. You are in the habit of hosting little interior debates with the declarations posted on the illuminated marquee, arguing the finer points of theology, but today the message is

WHATS MISSING FROM OUR CH CH?

UR!

and you suppose you can't argue with that.

The yard is dotted with dozens of elms and willows, clustered together so that their trunks lean against one another and their branches interlace. The bird-haunted stillness of the place makes you want to rest there for a while. You find a bench beneath one of the willows and sit down. You begin to feel tired and lie back with your feet dangling off the end, staring up into the canopy of branches. The openings between the leaves keep shrinking and expanding as the trees dance slowly in the wind, lending a beating quality to the sunlight that you find almost hypnotic.

Once, you were staying in a cabin with your family when the electricity went out. You were four years old at the time, and afraid of the dark, and when you started to cry, your parents brought you a camper's flashlight, the kind with a broad, flat base and a lens as big around as a lantern. You stood it upright on your chest, pointing the beam at the ceiling, and it was not long before you noticed the light shifting its center back and forth between a pair of wooden rafters. Gradually you came to realize that what you were seeing was your heartbeat, its pulse transmitted by the flashlight, throbbing above you just as the sunlight is now throbbing between the leaves of the willow.

You can't recall the last time this incident occurred to you, though the memory is a good one. Why is it that certain moments come to your mind every few days and other moments almost never? It is a mystery to you. Then your heart opens up in your breast, and the mystery does not concern you anymore.

Turn to page 146.

"Oh, I'm wasting my life all right," you answer. "I'm just not wasting it *that* way."

What is it about her voice that allows you to hear that she is smiling? There is a tightness to it, a pleasing elasticity, not the same kind of tightness you can hear when she is angry, but not entirely dissimilar. "And how are you wasting it?" she asks.

"You know. The usual. Mooning and nostalgia."

"Mooning? You're wasting your life *mooning*?"

"Not *that* kind of mooning. Mooning as in 'mooning away.' 'I'm mooning away for the hills of old Virginia.' You know what I meant. Pervert."

The two of you fill the next ten minutes talking about nothing of any real importance—a song with lyrics you can only half remember, the movies you have both been waiting to see, whether she should buy a new computer, and if so, whether it should be a laptop or a desktop. It is the best, most intimate kind of conversation, its true subject nothing more than how proficient the two of you are in your friendship, but it's interrupted when a call comes in on her other line. "Can you give me a second?"

"Of course."

You hear your clock ticking and then your wristwatch, slightly out of time with each other. You hear the keening of a fire engine. Unconsciously, you have been scratching out a drawing on the back cover of a magazine, and you hold it up to the sunlight to examine it.

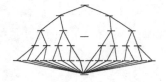

It looks like a flying saucer, you think, or maybe a chandelier—an umbrella of lines branching out from the tip, flaring wider and wider, then converging suddenly at a common point, with a little window to nowhere floating in the center.

Susannah clicks back over. "Hey, I'm going to need to take this call. We'll talk later, okay?"

"Okay. Later."

The phone settles neatly into its cradle. You pivot your head around in a long, low-swinging circle, trying to work a tight spot out of your neck, and when you yawn, there is a rush of wind in your ear. It happens just as unexpectedly as it always does: some membrane of fluid breaks open, and everything is twice as loud.

If you would like to go out and test the air,
turn to page 122.

If you are comfortable where you are,
turn to page 144.

McDonald's is nearly empty. The early-morning coffee drinkers have already come and gone, and the late-morning breakfast crowd has yet to arrive. There is only an old man standing at the condiment shelf, a woman feeding cookies to a small boy in a booster seat, and a man in a jogging suit talking loudly to himself by the trash bins—or so you think, until you see the headset curled around his ear like the shell of a mollusk. It is a testament to the restaurant's indomitable spirit of mechanism that you can feel such anonymity in so sparse a gathering.

You order a Coke and sink it at the counter, then order a refill and take it to a booth in the back corner. The bubbles seem to spark and leap against your tongue, leaving a pins-and-needles feeling behind them. The cold travels through you in isolated pulses.

After you have drained the cup, you slip a chunk of crushed ice between your lips, holding it against the roof of your mouth while it melts, as your mother used to do. She used to be young, wearing her hair in a long, limp curtain that fell halfway down her back. She used to clip UPC symbols from cereal boxes and send them in to sweepstakes contests. She used to sing Olivia Newton-John songs in the car and watch *Dallas* on Friday nights. It all seems like such a long time ago now.

You remember visiting the McDonald's down the street from your house with her when you were growing up: the burgers that came in Styrofoam clamshells and the fries that came in white paper sleeves. The walls in the restaurant were decorated with representations of all the McDonaldland characters—Ronald, Captain Crook, the Fry Guys—but you were a peculiar child, overanxious about the littlest things, and for some reason you were never truly happy unless you got to sit beneath the picture of the Grimace.

You think about the drinking straw dispensers that used to fascinate you when you were that age, the way the straws fell so neatly into the stainless-steel rack, like coins dropping into a piggy bank. You think about the fat sound of raindrops smacking against a canvas tarp.

You cannot name the feeling that passes through you. It is a pale, nimble thing that floats out of the corner of your mind and disappears into the darkness again, fading away like a wisp of fog, but it leaves you weak in the knees, as if you have taken a fast-rising elevator to the top of a tall building where the door opens directly onto the starlight. You wipe the moisture from your hands with a napkin. You swallow a mouthful of ice.

Do you throw your cup away and leave?
If so, turn to page 112.

Do you stop to buy another Coke?
If so, turn to page 138.

One of the bathrooms at Sufficient Grounds was damaged by vandals a few weeks ago—the mirror shattered, the paper towel dispenser ripped off the wall, and the toilet fractured into two large pieces as oddly and neatly divided as the halves of a peanut—and for the time being, the other bathroom has been converted into a unisex.

There is an emblem on the door of a straight-lined man holding hands with a triangular woman. The lock is broken, so you knock and call out hello, then slowly open the door to make sure the room is empty. More than once you have been only half-finished with what you were doing when someone came bulling into the bathroom and you had to arrest the door with your foot, offering a disconcerted "I'm in here," and waiting for whoever it was to go away.

The light flickers on automatically. You go to the sink to wash your hands. The soap spurts out of a silver nozzle on the counter. It is a pale red foam that smells like cherries, or at least that is meant to remind you of the smell of cherries, that smells like some chemist in a design lab must suppose cherries smell. On the lip of the sink is a hardened white powder that looks like the crust you find every so often in the battery well of a flashlight when it has been left running too long. You avoid touching it.

Your image is kinked in the mirror, and you put your hand to it to probe for a flaw. The sight of your fingers approaching themselves from the other side of the glass makes you feel dizzy again, and you reach out to steady yourself against the wall. For just a moment, you imagine that the mirror is a gate to some other world, that the kink in the glass is a keyhole and, were the tumblers to turn, your reflection would wheel open in a spray of silver light.

This was one of your favorite fantasies when you were growing up: you would enter some small, ordinary-looking room—a closet or an attic, a coat room or a pantry—and inside you would find a door to a place where your life would be utterly transformed, like Alice in *Through the Looking-Glass* or the Pevensie children in *The Lion, the Witch, and the Wardrobe.*

You close your eyes and try to catch your breath. Your head is spinning. Your left arm has gone numb. You hear someone knocking on the door. "I'll be done in just a minute," you mean to say, but you can't find your voice to answer.

The taste of copper fills your mouth.

Your heart stops short.

The door opens.

Turn to page 146.

You spray the glass with Windex, then wipe it dry, taking special care with the white dots of toothpaste foam above the sink, the dust beneath the light fixtures, and the fingerprints on the handle to the medicine cabinet. The overlapping circles of the washcloth leave moisture trails that look like the fossils of trilobites for the few seconds until they evaporate. The scent of ammonia blasts your sinuses clear.

You have always disliked meeting your gaze in the mirror. You avoid it as a cat will, and probably for the same reason: you are too proud, or too meek, to accept that the creature inside it is you.

This morning is no different. You manage to clean the entire mirror without once looking into your eyes. The process takes no more than ten minutes, but when you are finished and set out to return the Windex to the kitchen, you find that you have to sit down at the top of the stairs and catch your breath.

You should get more exercise than you do—you know that. Still, you can't believe that such little exertion has left you so winded.

A picture surfaces in your mind of a tattered coat draped over the back of a chair. Although it seems familiar to you, you do not know where it comes from. A painting, maybe, or a photograph. You hold on to it for a moment and then let it go.

You become a little dizzy when you stand up, and, bracing your hand against the wall to keep yourself from stumbling, you accidentally bite the inside of your cheek. You probe it to see if you have punctured the skin. A small, ragged flap meets the tip of your tongue. For the past few years, you have had to endure a series of mouth ulcers, some of them as large around as a thumbtack, and often as piercing, and you have learned how opportunistic they can be. Any time you aggravate your gums or your cheeks, your tongue or the roof of your mouth, wounding the flesh in any way, you know that the tissue will ulcerate and for a week or more you will feel as if you are holding a hornet inside your mouth. You will find it painful to eat, sing, talk, or even smile. The hornet will sting you if you twitch so much as a muscle.

As a child, you could never have anticipated how careful you would one day have to become with yourself. You are like a climber scaling the broad face of a rock, testing every mole and furrow to see if it will hold your weight. There are times when your whole life seems to bend itself to the worst instincts of your imagination.

You imagine your stomach is burning, and you clutch your abdomen, dropping the Windex bottle onto the stairs. You imagine your legs have lost feeling, and you sink to the floor. You imagine your blood has stopped pumping, and your heart turns to concrete.

Turn to page 146.

You are three-quarters of the way through a novel called *The Baron in the Trees*. It tells the story of an eighteenth-century Italian nobleman—Cosimo Piovasco di Rondò—who spends the whole of his adult life in the trees surrounding his village, never once setting foot on the ground. From the branches of the various oaks, elms, and ilexes, he is able to hunt and travel, conduct love affairs and educate himself, as well as engage in a series of duels with a creed-bound Spanish Jesuit. Your favorite passages are the ones that detail Cosimo's encounters with the outlaw Gian dei Brughi, whose book addiction he first initiates and later feeds, but you also find yourself lingering over the paragraphs that describe his long romance with his childhood neighbor Violante.

You settle into the couch and continue reading the novel, holding the pages up to a patch of sunlight. A fire truck begins whirring its siren somewhere, but you barely notice it. What most amazes you about the book is how rich it is, how sensitive to the constitution of its characters' souls, how beautiful and moving without being anguished or hopeless. It is certainly not blind to human suffering, featuring poverty, loss, aging, and death, but its mood is overwhelmingly one of celebration. There is a tenderness and a brio to the story. The writer extends his sympathies so widely that even the trees and the hills seem to sing with the joy of existence.

You bought a copy of the novel after you heard an interview with a Pulitzer Prize winner who described its author, Italo Calvino, as the finest writer of the twentieth century and this book, in particular, as the best one he had ever read. You were skeptical of such a lavish claim—who wouldn't be?—but damned if it might not be the best book you have ever read: a short, crystalline novel with all the grace and poetry of *The Great Gatsby*, but fantastic rather than realistic, and joyful in its elegies rather than plaintive. At one point, you are so touched and delighted by something you read that you actually laugh and kiss the page—a completely unself-conscious gesture that you don't even notice yourself performing at first, and which, when you do, strikes you as both ridiculous and somehow wonderful.

It does not take you long to read the last few chapters. You finish the novel, above all else, with an impression of a robust and loving comic energy. You feel as if you have been immersed in life—both your own life and the particular lives of the book's characters—and that life, for all its misfortunes, is a pretty good place to be.

If you find a place for the novel on your bookcase,
go on to page 116.

If you leave it sitting on the arm of the couch for now,
turn to page 142.

"I'm sure somebody has," you say. "There are just too many of us walking around."

Outside the man who strolls up and down the plaza selling yo-yos stops at a bench to tighten his shoes. He is your city's version of the dandy in the double-breasted suit who roots through the garbage scavenging for recyclables, or the old couple with sombreros and ukeleles who sit in the park singing songs about their sex life—recognized by everybody, the object of a thousand jokes, but so lasting a feature of the landscape that they inspire as much affection as anyone you could mention. You watch as he finishes tying his shoes, loops a pair of yo-yos around each of his index fingers and another pair around each of his ring fingers, then sets them spinning in an elaborate Gordian whirl.

"There," you say, pointing to the man. "He has. There's a man who's been happy his whole life."

David gives you a *yeah-well-about-that* grimace. "I hate to break it to you, but the guy comes in here for a steamer sometimes, and he sounds pretty miserable. He's always complaining about his wrists. He's worried he might have carpal tunnel. Uh-oh, she's about to unleash one of her whistles on me."

This swerve in his comments perplexes you until you spot his manager eyeballing him from behind the dessert counter.

"Believe me," he says, "you don't want her to whistle. You could be dead twenty years and that thing would wake you up. I'd better get back to work. Take it easy."

David glides away balancing a tray of empty plates on his palm, sheering around the banister of the staircase and using his free hand to bump the kitchen door open. You collect the last sip of chai on your spoon. You hear a few chirps of noise, followed by a seesawlike ululating sound, and look up to see an ambulance racing away from the corner. It vanishes behind a cluster of red gums, but for a long minute the siren continues to cut through the air, howling like some great beast fleeing a terrible calamity. You listen as the sound gradually fades away, then you get up and pay your check.

The pleasant weather has brought a surprising number of people out this morning, and by the time you reach the cash register, your chair has already been taken. After the cashier runs your credit card, you have to weave your way through a clutch of power walkers in nylon tracksuits to get to the door. Outside, the sunlight is sending shards of glass off the bike racks and parking meters. The chestnut leaves are ticking against one another like fingernails. You feel a touch of heartburn coming on. You give your chest a thump. It would do you good, you imagine, to take a little walk.

If you decide to go left,
turn to page 134.

If you decide to go right,
turn to page 162.

THE LADY WITH THE PET TRIBBLE

for Justin Turner

I.

On Sirius all the days seemed to melt together in a single formless three o'clock. The Keptin had been at the resort for the better part of two weeks, and in all that time he had acquired only one memory to speak of: an image of himself sitting in a chair at the edge of the plaza, sipping sapphire wine and basking in the light of the multiple suns. As soon as he had drained his glass, one of the drink girls would arrive to fill it back up for him, bending at the waist as she poured. He knew that if he brushed her wrist with the backs of his fingers, she would sink toward him like a blade of grass pooling over with water and forget to charge him for it. The Keptin was fully aware of the effect he had on women. Ever since boyhood, he had been blessed with a certain carelessly sensual charm, though he had never used it for anything other than to be charming.

It was late in the afternoon when he saw an unfamiliar person walking beneath the trees: a lady with a pet tribble. The light picked her out as she stopped to slide her fingers through the grass and then moved slowly across the plaza toward the public fountain. She was a vision—her long skirt belling out in the breeze, the tribble nestled delicately between her palm and her stomach. The Keptin had been sitting in his chair for so long that the blood rushed to his head when he stood. Thousands of exploding white holes appeared in the air around him, and by the time his eyesight cleared, the lady was gone. This was Sirius, though. He was certain he would see her again. He made up his mind that he would introduce himself to her at the first opportunity.

That opportunity came the very next evening, while he was dining in the open-air Sandorian restaurant by the Oxbow Lake. The lady with the pet tribble took a bench on the far side of the patio. After the Keptin had settled his bill, he approached her and asked if she would mind some company. She was no longer wearing the skirt he had seen her in the day before, but a bright yellow dress—something like a pinafore—that bared her arms and shoulders.

"Please," she said, gesturing at the bench, and he sat down. The lady put her hands together on her knees and asked him, "What's your name?"

"I'm James," the Keptin said.

"I'm Raïssa."

She had yet to meet his eyes. He watched her without speaking until she looked at him. A smile stole over one corner of her lips, making a comma-shaped dimple in her cheek, and though the expression vanished almost immediately, he knew right away that she would say yes to him when the time came. At the beginning of any relationship, there was a moment of flirtation when a woman either gave her assent or barred the door. The Keptin had become skillful at predicting which sort of woman was likely to be which. He could barely remember the last time he had heard a lock clicking.

"Are you here alone?" he asked.

"Yes. My husbands are back on Arcturus."

"Husbands?"

"Two of them. My people practice multiple marriage."

"I see. And are you enjoying your stay?"

She sighed. "The answer you're supposed to give is 'of course.' But . . . well . . . I was going to say that this place makes me tired, but the truth is that every place makes me tired." And though he had failed to notice it before, there was definitely a weariness in her manner, a fragile unbraided quality that reminded him of those stray plasma streamers he sometimes saw drifting slowly apart in the interstellar winds. " 'Sirius, the Pleasure Planet,' " she quoted. " 'Where life is one endless cocktail hour.' "

He smiled. "I like to think of it as the endless three o'clock."

" 'The endless three o'clock,' " Raïssa said. And then, "James is a clever man."

Her tribble was resting on a little pillow on her lap, purring, and a tremor passed through its pink fur as she stroked it.

They decided to take a stroll along the promenade, where he asked her about her husbands. The first one was a trader, gone for months at a time in his slow-moving mongrel cargo ship. She had married him mainly as a way of solidifying his relationship with her father's import-export business. The second husband was a more complicated matter. She had been in love with him once, she said, when they were both young and thought they would never change, or at least that they would always change for the better—but then he had broken one of his legs in a climbing accident, and he had never fully recuperated, and slowly all the happiness had leaked out of him. Now he rarely spoke to her except to say that she was the only thing he had left in the world. She could hardly sit in the same room with him without feeling a sense of paralysis. But she could never leave him. And she could never marry again.

"Why not? Isn't that one of the advantages of multiple marriage—that you *can* marry again?"

"Yes, but he would think I was abandoning him," she said. "It's complicated. He still loves me, you see, he just no longer loves himself." For a moment she was lost in reflection. "You wouldn't have guessed that would change the way I feel about him, but it does somehow. Strange."

"And how is it that you're not back on Arcturus with him now?"

"I wanted some time away, and he suggested I try Sirius. He said I should take as much time as I needed. I doubt he can do without me for more than another week or so, though."

After that, they turned the conversation to more pleasant topics: the music they liked, the novels they had read, the smell of the breeze as it rose off the lake. He put his hand to the small of her back to guide her around a broken stone in the walkway, pressing a little bit harder than was strictly necessary, and felt her respond to his touch by jerking away in a moment's surprise before she eased back against him. At the end of the evening she stopped at a grocer's cart to buy some grain to feed her tribble. Then the two of them parted, promising to meet again the next day.

The Keptin had been a faithful officer for more than half his life. He was married to his job, his commission, and it was not the sort of career that encouraged multiple marriage. But the service had never frowned upon the occasional love affair. And in fact his duty to his ship and crew had always offered him a convenient escape hatch from his relationships with women, one that was less likely to hurt them when the mysteries of their personality dissolved and inevitably they became plain to him. That night as he lay in bed, he thought with satisfaction of Raïssa. She was a depleted soul, it seemed, locked in a pitiful marriage, but she was beautiful, with her long, vase-shaped legs and her perfect white skin, and he looked forward to seeing her again.

The poor thing, he said to himself. It was the last thought he had before he fell asleep.

II.

The Keptin spent much of the next day with Raïssa, and every day thereafter until his leave came to an end. They would meet in the late morning in one of Sirius's many restaurants, where they would sit over cups of tea and plan their day together: hiking the resort's nature trails or soaking in the reyamilk baths, picnicking on the lakeside or taking in a holoconcert. The Keptin ran his finger along her jawline every so often, took the soft crook of her arm as she sat down, rested his hand on her waist as they walked. Slowly she relaxed into his touch. She was so young, barely out of her childhood, and with her hair coiled into a chaplet she reminded him of one of the girls he had been involved with during his time at the academy.

"Why do you have that look in your eye?" Raïssa asked him.

"You make me think of someone I used to know, a long time ago," he said, squeezing her hand, and when he told her about the girl he had in mind, Ruth, she blushed and then smiled. Her earrings swayed as she turned her head. She was young, and she made him feel young, too.

The two of them never separated until well after the suns fell. One evening, they were walking past the *jamaharon* center when Raïssa said, "You never talk about your work with me. What did you say the name of your ship was—the *Endeavour?*"

"I'm on Sirius to get away from my work. That's why we never talk about it." But he had to admit to himself he thought about his ship and his crew all the time. He wondered whether they had fought off any battle cruisers. He imagined all the new civilizations they might have encountered. He should have been there, on the bridge, watching the stars turn into white streaks in the main viewer. Why couldn't he put the idea out of his mind? Why did he wake up every morning worrying about his crew? He knew how unnecessary it was. He had left the ship under the command of his science officer, Commander S., and if there was one thing you could say about him, it was that he knew how to keep his wits about him in a crisis. He was all logic and no emotion—duty stripped entirely of passion. He was like the speed of light in normal space: he never changed.

"And when you're back onboard your ship," Raïssa asked, "will you stop thinking of *me*, too?"

That was the Keptin's intention. Instead of answering, though, he gave her his most appreciative smile, slipped his arm around her waist, and led her out of the trees into the plaza.

The sky was just beginning to dim. A gust of wind whipped through the air and made the fountain throw off a curtain of spray. They watched as a small boy who had been prodding a boat across the water caught the spray full in his face and staggered off crying, his arms held out like tree branches. The Keptin started to laugh, expecting Raïssa to join him, but instead she stopped midstep and said passionately, "I don't want to go back home. You don't know what it's like for me, James. I want to stay here with you, here on Sirius, but my husband, my husband—"

She leaned into him, and without thinking he kissed her, running his hands behind her ears and gripping the back of her head. It happened the same way every time: his legs became rooted to the ground, taking on an almost impossible heaviness, while his upper body seemed to thin out and rise into the air, as long and loose as a streamer, so that he had the peculiar sense that he was two separate people, two separate creatures, attached to each other by only the slightest thread. He let Raïssa go, then kissed her again. He watched as she looked around to make sure no one had seen them. The only person nearby was a trader with an Orion slave woman draped over his arm, her glossy green skin reflecting the last of the sunlight like the still water of a deep lake. The trader was paying no attention to them, of course. He had other things on his mind. And besides, the sight of two lovers kissing on the street was as common as grass on Sirius. "Take me back to your room," the Keptin whispered, and he followed Raïssa across the city to her hotel.

She could be so terribly naïve at times, like a little girl experiencing everything from the empty chamber of her own innocence, but then something would topple over or come together inside her—he was never sure which—and suddenly she would seem so perceptive, so worldly, like a woman twice her age. She gave herself over to him with that perfect mixture of purpose and abandon that could only be the product of long experience or unassailable instinct, but then, after they had dressed and the Keptin had borrowed her sink to wash his face and hands, she began to cry. He gave her a moment to compose herself. There was a basket of moba fruit on the table by her window. He sat down and slowly peeled the rind off a piece until he had unplugged the vent in the bottom and the fruit released its thick mist of red perfume. He spat the seeds out one by one into a small silver dish. The fruit was so good that when he was finished he peeled and ate a second one.

"My husband would never leave our house again if he knew that I had fallen in love with someone else. He would never leave his bed," Raïssa said. The lines of her tears still glistened on her cheeks. "What are we going to do?"

In the long life of the Keptin, many women had declared their love for him, but he had always known that he could never jeopardize his commission with a long-term romance, and known that he had a lifetime of such commissions in front of him, and so even at those moments when he felt his heart stir at the sound of the word, he had never felt free to declare his love in return.

He sat beside Raïssa and took her in his arms. "What *can* we do?"

"You don't understand," she said. "You're a good man. You're kind to me. You try to pretend you're some kind of rake, but I can see you more clearly than that. I know that it's only a facade. But I—I don't know what kind of woman I am anymore. I used to think my life was going to be so simple. But now I'm stuck. That's the awful truth—I'm stuck. I hate what I'm doing to my husband. And if you could see what I'm doing to him, you would hate me, too."

"I don't hate you," the Keptin said. But he didn't understand her, either. Why was she so overturned by what had happened between them? Couldn't she just accept their time together for what it was? He looked at the tribbles on her dressing table. There were eight of them now, piled together in a variety of colors, purring in the light of a small, dim table lamp. The day they met he had seen only the one. He could not remember her mentioning any others. Perhaps there was a tribble dealer somewhere on the planet.

"We'll have to say good-bye in a few days," Raïssa said. "We'll have to say good-bye and never see each other again. It will make us so unhappy, but it's the only answer."

"Everything will be all right," the Keptin told her, and he lay back on the bed with her head resting on his chest until gradually they both fell asleep.

The next day they took a floater out to the waterfalls at the edge of the city, where they spent the afternoon following the paths that ran beneath the line of cascades. The light seemed to change as it traveled through the water, softening to a pale green and taking on hundreds of closely packed twists and folds that looked like spaghetti strands twined together inside an eggbeater. As soon as the two of them crossed back into the open air, everything looked just as it had before, fixed and steady, shining inside its own sharp outline. They might have been on a completely different planet. The sky was blue, the leaves were green, and the seams of clay that showed through the hillside were red and yellow. How many planets was any one planet likely to contain? the Keptin wondered. Hundreds probably, if not thousands.

Raïssa was tired that day—tired much of the time, in fact—and as they made their way down the hillside, she kept pulling him aside so that they could stop and rest for a while, commandeering this or that bench or outcropping of stone. Occasionally, some hidden reservoir of vitality would open up inside her and she would seem as vivacious as she had the first time he saw her, bending over to slip her fingers through the grass, but before long the reservoir would seal shut again, her limbs would go slack with exhaustion, and she would rub her temples or close her eyes, taking long, soft, slow, deliberate breaths of air. He was surprised to discover that it was not when she seemed so strong and full of energy that he was most attracted to her, but at those moments when she looked as though she were stifling some infinite sigh. There was something about her weakness, her fragility, that made him want to hold her in his arms and shore her up.

They were walking by the chain of pools next to the field where they had left the floater when she turned to him and said, "This is my favorite time of day on Sirius."

"Why's that?"

"Everything is so tranquil here when the suns are going down. On Arcturus, the longneedles come out at sunset. You have to wave your arms around the whole time to keep them from biting. You can never simply stop and enjoy yourself."

The only insects the Keptin could see were making small circles on the surface of the pools, where the fish snapped at them and sucked them under. The insects made circles on the water, and the fish took them into the circles of their mouths, and then the birds ate the fish, and the wildlife ate the birds, and the soil consumed the wildlife, nourishing the plants that the insects ate. And so everything was a circle. He wondered how many people before them had stopped in that same place at the end of the day to watch the water trickling through the pools, thinking, as he was, about their moment in the circle, and how many people after them would do the same.

A Cossack in full military uniform stopped and glared at them, his eyes glimmering like drops of black oil beneath his cranial ridges. He didn't say anything, just harrumphed and moved on, and as he vanished up the trail, the Keptin and Raïssa looked at each other and began to laugh. Soon one of the suns slipped below the horizon. Raïssa leaned casually over into an embrace. The Keptin could feel the curve of her rib cage rising and falling beneath her shirt. "It's getting late," she said, and it was.

Two days later, shortly before his ship was scheduled to arrive back in orbit over Sirius, Raïssa received a brief transmission from her husband that made her decide to return home. The transmission was a simple low-frequency voice message, crackling with interference from the solar flares, that was waiting for her when she arrived in her hotel room: "Hello, dear. I missed the sound of your voice, and I was hoping to"—here the message either skipped or he repeated himself—"the sound of your voice, and I was hoping to hear it again. But there's nobody there to talk to, you see. What a mess." At that, he began to cough, and the transmission ended.

"It's worse than I thought," Raïssa said. "He's been drinking."

"How can you tell?" The Keptin was a skilled interpreter of tone and inflection, but he had been unable to determine anything about the man's character through the popping and hissing of the signal.

All she said was, "I can tell." Then she pulled out her suitcases and began to pack.

The Keptin had spent almost every minute of the last seven days with Raïssa. They had stayed in her room one night, in his the next, touching even while they slept. Over and over again she had told him how kind he was to her, how tender, and how she was failing them both, failing everybody, by being too weak to resist him and too guilt-ridden to leave her husband. "I don't see how either one of you can love me like you do," she said. But the Keptin knew that though he had been kind to her, and though he had been tender, he had never loved her. She had a duty to her husband, she claimed, and she was probably right, but he had a duty of his own, a duty to his commission, and he would not allow that duty to be frustrated.

A ship was leaving for the Arcturus System that afternoon. He stayed with Raïssa to help her pack, collecting her shoes from the closet and then folding her dresses for her as she knelt by the bedside cabinet stuffing dozens of tribbles into a suitcase. Together they walked to the transporter room. As they waited for the engineer to program the sequencers, she clasped his hands and said, "I'll miss you, James. I'll never see you again, but that doesn't mean I'm going to stop missing you. The way things are, we didn't stand a chance. In some other universe maybe, but not in this one." Then she kissed him. Her eyes were glassed over with tears, and the Keptin could see the subtle tightening of her features as she tried to restrain herself from crying. The speech she gave had obviously been rehearsed, but he was touched by it in spite of himself, and because he was touched by it, he was also irritated. It seemed to him that she was making their separation more difficult than it ought to have been, that she was prodding him with the sharp edge of her own misery as a way of saying, "Remember me. Remember me."

"We're ready for you now, ma'am," the engineer said, and Raïssa pressed one hand to the Keptin's chest and let the other slip from his fingers. Then she stepped up onto the transporter pad. He felt a curious mixture of relief and sadness as her body turned to energy inside the confinement beam.

Afterward, he stopped for a drink of sapphire wine in the bar by the plaza. He had barely finished his first glass when Commander S.

contacted him to tell him that the ship had arrived in orbit, and as he gathered his things at the hotel, he thought about Raïssa and the time they had spent together. Already she was receding into his past—just another episode in his life, just another romance. Soon his recollection of her would be stripped of all its living breath, like the cloud of gas cast off by a collapsing star, and he would think of her, when he thought of her at all, as only a glittering pinpoint of what she had really been, a speck glowing somewhere far in the distance of his memory. She was returning to the harness of her marriage, and he was returning to his ship and his crew, and that was the way it should be.

For the first time since he had arrived on Sirius, he felt a slight chill in the air. He flipped open the antenna grid on his communicator. "One to beam up, Commander S."

III.

The Keptin resumed command of his ship, settling quickly back into his daily routine. Each morning, from his chair on the bridge, he directed the navigator to lay in a new set of coordinates and watched as the stars tunneled toward him in the main viewer, fixing into fresh constellations as the ship reached warp speed. He called down to the engine room at the top of every hour to make sure the propulsion system was running smoothly. Whenever he received a message from a passing starship, he told Lieutenant U. to patch it through to him on the intercom, and whenever he detected a bird of prey decloaking nearby, he initiated a red alert. He never knew who he was so surely as he did at such moments, with his tricorder in his palm and the bridge ticking like a clock all around him.

Nothing had changed while he was away. The science labs, the corridors, the onboard lighting—they were all the same. The

Keptin ate his meals in the mess hall. He practiced his target shooting on the phaser range. He played cards in the recreation lounge. He knew exactly where he would find his crew when they were off duty: his science officer would be meditating in his quarters, the doctor reading in the ship's library, the helmsman pruning his plants in the botany lab. At night, as he lay with his head pressed against his pillow, he could hear the quiet, pulsing hum of the warp nacelles through the hull of the ship. The sound reminded him of the ocean waves along the California coastline, just a few blocks from the Academy. He would fall asleep imagining what it must have felt like to be one of those fish that lived in the shallows, sailing in and out with the changing of the tide.

In short, he became absorbed again in the details of his life. The weeks moved forward with a singular swiftness. One day he was surmounting a few minor difficulties to deliver a shipment of vaccine to the Tau Ceti system, and the next he was evading a fleet of battle cruisers on his way to a rendezvous with the starship *Potemkin*. He attended a performance of a Shakespeare play, led a landing party through the rocky cliffs of Planet M-220, and docked at a starbase for deflector repairs. He challenged Commander S. to a game of three-dimensional chess, and when the Keptin lost, as he usually did, he congratulated the Commander with a glass of spice tea, though in the privacy of his heart he had to admit that he found the look of joyless accomplishment on his face infuriating.

He was sure that he would stop thinking of Sirius soon, and yet, as the months passed, he realized he was dwelling on the memory of his visit there more and more. He would be riding the turbolifts or standing over the tactical console on the bridge, and suddenly he would hear the fountain trickling in the plaza, smell the strong vanilla scent of the perfumery, see the shadows of the trees swaying like the long necks of water birds, and it would seem to him that he was there again, on the Pleasure Planet. He knew that he had been bored for much of his stay there, bored and listless, slowly growing drunk as he drowsed in the heat of the multiple suns, but in his memory the resort was purged of all its tedium and hollow agreeability and it became something extraordinary. There was the Earth restaurant across the street from his hotel, for instance, which served the best grilled mushrooms he had ever eaten so far from home. There was the gentle breeze that cooled him as he walked along the beach. And most of all there was Raïssa. He thought of her constantly. He would look back on the afternoon they spent walking beneath the waterfalls together and remember how the mist had made her skin glisten when she crossed into the light, how her voice had sounded in the stillness of the mountain trail, how she had stopped by the chain of pools just to tell him that it was her favorite time of day. He would remember these things, and he would smile to himself. He couldn't help it. He would smile again as he thought about the way she rose onto her toes the first time he kissed her, as though she wanted him to toss her into the air. Sometimes his collar would kink against the back of his neck when he turned his head, and he would imagine he felt the touch of her fingers there, tickling him from behind, her pet tribbles purring in the background as she gave him a massage. Could it really be that he was destined never to see her again? He had been so brusque with her, so unresponsive, but for the life of him he couldn't remember why. When he thought of her now, he felt nothing but love. "You're a good man," she had said to him. "You're so kind to me, so tender," and he knew that it wasn't true. She was the kind one, she was the good one. But now that she was gone, he wanted to be the man she had deluded herself into believing he was. He wanted a second chance.

He began to dream about her. He imagined they were married and raising two children, who were also named James and Raïssa, and the tenor of his dreams followed him into the waking world. Once he was on a shuttlecraft with his chief engineer, embarking toward a vessel that was in need of transporter repair, when he found himself fantasizing about what it would have been like if he had never become an officer and she had never married her husbands back on Arcturus. The engineer had to call his name several times before he heard him. "Sir? What are your orders, sir? Earth to James."

The Keptin was embarrassed. "Full impulse, Scotty. Maintain current heading."

"Aye, sir," Scotty answered, and though he did not say anything more, the Keptin could tell that he was wondering what was wrong with him.

There was no one he could talk to about Raïssa. Sometimes, walking through the recreation lounge, he would overhear some of the ensigns bragging about their romantic conquests and he would long to join in, to say to them, "I met the most amazing woman on Sirius last summer. The way she looked in the morning, with her hair all in a tangle—my God, if only you knew," but it would have been a breach of decorum to mention it, as well as a breach of integrity. He began to experience stomach cramps—hard, lancing pains that seemed to come from out of nowhere. He scheduled a visit to sick bay, but the doctor couldn't find anything wrong with him. He gripped the Keptin's shoulder as he was leaving. "Jim?"

"What is it, Doctor?"

"I say this to you as the ship's chief medical officer. You should take it easy on yourself."

"Understood."

What was wrong with him? He had experienced some of the finest moments of his life onboard his ship, and yet somehow it wasn't enough. Everything seemed thinner than it had before, as insubstantial as tissue, as though he could take hold of the world he knew and with one good tug it would all fall apart. The whole of space was visible outside his window, and yet it was entirely without meaning.

So it was that when ordered to take the ship to a cometary cluster that was passing within a light year of the Arcturus System, he hesitated only a moment before directing the navigator to make a short detour. "Bearing three twenty mark fifteen," he ordered, and then, "At the helm, Lieutenant. Warp Seven."

"You realize that if you follow that heading, you'll be taking the ship to Arcturus," the science officer told him.

"I'm aware of that, Mr. S."

"Arcturus is not on a direct course with the cometary cluster, Captain."

"We should have time to make a brief stop."

The Commander raised an eyebrow but made no further comment.

The Keptin wasn't sure what he would say to Raïssa. Perhaps there was nothing to be said at all. He knew only that he wanted to see her again.

She had given him her address before they parted on Sirius, saying, "I'll never go anywhere, and you'll never be able use it, but I'll feel better if you know where I am," so he was able to find her house without difficulty. It was constructed of a local stone he had never seen before, red with a powdery-looking texture, the blocks fragmented with dusky green veins that he mistook for creepers of moss at first, though they were actually streaks of clay. It was a carnival house, he thought, twice the size of the other buildings on the block, the house of a person who had a great deal of money to spend but very little taste—her first husband, the cargo trader, he presumed.

And yet the idea that she was there inside it somewhere, padding through the kitchen, perhaps, or sitting behind the yellow window on the second floor, gave the house an aura of mystery and fascination, as though some formative religious ritual were being enacted behind its walls, a sacrament from which centuries of observance would descend. To the Keptin it was the most important building in the city. He considered knocking on the door, but it occurred to him that one of her husbands might answer, and he didn't know how he would explain himself if that happened. Also, he couldn't help but think that simply arriving on her front porch after so long, waiting with his hands behind his back like a salesman or letter carrier, lacked the proper sense of drama. He wanted to see the changes that took place in her face when he appeared someplace she would never have expected to find him. Only then, he thought, would he know what to say to her.

As he stood across the street trying to decide what to do, a woman came out of the house hauling three large black plastic trash bags. A few tribbles fell out of the neck of one. She stooped over to jam them back inside. She was straightening onto her feet again when he approached her. "Excuse me. Can you tell me whether the lady of the house is in?"

"You don't really think anyone would be at home on a day like this, now do you?"

"Why?" he asked. "What's happening today?"

The trash bags were wiggling in her grip, and he could hear a faint gobbling noise coming from inside them. "It's the first day of the festival, of course. Miss Raïssa is there along with the Misters. Nobody would miss the first day of the festival, only a poor cleaning woman like myself."

He thanked the woman and set out at a brisk walk. At the end of the block, he caught a hovertrain that ferried him over the city and dropped him off at the festival gate. It was an outdoor event with rides and games and concession stands where craft vendors sold jewelry and clay pots from open-walled tents. Above him he could see rows of lights glowing by the hundreds, tied to thin white strings that crisscrossed over the pathways in a jiggling net. A man in a credit-exchange booth called out to the passing crowds. A barker in a striped red suit stood next to a wheel of fortune, spinning it around so that it clacked to a stop after one or two lazy rotations. A child ran past the Keptin licking a confection of bright yellow sap from a stick. All in all he was reminded of the state fairs he had attended as a boy in Iowa.

It took him more than an hour of wandering from tent to tent before he finally spotted Raïssa. She was standing between two men at a ring-tossing booth, an older gentleman, with thin legs and a barrel-shaped chest, who must have been her first husband, and a younger one, with a wooden crutch under his arm, who must have been her second. While the first husband paid for a set of rings, the Keptin watched Raïssa take the other's sleeve and point out something she had seen across the distance of the fairway. She leaned into him and smiled. For a moment the Keptin was convinced that she had fallen back in love with the man, that she had forgotten their time together and that he was now dead to her, but then her husband nodded dourly and turned away, and the tiredness seeped back into her posture. The effect was so familiar to him that he regained his confidence. He moved into Raïssa's line of vision and winked at her. She brought her hand to her throat in astonishment, took a half-step back, and dropped the carved wooden *sehlat* she was carrying. She was about to say something, it seemed, but then she looked in terror at her two husbands and quickly back at the Keptin with a nervous, excited, bewildered, appraising glance.

He motioned for her to follow him. He kept walking across the lane, weaving past a cigarette trader and a group of Rigelian tourists. Then he stopped behind a refreshment booth. After a moment Raïssa came after him.

"What are you doing here? You can't be here."

His heart was pounding. "Don't be angry with me. I had to see you."

"Angry? I'm not angry." Tears welled up in her eyes, and she made a gesture he had never seen her make before, cupping his chin in her palm and shaking her head. "But if my husbands find out about you—if anyone sees me with you and tells them—oh God, what are you doing here?"

"I've asked myself the same question, believe me. I thought I would know what to say when I saw you, but now . . ."

"Where's your ship? Your crew?"

"I left them waiting in orbit."

She sounded crestfallen. "You're not staying then. You're going to leave me."

"Do you want me to stay?"

"Yes, oh yes, James, but you can't. It's too hard. It would hurt too many people. I've wanted to see you again ever since the day we left Sirius. You're the only thing I've thought about. A hundred thousand times I was sure I glimpsed you out of the corner of my eye, but it was always somebody else, just a trick of the light. Those have been the only meaningful moments in my life since I came home—the times when I thought I saw you and my heart started racing."

It was late afternoon, and the longneedles were biting, but the Keptin hardly noticed them. As he stared at Raïssa, she seemed to become the still point of the swirling crowd, all those vendors and carnival barkers and endlessly moving families. In that same instant he understood that he was in love with her. He wondered how it had happened. She was no different from the thousands of other women he had known, or so it seemed, and yet the sound of her voice, the globe-shaped earrings that bumped against her neck when she turned her head too quickly, the split-second smile she gave when-ever he said her name, meant everything in the world to him. To think that when they said good-bye on Sirius he had imagined he would soon forget her, and that he had greeted the prospect not with dread but a feeling of liberation. He kissed her, and once again he felt himself becoming two separate people—one infinitely heavy, the other as thin and light as air. But she broke the kiss and pulled away.

"We can't. There are too many people."

He felt a terrible cold sensation of emptying out, as though everything inside him, his heart and his blood and his bones, had been phased suddenly out of his body, dematerializing in a long stream of matter. "I don't want never to see you again," he said.

It was the closest he had ever allowed himself to come to a declaration of love.

"Then I'll visit you. I'll charter a ship, and I'll visit you. But my husbands will be looking for me soon. You have to leave now," she pleaded. She squeezed his hand, holding it to her chest for a second. "I don't see how either one of us will ever be happy again. But I promise I'll come, James. I promise," and she hurried off into the motion of the fair.

For a moment the sunlight struck her orange dress from behind, and he could see her legs scissoring away beneath the fabric. He watched as she waded into the crowd, becoming a lifted neck and a curved wing of shoulder, the few stray pieces of her he was able to glimpse through the interspaces of all the other bodies. Then finally, inevitably, she disappeared.

IV.

There was a part of him that had never returned from his visit to Sirius, a certain presence of mind he had never been able to recapture, and following his trip to Arcturus, he began to wonder if he would ever see that part again. For some reason he had imagined that it would be easier to rejoin his life onboard after he spoke to Raïssa again, but it soon became obvious to him that he was mistaken. The only time he was entirely at home with himself was when she was onboard the ship with him.

She was able to visit him a few weeks after he saw her at the fair, and again a month later, and after that whenever he was traveling close enough to the Arcturus System for her to make the trip without arousing the suspicion of her husbands. Though he could not conceal her presence from the crew, he made it clear that he was reluctant to discuss her with them. It was not that he was ashamed of their relationship, or uneasy about its consequences, but that she had become the most precious thing in his life on a foundation he only barely understood. He had adopted the habit of silence as a convenience when he believed he would never see her again, and he was afraid that changing that habit, changing anything at all, would tear down some secret bearing wall and leave the two of them in ruins.

He was always surprised by the feeling of loneliness that came over him after she left. She gave him one of her tribbles as a going-away present—to keep him company, she said—but though it was soft in his hands and it purred whenever he stroked it, it was a feeble substitute, and he shut it in his spare room along with a few large bags of grain and forgot about it. Whenever Raïssa was gone, he missed her, and whenever she was onboard the ship, he thought about her continuously, anticipating the moment when he could hand control of the bridge over to the duty officer and meet her in his quarters or the recreation lounge. What was she doing? he wondered. What was she doing right now? Was she painting in the art studio? Was she thinking of him?

These were the questions he was asking himself the afternoon an unusual energy jet appeared a few thousand kilometers off the ship's port bow. He looked at the image in the main viewer. "It seems to be some kind of complex plasma pattern," Lieutenant U. said.

"Or it could be a noncorporeal life form," proposed Commander S. "May I suggest we scan the phenomenon with an ionizing beam."

The Keptin ordered his helmsman to make the scan. After the computer had completed its analysis, he told him, "Energy scan shows no sign of sentient activity, Captain," and the Keptin said, "Nevertheless, we should exhaust every option. Lieutenant U., open a channel to the phenomenon on all hailing frequencies."

And all the while he was wondering whether Raïssa was reading a book or watching the stars pass outside the window, napping in his bed or taking a sonic shower.

He had another life hidden beneath the surface of his life as an officer, and it seemed to him that that other life contained the best part of himself. He was a smaller man there and a better one—a man who experienced everything not with more depth but with more exactness, as though his ego had been polished away until it exhibited the world like a fine lens. And yet this better man was concealed from everyone around him, concealed even from Raïssa, though he was fastened to her by a thousand strings. The Keptin was someone other than who he appeared to be when he was striding through the ship with his phaser in his belt and his shoes tight on his feet, filling every corridor with the sound of his voice. His crew did not really know him. Neither did his family, and neither did his closest friends. He shone at his brightest only when no one was watching—and so, he presumed, did everyone else.

When he got back to his quarters that evening, Raïssa was laying out a meal of roast fowl and egg broth. Her face was pale, her features tight with sadness, and for a moment she would not meet his eye. She put the last plate on the table, came over to the bed where he was taking off his shoes, and embraced him. It was the third day of her visit, and they both knew she would be going home soon. "Oh, I wish I could stay with you," she said, tightening her arms around him. "Why does it always have to be this way?"

And he said, "There, there, my dear," resorting to the same helpless phrase every father in the world used to console his daughter after she scraped her leg or crushed her fingers in a door, because why *did* it have to be this way?

He began to stroke her hair. That was all it took. Experience had taught him that the longer he held her, the harder she would cry, and so he drew himself slowly away and finished changing out of his uniform. He sipped at the glass of wine she had left on the table and then went to the mirror to comb his hair. There were three gray strands above the temple. He plucked them out and examined them in the light. It was obvious to the Keptin that he had turned a corner in the past year. His eyes were dimmer than they used to be, his waist thicker, and just a few days ago he had discovered a small rough mark the size and color of a brown cherry on the underside of his arm. He had jettisoned his youth so suddenly. He had learned to love too late. Why couldn't humans be like his science officer, he wondered, with a life span of centuries? Raïssa sat at the foot of the bed sniffing back a few last tears. She seemed so young, and yet soon her own eyes would grow tired, her skin would lose its luster, and there would be no going back for either one of them. If only they could have known each other as children, he thought, when a different sort of life might have been possible—or if only he could leave his commission, and she could leave her husbands, and they could make a different sort of life together now. But he knew that there would be no other life for the two of them. They had not been young together, and they would not be old together, either.

Yet still he went to the bed and kissed her and said, "Are you feeling better now? Don't worry. We'll think of something."

"What, though? What?" she asked.

He did not have an answer, would never have an answer, and she looked at him and gripped his hand and gave a brokenhearted sigh. In the silence that filled the room, they could hear a purring sound, the same quietly rolling buzz the Keptin had been listening to as he fell asleep for weeks. After a while, Raïssa said, "Well, at least you have your tribbles to keep you company while I'm away."

"Tribble," he said. "You gave me only the one. And I've barely touched it."

A straight line creased her brow. "Tribbles are born pregnant, and they reproduce exponentially. I thought you knew that."

"I didn't."

The Keptin got up and opened the door to his spare room. Inside there were thousands of tribbles, maybe tens of thousands, heaped together in a single great pile that held the high, flat shape of the door for a second before spilling over onto his legs. There were so many tribbles that the air seemed to vibrate with their purring. He was astonished that they had been able to accumulate in such numbers without his awareness. He could not imagine how he would ever get rid of them all. And as Raïssa came up behind him and said his name, locking her arms around his waist, he understood that a long time of difficulty lay before them and their troubles were only just beginning.

—Pavel Chekov
Stardate 6823.6

A FABLE CONTAINING A REFLECTION
THE SIZE OF A MATCH HEAD IN ITS PUPIL

Once there was a city where people did not look one another in the eye. It had been that way for as long as anyone could remember. Old married couples lowered their heads like swans as they sat on park benches together. Young mothers stared sweetly at the folds of their babies' necks. Whenever two people met in conversation, each would rest his gaze on the blank surface of the other's shirt, and though occasionally, in a fit of daring, the most intimate of lovers might go so far as to watch each other's lips move, to venture any higher was considered the gravest of social transgressions.

The people who lived in the city were no less curious about one another than you and I. They had the same longings, the same anxieties, the same slowly building affections that seemed to take their hearts over little by little like waves spilling across a beach, but at some point in the distant past the belief had grown among them that eye contact was dangerous. Every child was taught that the eye was where the spark of life was located. That spark was always hungry, they learned, and it fed on the things it saw. It stood to reason, then, that to look into someone else's eye was to risk having your spark consumed, if not devoured in a single swallow, then eaten away a piece at a time. The common understanding among the inhabitants of the city was that people were born with only a small amount of life in their eyes and that when it emptied out, it could not be replenished. This one thing they were certain of above all others: just as staring into the sun would eventually steal their sight from them, so, too, staring into another pair of eyes would eventually steal their souls.

Because the people of the city lived in fear that they would unintentionally meet someone's gaze, they developed the habit of shutting their eyes whenever anything took them by surprise; they might be walking down the sidewalk in all innocence when a car engine would backfire or a metal door would slam. The noise would startle them, and instinctively they would twist around, and then—and then it would happen. So they closed their eyes and they waited for the shock to pass. The children of the city received this lesson early. Before half a dozen years had gone by, they knew without thinking to screw their eyes tight during any moment of tension or uncertainty. The custom followed them into their adulthood, so that every time a hospital phoned with a diagnosis, every time a lecturer stepped up to a microphone, every time one person said "I love you" or "I want you to love me" to another, they would fasten their eyelids shut like penitents kneeling at an altar. The risk was just too great.

Occasionally, of course, in spite of all their precautions, someone would accidentally have his gaze arrested by someone else. It was inevitable. Whenever it happened, the two people involved would feel a hard current of energy passing between them, flowing as smooth and fast as a river. They knew that if it was not the life draining out of their eyes, it was something no less powerful or disturbing, and they turned away with a shiver of nameless emotion.

You might imagine that in a city such as this even the closest of friends would often walk past each other without recognition, but somehow everyone made do, finding ways to distinguish the people they knew by their voices or the sound of their laughs, their gait or the cut of their clothing. They met in restaurants where all the diners kept their eyes fixed on their plates. They went to clothing stores where all the mirrors faced empty corners. They drove to work and fell in love, grew ill and slept in on Saturdays, filling their lives in all the ways that people everywhere do, and yet their reluctance to look one another in the eye could not fail to affect them. Sometimes a painful shyness would overtake them, sometimes a free-floating nostalgia. They made sure never to look directly into the camera when they were having their pictures taken, and on their desks and in their wallets you would see photo after photo of people staring thoughtfully off to the side, tilting their heads as if they were trying to remember the formula for converting grams to ounces.

Doubtless it was because they could not meet face-to-face that they remained such riddles to one another. Every mother was a mystery to her child, every husband a mystery to his wife. Even the simplest of souls was like a brightly painted house that on the inside was full of shadowy spaces and hidden rooms. From the minute they were born until the minute they died, the people of the city took great care to avoid staring too closely at those they loved, and as a result, at wakes and at funerals, it was not at all uncommon to see bereaved men and women clutching at the face being laid to rest, prying its eyes open now that they could finally look into them without fear of what they would find there.

It was true that, at one time or another, everyone was tempted to examine the features of someone who had fallen asleep—nurses tending their patients, children playing truth or dare at slumber parties, parents whose babies had suddenly gone quiet in their cribs—but there was always the danger that the sleeping person would wake, so no one gave in to the temptation very often.

In the city where people did not look one another in the eye, signs and paintings that might ordinarily have been fixed some five feet above the floor were instead placed at knee level. The trellises in public gardens rose no higher than bicycle racks. The peepholes on front doors were drilled at a slight downward angle, revealing the clasped hands or belt buckle of whoever stood in front of them. As a result of these and other such measures, the men and women who lived in the city had long since taken up the habit of dipping their heads whenever they stepped out in public. They did so in sunlight and in darkness, and regardless of the danger of meeting someone else's eye, a custom that lent them the humble if not pious bearing of virgins in medieval portraits.

It is one of the curiosities of life that putting on a smile can make you happy, just as putting on a scowl can make you angry and putting on tears can make you sad, and in much the same way, adopting the postures of modesty had made the people who would not look one another in the eye uncommonly reserved and timid. They found it difficult to begin romances and just as difficult to end them. Words such as *love* and *need* and *miss* came slowly to their lips, however quickly they came to their hearts. Long after their youthful friendships had hardened and died, they would continue carrying them across their shoulders like laborers hauling sacks of gravel. They cringed at the thought of bringing hurt to one another, no matter how unwittingly, and often they would lie awake at night silently chastising themselves for some tiny slip of manners they feared might have wounded someone.

And so it went on, with the years laying their winters down flat upon their summers, and everyone passing within inches of one another, and everyone looking away. Bartenders kept their heads bowed to their beer taps. Teachers addressed their lessons to the back corners of their classrooms. Occasionally, in the fever of adolescence, boys and girls of a certain character would meet in the alleys behind convenience stores to get drunk and participate in staring contests. Just a few seconds of direct scrutiny was enough to make their knees go weak and a cocaine-fizz of light suffuse their heads. There was so much life in their eyes, they hardly knew what to do with it all. Why not throw a little bit away? Though most of them were able to kick the habit as they grew older, the ones who couldn't spent the rest of their days in confusion and misery, coming together for quick liaisons in forgotten stretches of city parks or attending slash films in dank theaters where the actors stared directly out of the screen. They usually died young, such people, and there were never very many of them, but more than a few of the city's residents enjoyed stepping as close to the margins of the taboo as they could without actually violating it. Fashion models would almost but not quite lift their eyes from out of the pages of lingerie ads. Motivational speakers would initiate trust exercises coaxing whole sales teams into holding still while one of their coworkers wove his line of vision between their heads. Young lovers overcome by curiosity about each other would play the old erotic game of closing their eyes so they could take turns running their gaze over each other's faces, poring over their lips, cheeks, and temples in all their harmlessness and tranquillity. Afterward, they would feel as if they had woken from a strange and wonderful dream. They might be sitting on a couch together, or lying front to back in the center of a king-size bed, but in their minds they were still tracing the soft blue curvature of each other's eyelids, gasping audibly with every flicker of their lashes.

The city where no one looked anyone else in the eye produced its fair share of human happiness, but it was a cautious sort of happiness, never spilling too far past its own boundaries. If you had stopped people on the street to ask them whether they were happy, they would have had to search their feelings carefully for an answer, and as often as not they would not have found one waiting for them. So, too, if you had asked them whether they were desperate or fearful, hopeful or contented. They kept their passions hidden, even from themselves, for they had grown accustomed to their lives and did not wish to see them overturned.

And yet, though most of them were at peace with the custom of turning their gazes away from one another, every so often someone would realize that he had become tired of treasuring up the sparks in his eyes and fall silent for a day or two. It happened not only to teenagers groping toward their futures, but to grown men and women who had already come into the fullness of life, and occasionally even to those nearing the end. They had never stood on a stage under the surveillance of a crowd. They should not have known what it felt like to spend long minutes staring longingly into someone's eyes. Yet something inside them missed those things terribly.

When it got to be too much for them, they would lift their heads—uncertainly at first, and then with a poise that surprised them—and begin looking for a pair of eyes that was willing to meet their own, no matter the consequence, for however long it took until they expended the last of their souls.

As for the rest of the city's residents, they went on with their days exactly as they always had. They worked and they slept. They wrote letters and they talked over dinner. Sometimes they married. They never knew if they could have been more to each other than what they were, but on the other hand they were already so much—too much to fathom or bear sometimes. Every one of them was like a sealed box with an impenetrable mystery at its center.

As are you, and as am I.

And I do love you, you know.

HOME VIDEOS

People aren't funny. I work for one of America's longest-running family television series, a show you would certainly recognize if I told you the name. Each week we broadcast a full hour of home video footage featuring the blunders and foul-ups of our ordinary (oh, how ordinary) viewers, awarding a cash prize to the contestant who provides the funniest clip of the evening. My job is to screen the four or five hundred videos that arrive at our office every week and, along with the other associate producers, separate out the ones that are most likely to get a laugh. So I know whereof I speak.

The following is a short list of subjects that people seem to find funny: athletes failing to make a catch, babies with sloppy eating habits, good weather turning bad, actors flubbing their lines, children sitting on the toilet, pets sitting on the toilet (the kids in the toilet videos we receive are almost always reading or singing or engaging in some other commonplace activity—singing is the most popular—but the animals just sit there with these imperturbable looks on their faces, like figures on a totem pole), pets falling off pieces of furniture, children falling off pieces of furniture, and people—usually old people or fat people—snoring.

Also small objects being crushed by bigger objects.

Also grown men being jabbed, smacked, or buffeted in the genitals.

It's not often that we receive something truly extraordinary, something we've never seen before, much less anything that can chip out an honest laugh, so when Pram called the rest of us over to his monitor one afternoon with "I've got a live one here, you guys," I think it's fair to say we were all pretty skeptical.

Pramoedya—Pram—came on staff about a year ago. The other associate producers are Karen, Leo, and myself. I've been with the show from the days when it was just a one-hour special airing opposite *Sister Kate* and *My Two Dads*. My name is fifth from the top now when the closing credits roll. I can still remember when it made the climb from thirtieth to twenty-seventh. I may have wasted my life.

The video Pram was screening knocked me sideways. A man was posing nude on a stool in front of what looked like a college-level drawing class. A full-colored erection was bobbing up from his crotch. His eyes were twisted shut in the earnest, jittery way of a little kid counting off numbers in a game of hide-and-seek, and I could tell that he was trying, really trying, to quell the erection, but without much success.

Now, we receive what we call "do-it-yourself pornography" at the show all the time, sometimes from exhibitionists, sometimes from people who just forget they've taped the honeymoon along with the wedding. But what made this video so unique—and, yes, funny—was how accidental the whole thing seemed. The instructor was talking to the class from off camera, saying something about how she wanted them to concentrate their attention on the ten major muscle groups. Then she must have noticed the model's condition, because suddenly she stopped and puffed out the words, "Oh my. That's no good." I should say here that the model was not an attractive man. He was all folds and rotundities where no folds and rotundities should be. In the foreground of the shot—and this was best of all—a student's hand was working to add a very adroit rendition of the model's penis to a very clumsy rendition of the rest of the model, as though some Rembrandt had suddenly risen up inside her.

By the time the screen went blank, we were laughing as loudly as our idiot viewers. Pram rewound the tape and we watched the model's erection wither away like a flower closing up on itself in one of those time-lapse nature documentaries, which made us laugh even harder.

Pram did a little flourish with his hand, taking credit for the discovery. "Thank you. Thank you very much, ladies and gentlemen. A shame we can't broadcast this."

He was right, of course. The network would never allow it, even if we eclipsed the offending parts behind a solid black bar. One of the unspoken rules of prime-time television: you can show the sexual organs experiencing pain, but you cannot show the sexual organs experiencing pleasure.

"Still," said Leo. "Can you imagine the reaction we would get?"

Now, you would think a guy named Leo would have a rumble to his voice, like cement revolving inside a metal drum, but our Leo sounded like a twelve-year-old boy who wouldn't hit puberty for another three years, the perfect voice for the impersonation he did. " 'And how many times have you good people been out tending your gardens when this happened to you? Hold on to your watering cans, folks.' "

Inevitably, we heard a shuffling noise behind us, and when we turned to look, the Second Goofy Man was standing there. "Hey, that's a real laugh," he said, showing a good two dozen teeth. "Joke's on me. Maybe you folks should get some work done now. Or am I the only one with a job to worry about? Gotta pay the old bills, right?"

The resemblance was uncanny.

The Second Goofy Man has been the show's host for the last two seasons, ever since the Ken and the Barbie who replaced our original host, the First Goofy Man, were fired by the network. "Do we hear each other?" the Second Goofy Man asked.

Karen answered for the group of us. "Aye, aye, mon poltroon." She's usually pretty deferential toward the guy, if not actually respectful, but occasionally she lets one slip through. Of course, the Second Goofy Man would never admit that he didn't know the word. "Okay," he said. "Good deal," and went scuffing off down the hallway, hands jammed into the pockets of his blue jeans.

Let me tell you, the First Goofy Man was a prince—generous, smart, with a natural amiability about him that made him seem compassionate, vulnerable, and only slightly absurd. The Ken and the Barbie were a bit flimsy in the head, perhaps, but essentially harmless; you got the sense that their beauty had gradually rendered them inept, like those luxury cars that sit so long in the showroom their tires go flat. But the Second Goofy Man is a terrible human being. Completely, irretrievably terrible. I once saw him hurl a stapler at his personal assistant, Rachel. We listened for his footsteps to fade away, and then Leo asked Karen, "What did you call him? A poltroon?"

"*Poltroon*," she said, "from the medieval Latin *pultro*, meaning 'a worthless wretch.'"

Pram had removed the videotape from the player and was preparing to put it in his sorry-but-we-must-decline box. "The video. What's the name on the package?" I asked him.

"So to speak?" He turned the cartridge over in his hands. "Well, the tape is unlabeled, but—" He fished a bubble-envelope out of the trash. "Here we go. Ann Wilson. No return address."

"Let me see that." I took the envelope from him. Sure enough, there was only the name: Ann Wilson. The mailer itself was empty, with no notes or shipping instructions enclosed, despite the fact that the show requires an address and telephone number from all its entrants, along with a description of the clip under consideration. There was, however, a cancellation stamp in the upper right-hand corner of the envelope. It was perfectly legible: AUSTIN, TEXAS. 08 SEP 2003.

Two hours later and we'd found exactly four yeses and one maybe. The maybe was a near duplicate of one of the yeses, both of them examples of that dismal subcategory of videos in which babies use their fingers to eat things that are normally eaten with silverware—in the one case chocolate pudding and in the other spaghetti with marinara sauce. Since there was no return address on the Ann Wilson video, I put it in the top drawer of my desk, thinking that we might want to watch it again one day when we needed to be reminded that there was honest-to-god comedy in the world and not just thousands upon thousands of cute animals and hammy little kids, and I took the five videos we had selected down the hall to our production coordinator, who would edit them, splice them together, and return them to us the next day so that we could come up with some voice-over patter for the Second Goofy Man, which he would invariably reject in favor of his own threadbare gags. Then I left the building and got in my car and drove to the planetarium.

It was one of my favorite rituals. The planetarium presented its Wonders of the Visible Universe show every Wednesday and Saturday night, and I tried to make it out to the park for one of the early evening screenings as often as I could. Sometimes, it was true, I would miss a week or two during sweeps period or when I was dating someone, but I never went longer than a month without driving up to the big dome of the observatory, buying a ticket, and leaning back in one of the deep, yielding seats to take in a show. It was a comfort to me, a restorative. Some people have basketball games, some people have opera, I had the Wonders of the Visible Universe.

The program always began with a close shot of a blade of grass, an insect the size and color of a pumpkin seed crawling along the broad part of the leaf, filmed with such remarkable clarity that you almost imagined you could touch it. Then the camera would lift off in a dizzying ascent that allowed first the neighborhood and then the city and then the entire continent to take shape. The blue-white marble of the Earth would come together from the edges of the projection dome, spinning and receding into space, and you would see the moon sailing around it like a tiny paper boat, and suddenly everything would seem to slow down as the vast expanse of stars came into view, and, if you were anything like me, a tremendous, full-bellied feeling of contentment would wash over you. After the opening shot, the film would gradually make its way through the solar system, one planet at a time (*Mother Very Easily Made a Jam Sandwich Using No Peanuts*), before it ventured out into the wider universe, traveling straight into the core of the Milky Way, then skipping out through the girdling of stars into the deepest regions of space.

This was was why I came—this last half hour of footage. The planetarium updated it every few months to incorporate the newest images from the Hubble Space Telescope, pictures of brilliantly colored nebulas and stars with great quills of light extending from them. Have you ever seen these images? If you have, then you might understand what I mean when I tell you that that's where I want to go when I die.

This particular night a woman had brought her son to the show. The pair of them sat directly across the aisle from me, a thirtysomething Hispanic woman and her thin-limbed ten-year-old boy. Even before the lights fell and the kid began asking his two thousand questions, I could tell that he was blind. It was something about the way he held his face, as though all of his features had been permanently kinked toward his ears. It made for a nice little theory—that people's faces become concentrated around whichever sensory organ they use the most. I wondered briefly if my own face had been hitched toward my eyes from so much watching.

About twenty minutes into the program, long after the blade of grass with the insect crawling toward the tip had fallen away, I heard the blind boy ask his mother the first of many questions: "What are they showing now?" He waited out her answer in the quiet of the theater.

"That's Andromeda. It's a galaxy, like the Milky Way Galaxy— a big group of stars all crowded together in one place. It spirals around in space like water going down the drain."

"Where does the drain go?"

"It's not a real drain, honey. It doesn't go anywhere that we know of."

"Oh. Now what are they showing?"

"Now they're showing the Crab Nebula."

"What's a nebula?"

"It's a big dusty cloud in outer space. Sometimes it's dark, and sometimes it's full of colors."

"Oh. What's a crab?"

"Crabs live on the beach and scuttle around in the sand. They have claws that snap together like Auntie Nina's salad pincers."

"Like Red Lobster!"

"No, a lobster is bigger than a crab. You take a hamburger and put lobster claws on the end of it, and then you have something like a crab."

"That's funny. That's a good joke. 'Knock-knock. What do you get when you take the claws off a hamburger? A lobster!' No, wait. How does it go?"

"Now they're moving on to a bunch of galaxies near something called the Great Attractor. It's—oh!"

"What? Mom, what is it? What are you looking at?"

"The stars. It's hard to believe how many there are. You live in the city so long, you forget what's up there."

They went on like this for a full half hour, until the footage dead-ended against the Great Light Barrier and the camera made the reverse journey back to Earth, stopping at the same blade of grass from which it had started. I had closed my eyes for a few minutes to see if I could use the mother's descriptions to picture what was happening on the curved ceiling of the planetarium, but the test was rigged in my favor. The truth was I knew the program so well I could have visualized the entire thing without any cues at all. After the lights came back up, I heard the boy ask his mother, "Can we stop for hamburgers on the way home?" to which she said, "Grammy's already got something cooking on the stove for us." Then their voices were lost around the corner as they filed out of the theater.

I sat there for a while, as I always did, while the aisles emptied out and the doors closed and the silence crept back into the room. I let my eyes rest on the starmaker that stood in the center of the floor, that curiously tilted mechanism with the thousand-eyed globes at either end, as alien as any creature I was ever likely to encounter, until the ushers began sweeping between the seats and I knew I had to leave. Then I drove home and made a late dinner for myself and went to bed.

The next day was the last of this month's broadcast cycle. There is always a two-week lag between our work in the production office and the actual telecast of a show, which means that the videos we select one week will be screened for the in-studio audience a week later and aired during prime time a week after that. Nevertheless, we had to finish the packaging process by the end of the day, and we still had a good six minutes left to fill. There were weeks when we found more than enough material for the show, but usually, come Thursday morning, we were faced with anywhere from two to twelve minutes of empty programming time, and this led, perhaps inescapably, to a falling off in our standards.

I suppose I should tell you about the difference between funny ha-ha and funny peculiar. These are the two most comprehensive varieties of humor on our show. Funny ha-ha is exactly what you would expect it to be: videos in which children drop their pants at weddings, tuba players suffer accidents involving clumsy waiters and meatballs, construction workers get their feet jammed in buckets of paint. Funny ha-ha usually involves some small element of human suffering, though never anything too permanent or deeply wounding. Funny peculiar is a different animal altogether. The funny peculiar video is distinguished by its lack of an obvious comic trigger: it's more odd than ridiculous, more playful than farcical; you're not exactly sure why you want to laugh when you see it, but you do. After such a video has ended, you're likely to think, or even say, "What the—?," take note of its absurdity or incongruity, and then, after a few seconds have passed, experience a slowly rising feeling of glee that will plateau in a single vocalized "Ha!"

Funny peculiar is often, strictly speaking, funnier than funny ha-ha. My favorite of the many thousands of clips we have broadcast, for instance, is a funny peculiar video in which a McDonald's cashier, obviously a trainee, keeps putting an absentminded look on his face and wandering away from the register whenever a customer approaches. He must do this a dozen times before the camera finally cuts off.

In addition to funny peculiar and funny ha-ha, there is also funny adorable—i.e., not funny. Think of the sort of greeting card you would be likely to send your favorite aunt. It might feature a photograph of a baby clapping his hands together or a puppy wearing a birthday hat. Inside, the message would read, "Wishing you the best on your very special day." Funny adorable.

By the time the office shut down for the evening, we had managed to come up with twelve yeses and a promising maybe—a good day. Nine of the videos were funny ha-has, one was funny peculiar, and we rounded the selection out with a couple of funny adorables. The best of the lot was a video that Leo discovered, a funny peculiar in which a minister was delivering the sermon at his church's Easter service. The minister paced in front of the altar with a tack-size microphone clipped to his collar, testifying, "With Jesus, there's no need to be sorrowful, brothers and sisters. With Jesus, there's no need to feel weighed down. For two thousand years ago, Jesus, our Lord and Savior, Jesus defeated the grief of this world. Jesus cast aside the stone and ascended into Heaven. Jesus rose, brothers and sisters! Jesus rose!"

There's nothing particularly funny about this, I know. But the minister was battling a truly alarming case of the hiccups, and each hiccup landed smack on the word *Jesus*, so that his sermon sounded something like this: "With J*a-hup*sus, there's no need to be sorrowful, brothers and sisters. With Jes*a-hup*, there's no need to feel weighed down. For two thousand years ago, J*a-hup*sus, our Lord and Savior, J*a-hup*sus defeated the grief of this world. Jes*a-hup* cast aside the stone and ascended into Heaven. J*a-hup*sus rose, brothers and sisters! J*a-hup*sus rose!"

"What do you think?" Leo asked after he had screened the video for us. "Can we air this on a Sunday night? We won't piss off the family values crowd?"

"It seems pretty benign to me," said Pram. "Hiccups are a family value. I say we run with it."

"Run with it," Karen agreed.

I told him, "Take that sucker and run with it."

We received the next Ann Wilson video early the following week. It arrived exactly as the first one had, bearing no return address, only a gray cancellation stamp in the upper right-hand corner: AUSTIN, TX. 11 SEP 2003. Another arrived two days later, and another the day after that. We clustered like beetles around one another's monitors to watch. The videos were simultaneously amusing and disquieting, even a little gruesome, "like a bear humping a Volkswagen," as Leo put it, by which he meant more interesting than the sights you usually saw, but not the sort of thing you could broadcast on network television.

One of them presented footage of a small girl trying to suck what we thought was a raisin through a straw, until the raisin started to crawl. Another showed a team mascot of some kind, a man in a pirate costume, weeping uncontrollably into his hands. In the final video, a man with wire-rimmed glasses sat talking quietly into the camera. "People say that it must be craziness, which is what Aristotle thought, but that's not necessarily true, in my judgment. I think you have to ask yourself, on balance, do you bring more joy or more pain into the world? If the answer is pain, and pain is the only foreseeable answer, then you have every justification in the world, I should think. Notice that it's the pain of others I'm talking about, not your own pain. But even then, if you can posit a world where the suffering of any one individual is experienced by every other, your own pain would be reason enough. It's a principle I call 'the contamination of suffering.' "

Though he never used the word, we gathered that the man was talking about suicide. A gumdrop was affixed to the shining center of his forehead.

I put this video along with the others in the top drawer of my desk.

It was late on a Friday, that time of day when the afternoon becomes indistinguishable from the evening. We could hear the Second Goofy Man excoriating the interns who worked across the hall from us, peeling the flesh from their bodies in his folksy, mild-mannered, horribly exacting way. "Now, who heard what I said about my car? I count eight ears in here—nine if I include that growth on your cheek—so somebody must have heard me. What I said was *five o'clock, by the front door, without fail.* And what time is it now? It's sure as heck later than five, I can tell you that. You know, three people can accomplish nothing just as easily as four. A little food for thought. So who wants to hop outside and get that car for me?"

One of the interns came scrambling out of the office with a set of silver keys in his hand. A short time later, the Second Goofy Man strolled out wearing a little smile on his face. He was tending his hair with a small black comb and patting it into place with his palm.

"Witling," Karen muttered as he walked past our window. Leo didn't even have to ask her this time. " 'A person who fancies himself a wit,' " she said. " 'Chiefly derogatory.' "

I thought about the First Goofy Man as I made the commute home that evening. One of the things you remembered about him was the way he seemed so entertained by the little irritations of the world, never bullied or affronted but honestly amused by them, as though life were just the rags and sticks of an old traveling carnival and you couldn't expect anything more from it. I missed the guy.

The lights of the city, some four thousand square miles of them, cast a pale orange glow over the highway, thick enough to obscure even the brightest stars, and only the moon was powerful enough to burn through.

I made a dinner of salmon and wild rice for myself when I got home, and I ate it listening to one of my Iris DeMent CDs. I enjoy cooking—I always have. I've often thought that if I hadn't gone into television, I might have become a chef in a French restaurant, or even a short-order cook in some dive across the street from a pawn shop and a gas station—anything, so long as it gave me the pleasure of feeding people who were hungry.

I went to bed after the late news. The next morning I did some research. There were five Ann Wilsons in the Austin, Texas, phone directory.

"Hello, is this Ann Wilson?"

"Yes, this is Ann. Who am I speaking to?"

"This isn't by any chance the Ann Wilson who's been sending the videos?"

"Videos?" I heard a powerless little noise of escaped air. "Look, I don't want to receive any telephone solicitations at this number. Please place me on your do-not-call list."

"But—"

"I'm not interested. Don't call this number again."

"But I'm not—"

"Thank you," Ann Wilson said, and she hung up.

The second Ann Wilson supposed I was somebody named Rabbit. Try as I might, I couldn't disabuse her of the notion. "When are you coming by to see me again, Rabbit honey?"

"No, this isn't Rabbit," I said. "You don't understand. I'm looking for the Ann Wilson who's been shooting videos for television." I told her the name of the show. "Does that ring a bell?"

"I ain't never heard of it. I had to sell my TV. Don't you remember, baby?"

"You've never made a video of a man in a pirate costume? Or of a naked man in an art class?"

"No, no. No naked man, no pirate costume. But I'll try anything once. I didn't think I'd like sushi until I tried it, but then I did, and what do you know—raw fish. Tell you what, you bring the camera and the pirate suit, and I'll be waiting at my place, baby. Want me to phone out for a pizza or something? The cupboards are bare."

The third Ann Wilson had disconnected her telephone number and left no forwarding information.

At the home of the fourth Ann Wilson, a man with one of those deep, lazy voices characteristic of very small boys who are shocked to have come through the wheelworks of their adolescence as very large men answered the phone. "Yeah?"

"Hello, is Ann there?"

"Who that?"

I gave him my name. "But Ann doesn't know me," I said. "I'm trying to reach her because she might be the Ann Wilson who—"

"This is her boyfriend. How you know Ann?"

"I don't. I just want to talk to her so that I can ask her about some videos she might have sent my way."

"Man . . ." He pulled the word out like taffy. "I think you don't want to be calling here asking for another man's woman. That's what I think. Where you meet Ann anyway?"

"Like I said, I don't know her."

"Yeah, but where you meet her?"

"Maybe I should just go now."

"I think you better, bitch."

The fifth Ann Wilson did not answer my call, even after a dozen rings.

It was no mystery to me that people could react with disorientation when they were mistaken for someone else. I was on a first date once when a man presented himself at my table and said that he knew my work and just wanted to thank me from the bottom of his heart. I was too flattered to tell him that I couldn't have been the person he thought I was, a misjudgment that led to a great deal of disappointment and hostility when the woman I was with discovered a few nights later that I wasn't the sort of person strangers regularly approached with hosannas of adulation. Still, I have to say that the immense—and, as far as I could tell, genuine—bewilderment of the various Ann Wilsons I had phoned was a marvel to me.

The planetarium was unusually crowded that evening. The city had been experiencing the kind of perfect early-fall weather that

sends people out in their thousands to look at the stars. The observatory had added a few minutes of footage to the tail end of the
Wonders of the Visible Universe, including some new images of the
Eagle Nebula, a dark shell of dust that resembles, to my eye, an
owl rather than an eagle, but no matter. The nebula was illuminated from the inside by a dozen bright blue stars that set off the
gold and violet tones of the surrounding dust cloud. There were pillars of molecular gas inside that looked as solid as oak trees, so
sturdy I imagined I could climb them—and who's to say I wouldn't
someday? When the footage ended and the crowd had dwindled
away, the ushers came in with their long-handled maintenance
brooms and swept the floor, working in the silent, cadenced, grimly
efficient way of people who have no respect for what they do, but do
it well.

I took a walk through the grounds of the observatory after I left
the planetarium, heading for the slope along the back side of the
main building. I decided I might as well try to reach the fifth Ann
Wilson again, so I punched the redial button on my cell phone.

Someone answered on the second ring. "Yes, hello?"

"Ann Wilson?"

"Yes."

"I've been trying to track you down all day," I said. "I work for
The Painfully Familiar Video Hour," though I used the show's actual
name, which is not *The Painfully Familiar Video Hour*. "We've been
receiving submissions from an Ann Wilson who lives in Austin,
Texas, and I thought she might be you."

"Videos?" She laughed. "Where are you calling from?"

I was hiking through a stand of sugar pines where thousands of
fallen needles—many of them still green—lay lightly on the long
grass. "I'm at the planetarium," I said. I realized more or less immediately, of course, that this was not what she meant, but before I
could set my answer straight, she started laughing again, as though I

were a precocious child who had just uttered his first five-syllable word.

"The planetarium, huh? Man, I used to love those places."

"Me, too."

"The way the stars drift over the dome in that big arc."

"You should see the updated exhibits, the ones with all the latest technology. They use full-color video projection now, so it's not just the pinpoints of the stars like it used to be. Some of the images will knock the breath right out of you."

"You mean like from the Hubble Space Telescope?"

"Yeah, those are the ones. I look at them and I just want to take myself there. Really. They seem like some kind of Heaven." The sentiment in my voice embarrassed me a little. I felt as though I were making a connection between two free-floating ideas, though, and I continued talking. "You wouldn't need to go anywhere else. You could just settle in and enjoy the spectacle."

"Well, when you think about it, you're already there, aren't you? I mean, you're right in the middle of it. If there's another Hubble Telescope halfway across the universe—though they wouldn't call it the Hubble, would they? The Spock Telescope, maybe. The Cylon Telescope. Anyway, if there's another telescope up there, someone else is probably looking through it and wishing he were here on Earth."

"I guess that's true." The pine trees rustled, stirred by a breeze so high and attenuated I could not feel the slightest trace of it on the ground. "Funny it never occurred to me. In any case, I didn't mean to go on like that. So, do you happen to be the Ann Wilson I'm looking for?"

"Nope. I've never recorded a home video in my life."

"Damn," I said. "Well, I enjoyed talking to you nonetheless."

"Any time," the fifth Ann Wilson answered. "Sorry to disappoint," and she laughed again and hung up.

Some kind of night bird—it might even have been a frog—made a creaking noise overhead, and I paused to listen. A strong wind blew in from the south, carrying the smell of salt water and motor exhaust. I slipped the cell phone into my pocket, circled around the observatory, and made my way back to my car.

It was a little more than a week later that Leo was fired. We could tell something important was going on by the number of network big shots clacking up and down the hallway in their hard-soled shoes, and though we were all a bit curious, we spent the morning doing our usual work, sifting through the latest eructation of videos in our little office by the fire exit and the storage closet. The most promising entry of the day was a video in which one monkey stole up behind another monkey with an inflated paper sack and popped it. I forget who it was—it wasn't me—who said that the three pillars of comedy are monkeys, robots, and midgets, the reasoning being that monkeys, robots, and midgets are not quite normal human beings, but they all aspire to be, which is a condition that lends itself to comedy. Whether the theory is sound or not, I couldn't say, but I can tell you that we do receive a considerable number of videos every month featuring monkeys, and more than a few featuring midgets, and if the show is still on the air a hundred years from now, I have no doubt we will receive just as many featuring robots.

We were sitting at our own separate monitors, gradually cuing through our individual stacks, when the Second Goofy Man's personal assistant, Rachel, came to the door. "He wants to see you all in his office," she said. "And fair warning." She lowered her voice. "The big men upstairs just kicked him in the ass. He's ready to kick someone back."

We followed Rachel down the hall. I could see the tiny scar on the back of her arm where the stapler had nicked her before it went whirling into the filing cabinet.

The Second Goofy Man was waiting for us in his office, smiling his most avuncular smile and standing beneath an inspirational poster of a seacoast in fading sunlight, captioned "Perfection: The difference between ordinary and extraordinary is that little extra." He had long since removed the posters that had originally decorated the room, promotional photos of the First Goofy Man and the Ken and the Barbie. The last I had seen of them, they were stacked behind a set of metal industrial shelves in one of the tape libraries.

On the office television set was a twitching freeze-frame from the video of the hiccuping minister—his arms open to his congregation and his cheeks distended in a monstrous bulge. The question the Second Goofy Man asked was obviously a trap: "Who deserves the credit for this?"

It was a few seconds before I decided to risk an answer. I said, "We all deserve the credit. It was a group discovery." The video had aired on Sunday night. My guess was that someone from the Christian Right had organized a phone-in campaign the very next morning, the sort of wild-eyed protest we always get when we tiptoe into the dusty realm of religion: *no respect for our heritage of values, the liberal media, boycott your advertisers*—you know the script.

Leo must have been thinking the same thing, because he piped in with, "It wasn't a group discovery, it was my discovery. If you're looking for someone to blame, I'm your man."

"I'm glad you said that," the Second Goofy Man replied, and I knew all at once that the trap had been activated. He advanced the video a few frames, no more than four or five, and we were surprised to see what looked like a middle finger penetrating the edge of the picture, some petulant kid flipping the camera the bird. Another unspoken rule of prime-time television: you can intimate that the middle finger has been extended—inside a glove, say, or a foam hand—but you cannot display an actual extended middle finger.

Karen gave a single barking laugh. "Whoops."

"Whoops, indeed."

"You can't think we left that in there on purpose," said Pram. "We didn't even know it was on the tape." Which was true. Not only had nobody in our own office noticed, nobody on the entire production staff had noticed, nor had anybody in the in-studio audience. But clearly someone had—one home viewer with a DVD recorder and access to the Internet—and that was all it took.

"I'm sure you didn't," the Second Goofy Man said. "But to be honest, I don't give a good goddamn. Say *adios* to Leo, folks. He's out of here."

A silence spread through the room. "You're kidding, right?" Leo asked.

"I'm never kidding. Your position with this show is hereby terminated. You have until the end of the lunch hour to clear out your things. I suggest you get started."

Leo just stood there trying to blink the shock out of his system until the Second Goofy Man said, "Didn't you hear me? Scoot," and gave a dismissive little good-bye flicker of his hands.

Leo swung around to leave. As he vanished around the corner, the Second Goofy Man called out, "Stick that in your watering can." Then he turned to us with a big triumphant grin on his chops, as though waiting for our applause.

Somewhere in the back of my head, I suppose I was still trying to work out a defense for the minister and his hiccuping Jesuses, the only trouble any of us had been expecting, because what I said next was "Neurologically speaking, the hiccup is just the final stage of laughter."

Everyone ignored me, and rightly so.

"As for the rest of you good people," the Second Goofy Man finished, "consider yourself lucky. The next person who makes a mistake that gets me chewed out by the network will be in the same boat old Leo is in. You can bet on it." He straightened the knot of his tie, sat down at his desk, and made it plain by his silence and the posture he adopted that he meant for us to leave.

As we were heading out the door, he added, "And by the way, Miss Thompson"—Miss Thompson was Karen—"I do know what *poltroon* means. I can use a dictionary as well as the next guy. I'm not a complete ignoramus." He pronounced the word with a long *o* and a short *a*, like *hippopotamus*.

The next few days were uncharacteristically gloomy in our corner of the studio. Karen, Pram, and I tried to get on with our work, but without Leo it was hard going. The tapes overspilled their baskets: hundreds and hundreds of yellow envelopes, like a display of burst melons. One of the fluorescent lights kept dimming out in a way that made me imagine I was drifting off to sleep. Every video we watched seemed to spotlight some bright-faced little kid falling over for no reason at all. The room echoed with their bawling as they hit the floor.

Every so often one of us would ask, "So are we going to talk about this?," alluding to the incident with Leo and the Second Goofy Man, but there was little to be said. Karen announced that she had called Leo's home number a few times, and so had Pram, he said, but Leo wasn't there, or at least he wasn't answering the phone. I myself had dropped him an e-mail the day before, but had yet to hear back from him. We all hoped that he was on vacation on some warm, leafy island in the Mediterranean or the South Pacific, a place where the ocean never smelled like the highways, and not sealed away in one of the dimly lit bars he tended to frequent.

On Thursday evening, after the others had left, I stayed behind to pore over a few last videos. We still had a minute or so left to fill, and the production deadline expired at the end of the day—which usually meant six o'clock, but in this case meant whenever I managed to put everything together and pass it on to the production coordinator.

I had just decided to accept a clip of a squirrel being startled by an automatic sprinkler—fifteen seconds of funny ha-ha that could be stretched out, if need be, by five seconds of funny adorable on either end—when I set my hand on another Ann Wilson video.

My heart began to race. *Finally,* I thought, though until that moment I hadn't realized I was waiting for it. The truth was that I was half in love with Ann Wilson—in love, I mean, in that teenage way of a boy who spots a picture of a beautiful girl in his best friend's yearbook, a girl he knows he will never actually meet, though he can tell by the crookedness of her glasses and the way she hides her smile that he understands her more intimately than anybody else in the world ever could. The envelope was marked AUSTIN, TEXAS. 23 SEP 2003. I opened it and popped the tape into the VCR.

The footage began with a good half minute of darkness, salted with the sort of dissolving white sparks you see in unexposed videotape. I was about to fast-forward through it until I realized that the darkness was part of the film. What I was looking at was a cheap camcorder image of the night sky. It lacked the color and clarity of the Wonders of the Visible Universe, which was why I had failed to recognize it at first, but the night sky it definitely was. In the lower half of the image hundreds of what I suddenly saw were fireflies blinked out their messages to one another, giving off a cool greenish glow that was hard to distinguish from the light of the stars. Most of them remained below the horizon line, but occasionally one of the insects closest to the camera would go looping out into the field of stars and disappear like a meteor.

A grainy-sounding voice-over began: *I look at them and I just want to take myself there. Really.*

The speaker was obviously not a professional: that was my first thought. There was too much sentiment in his voice, a wobbliness to his intonation that you almost never hear outside of public radio or the least distinguished situation comedies. It took me a moment to figure out why he sounded so familiar.

The voice was my own—a Second Me—and the sentences I was speaking were from my telephone conversation with the fifth Ann Wilson.

Which meant that the fifth Ann Wilson had been the real Ann Wilson.

They seem like some kind of Heaven, I heard myself say. She must have recorded the entire audio track while we were talking on the phone, I thought. I wondered if she recorded all her conversations that way, a sort of Richard Nixon of the amateur video world. I tried to wrap my head around the idea.

There was just enough light for me to detect something moving a few feet away from the camera, a vague marshmallowy blur, and then a pair of sparklers lit up, the kind children play with on the Fourth of July, and two streams of leaping white sparks showered out of the burning tips, flaring so brilliantly I could see the faces of the boys who were holding them. They couldn't have been older than twelve or thirteen. They began waving the sparklers around in the darkness to create simple pictures out of the light, leaving trails and swirls and speckles in the air. The afterimages lasted just long enough for me to make out a five-pointed star and a set of breasts, complete with nipples.

You wouldn't need to go anywhere else, I heard myself say.

I couldn't shake the strangeness of my voice. It was like a stand-in for the person I knew myself to be, an heir or a successor, just as the Second Goofy Man was a successor to the First Goofy Man—though in my case the Second Me was in all respects the better one. I kept my eye on the video. After the sparklers tapered down, the kids ignited another pair, and then a third, and then a fourth and fifth. There were times when it was impossible to tell the stars from the fireflies and the fireflies from the glittering traces of the sparklers.

You could just settle in and enjoy the spectacle, my voice said.

I sat there watching the many twinkling lights, the stars and the sparks and the fireflies, watching the kids as they drew boobs and penises and also their own names over and over again on the glassy night air, until the video ended and the monitor filled with hissing snow.

This is the story of the day I lost my job. It was a Saturday afternoon, clean and bright, just a few hours before the show's four o'clock taping began. A small number of tourists were already waiting by the front doors to claim their seats in the audience, but most of the production staff was gone for the day, including Pram and Karen, and the studio was all but deserted. Only the people directly involved with the taping of the program came into the building on Saturdays, and most of them took a long lunch break prior to the show's final sound check.

Before anything else, I stopped by my desk in the screening office. In the top drawer, exactly where I had left it, I found the original Ann Wilson video, the one with the art students and the nude model and the erection that rose with a faltering slowness into his gut, as though attached to some powerful hoisting machine. I took it out of its envelope and cued it up on my VCR. Then I turned the lights off and shut the door and aimed myself toward the elevator. The editing room, where the final arrangement of clips for the show was composed, was one flight up and two doors down the hall. I knocked on the door and, when nobody answered, used my spare key to work the lock.

The room was empty, as I had expected. I located the video I was looking for without any difficulty. It was on the metal stand beside the monitors, the only tape in the tape carousel: CLIPS, SEASON 14, PROGRAM 7. I fast-forwarded through the first five or ten minutes, waiting for inspiration to strike, and stopped finally at the babies-who-look-like-celebrities montage. Most of the babies resembled the only celebrity any baby ever resembles, Winston Churchill, but a few of them were decked out in costumes that made them look like Elvis or Cher or Marilyn Monroe—a consequence of the wigs and clothing they wore rather than any real similarity, just as anyone will look like Groucho Marx if you put him in a pair of Groucho glasses and a mustache.

It was an easy enough thing for me to replace the baby montage with footage from the Ann Wilson video. I had filled in for our production technicians any number of times, and once you familiarized yourself with the editing equipment, duplicating material from one tape onto another was a snap. I rewound the clip video when I was finished and put it back in the carousel. I took the Ann Wilson video and stuffed it in my pocket. Then I locked the door, rode the elevator downstairs, and spent a while reading the newspaper in my office. There were hundreds of listings for grill cooks and chefs in the classifieds, and a handful for cooking institutes accepting new students in the spring.

The doors to the theater opened an hour or so later. The studio audience streamed into the building in their khakis and collared shirts, sandals and casual dresses, toting tiny plastic purses and shopping bags with the network logo printed on them. The ushers guided them to their assigned rows, and a few minutes before the taping commenced, I slipped through the door and joined them, finding an empty seat in the back of the theater where I could settle in to enjoy the spectacle.

At 3:55 on the dot, the Second Goofy Man took the stage, saying,

"Welcome, welcome, welcome, ladies and gentlemen! We're going to show you a good time tonight, so get ready to laugh!"

It would be another twenty minutes before he announced, "It looks like Bill Clinton has got a little competition from somebody—and I do mean 'little,' folks." I couldn't wait for the moment when his expression would pucker as he realized what had appeared on the screen behind him. It would be worth all the trouble in the world, every possible recrimination, just to see it rise.

THE AIR IS FULL OF LITTLE HOLES

The parchments proclaim it, and it is true: neglect is a friend to the weary, fame a friend to the strong. The year my photograph was taken, I was living in a refugee camp at the foot of the mountains. My mother and father had died in the bombing shortly before we fled our village, and for nearly half my life my grandmother had taken care of me. I remember watching as Yusuf, one of the boys in the camp, whipped his belt around like a whirlwind to churn the dust up from the grass. Insects the size and color of sesame seeds went hopping out of his reach in all directions. A clutch of them had just landed on my skirt when a man with a jacket that seemed to whisper against itself as he swung his arms—an American—said to me, "Girl, look here."

A little hole opened up in the air, and light came pouring through from the other side. For a moment I believed that the man had shot me and I was dying, and I thought of what my grandmother had always told me—that if ever death comes to take you and you believe he has arrived by mistake, you must meet him with defiance in your eyes. I refused to look away.

The man let the box he was holding fall to his chest, where it dangled from a flat black strap. His speech was bold and graceless, the words lumbering out of his mouth like brown bears, but even so, I understood what he meant. "I have moved you into the picture," he said. He smiled at me and set off across the camp, tilting his head one way and then another as he squinted at our tents and our cooking fires, at the warm stream spilling down from the mountain, at the pitiful ash tree growing by the garbage trench, its thin head enveloped in a shock of yellowing leaves.

Yusuf ran up to me, his belt snaking through the grass. "That man, what did he want from you?"

"Did you see the box he was carrying? I think it was a camera."

He sat down, took my hand, and began cleaning my nails with his index finger, carefully scraping the dirt away and letting it fall to the ground. My fingertips! If they had given off sparks, I would not have been more surprised.

After a while, Yusuf stopped grooming me and said, "You're getting older now. You don't know how beautiful you've become. I tell you this as someone who cares about you: maybe it would be best if you began to cover yourself like a woman."

When I fasten my memory upon that day, I cannot say what was more remarkable about it, that my photograph was taken by an American in a whispering jacket or that Yusuf, my Yusuf, found the courage to tell me I was beautiful.

I was fourteen when the war ended, fifteen when I married. My head was anointed with sandalwood oil, my hands and feet painted with henna, and the priest led me to the prayer tent and seated me next to Yusuf, instructing us to gaze at each other in the nuptial mirror so that we might see ourselves as God did, side by side and clothed in the brightest silver.

It was high summer when we left the camp for my parents' village in the foothills of the mountains, traveling down roads made rocky and narrow by a decade of bombs. By the time we arrived I was carrying the first of our daughters. She was born early the next year, just as the honeysuckles were beginning to blossom behind our house. We named her Nawar in their honor. The next few years brought three more flowers to our garden: Zahra, Izdihaar, and Nesayem. The sound of their voices, the sight of their little fists gripping their spoons with such ferocity, these things filled us with joy. Then one morning I woke to find our youngest, Nesayem, lying heavy in her cradle, and with one touch of her cold clay skin, I could tell that she was dead.

I had never forgotten the weariness that overtook me after my parents were killed, nor the savagery of my tears as I walked with my grandmother to the refugee camp, so I was able to meet my grief with a kind of recognition. I was aware that in time my heart would settle, like a pond after a thunderstorm, into a wistful stillness that might almost pass for peace.

Yusuf had no such familiarity with loss. His appetite deserted him. The straight lines of his bones began to show through his skin. It was all he could do to put his shoes on in the morning and head out with the other men to tend the terraces above the village. At night, as we lay in bed, he would cry in almost perfect silence, as if to keep me from hearing him, yet he would press himself against my body so tightly that I could feel his tears flowing down my neck. Did he want me to comfort him? I was too frightened to ask.

I tried my best to nurture him surreptitiously, keeping his hair clipped short, mending the frays in his clothes, and making the boulanee and yogurt sauce he liked so much. Even the girls seemed to sense what was needed, climbing onto his lap when he got home and asking, "Baba, will you make your tiger face? Baba, will you tell us a story?"

But it took the first deep snow of winter and its long days of smoke-scented isolation before the Yusuf we had known finally came back to us. I remember the moment well. We were sitting at the table listening to the ice hiss in the chimney when he said, "Did

I tell you about the rock we found in the wheat field last month? Rahi thought it was wedged in deep, but when he tried to pry it out, it came loose and he fell over backward."

Yusuf smiled into his chin, wearing that old expression of barely restrained amusement, and I knew that he would be all right.

The years that followed were surely the best in my life. There was the drought to contend against, with clusters of minnows spreading themselves flat in the puddles of the stream, and there was the wind that brought down the walnut tree in our front yard and the blight that killed the corn one summer, but through it all Yusuf and I were able to watch our daughters growing decent and strong, our home growing lush with memories, and with every year we had a greater sense of devotion to each other.

It seemed that our world would go on that way forever.

Then the American returned.

One evening Yusuf came back from a trip to the city and asked me to sit with him on the sofa. He took my hand and said, "There is a Westerner who has been inquiring about you in the market. It appears, my wife, that you have become famous."

The story as I came to know it was that the American, the one who wore his camera around his neck like a medallion, had arrived in the town where the refugee camp used to stand carrying a copy of the picture he had taken of me so many years before. He had spent several days showing it to the men assembled in the teahouses to drink and play chess. Eventually one of them had recognized me and taken him to see Yusuf's brother, who had in turn pointed the way to the city nearest our village, where the American had left word that he wished to meet with me.

"But why?"

"I believe he wants to take another photograph," Yusuf said.

"Apparently, the first one appeared on the cover of a popular American magazine. The people there are dying to know what happened to you." The idea was plainly ridiculous. I had to wait for the smile to fade from Yusuf's face before he continued. "So the first question to ask is, are you willing to meet with this man?"

A jacket that seemed to speak to itself and a hole blossoming with white light—that was what the American had been reduced to in my memory. I had no particular desire to see him again. But Yusuf was my husband, and I told him it was only proper that he decide.

"The man has traveled so far," he said. "There is custom to consider, yes, but there is also hospitality. In times like this, the parchments tell us to seek out our greater obligation. Do you agree?"

"If you wish."

He sighed and drew his brows together. "I will have to consult with the rest of the village."

That night I waited in the back room with my daughters while the men gathered around our table to discuss the matter. Izdihaar was suffering from a poisonwood rash that had just begun to lose its color, and she kept peeling little bits of her skin loose and flicking them at the other girls to aggravate them. I watched as Nawar and Zahra concocted various retributions against her, bumping her with their hips as they walked across the room or switching her name to Tafh Geldi, "skin rash," when they spoke to her. They were bored—nothing more—but it was all I could do to keep them from coming to blows. I was unable to overhear more than a few fragments of the men's conversation.

The meeting had been in progress for almost an hour when someone began to shout. "Enough! We should be ashamed that we are even discussing such a thing." It was Kashar, the youngest of the husbands, his voice leaping higher and higher like a wild goat scrambling up a mountain. "If we start exposing our wives to the eyes of any man with white skin and a wealthy accent, what will we have left? They've already taken the fish out of our streams, the coal out of our hills. Are we going to give them the last of our treasures, as well? We might as well throw our bones into the ground right now!"

A great din of curses and exclamations arose in the other room. The girls stood as quiet as owls for once, staring at one another out of the cool liquid depths of their eyes.

A short time later, after the house had been emptied and Yusuf had extinguished the candle in the *majlis,* he opened the door to us. "Tomorrow I will fetch the American," he said.

The next morning I watched from the window as he vanished into the trees, his brown shirt and olive green turban following the dusty thread of path that led from our village into the city.

So much can happen in seventeen years. The American had lost all but a thin sickle of his hair. He had replaced his jacket with a heavy leather coat that creaked at the shoulders and elbows. His stomach had grown tighter, and he had taken to wearing a small pair of glasses. His speech, however, had not improved at all. "Do you know who I am in the past?"

I was reminded of the way my grandmother began to talk after the wasting disease entered her brain, in the days before she finally took to her bed and yielded up her spirit. "Yes, I remember you."

"Good, good." He sipped at the sweet milk tea I had poured for him, set his cup down, and showed his teeth in a nervous grin, examining our home like an awed merchant entering a palace—the ceramic vase and the scarred oak table, the sofa where I sat next to Yusuf, the fine muslin curtains we had been given on our wedding day. "You cannot pretend the trouble I had to find you. I talked to I would not try to count the numbers of men. You were so much a child when I locked your picture, I'm surprised you can true remember."

"It's not the sort of day I would forget. It was the only time I ever had my picture taken." An image came to me of Yusuf dragging his belt behind him, then sitting beside me and patiently cleaning my fingernails. "And there were other things, as well."

"Would you like to see the picture?" the American asked.

I nodded. He opened the case he was carrying and handed me a magazine with a yellow border around the cover. The first thing I noticed about the picture was my head scarf. It had been scorched by a cooking fire and was riddled with holes, some of them embarrassingly large, like breaches in a bomb-damaged wall. I was about to explain what had happened when Yusuf, looking over my shoulder at the magazine, caught his breath. "Oh, how beautiful," he whispered.

I inspected the picture more carefully. The parchments teach us that we see the world only from the back, which is why everything appears so imperfect to our eyes. There is no leaf on a tree that is not a leaf seen from behind, no star in the sky that is not a star seen from behind, no man and no woman who are not souls seen from behind. But occasionally, by the grace of God, the world turns its face to us, uncovering its perfection, and though the glimpse we are given never lasts longer than an instant, we remember it for the rest of our lives. It seemed to me that the American had managed to capture my image at the exact moment my face—my true face—was revealing itself to him. I could hardly believe it had once been me.

"In my home, humans look at this picture and they never forget." His eyes were moist with emotion. "We get so many letters, even today, from those who want to childbear you. To childbear you? No, to adopt you. To adopt you or even to marry you. Your picture is like a badge to us. It shows the bravery of your people. I would like to know what has changed of you since then."

"What has changed of me?" I thought the question over and began to talk. I told him about my wedding day and our journey across the mountains, about our garden of flowers and that poor pale blossom, Nesayem, who had been plucked so early from the soil, about the seasons that had passed so reliably in the village, about the honeysuckle vines that luxuriated along the fence behind our house, about the years when the sound of a plane would cause a dagger to pass through my heart and the day when the terror suddenly lifted and I realized I was free.

He used a silver pen to write in his notepad as I spoke. When I finished, he asked if he could take another picture of me. I looked to Yusuf, who nodded his permission.

The American requested that I avert my body and pose with my eyes gazing into the lens of his camera, just as I had when I was a child. Then he asked me to hold a framed copy of the magazine in my hands. Finally he suggested that I stand with Yusuf and our daughters so that he might capture a portrait of our entire family. I called the girls to join us from the other room. Nawar and Zahra were unusually subdued, but I had to hoist Izdihaar into my arms to keep her from running away.

The image is as clear to me now as it was then: the American's flashbulb punching little holes inside our house, and behind him, through the break in the curtains, a cluster of men looking on like witnesses gaping at an accident.

It was not long before our neighbors discovered a way to demonstrate their displeasure. The very day Yusuf escorted the American back to the city, he returned to find a note tucked into our doorjamb with a quotation from the parchments: "Say to the believing woman that she should lower her gaze and guard her modesty." And the following morning, while he was out weeding the terraces, someone slipped a second note into his satchel that read, "The best garment is the garment of righteousness."

As the next few weeks passed, we uncovered note after note, in a variety of hands, all of them attempting to hold our family up to its shame. Almost every day, another slip of paper would appear like a pennant on our door. We found them battened inside the frame of the window, pinned beneath stones on the front porch, wedged between the slats of the fence. Even the children grew used to discovering them. One morning, Izdihaar came in from playing in the yard with a blank page that someone had torn out of a book and placed directly in her palm. Written on it was one word: "Repent."

"Who gave this to you?" I asked, but she was young enough that the men of the village were all just strangers and uncles to her, an indistinguishable mass of giants, and she could not describe him except to say, "He was tall, and he had a beard."

Yusuf told me not to worry about these incidents. "It is only Kashar and his friends. Soon they will find some new scandal to occupy their attention, and all this trouble will disappear." Every time one of us chanced upon another note, he would say, "Nothing more than clouds in the sky," and make a vanishing motion with his fingers, as if the wind were whisking the clouds away. When I closed my eyes, though, I saw something very different: a blanket of thunderheads stretching from horizon to horizon.

The entire growing season had passed and most of the corn had been harvested when a messenger arrived from the city carrying a copy of the magazine's newest issue for us. Yusuf answered the door, then came back and laid the magazine on the table. I saw myself staring out from the cover with a look of puzzled vigilance, using the tips of my fingers to support the photograph the American had taken of me so many years before. Embarrassed, I cast my gaze aside. "I have to finish the cleaning," I said, and left the room.

I ought to have been indifferent to the attention, and the bigger part of me was, but the next day, when Yusuf was away, I could not resist leafing through the magazine to look at the rest of the pictures. What was most plain to me was how inadequate they were. I had lived through so much since I was a child, been changed so deeply by the years, yet how little of my soul could be seen in my face!

My moment of shining presence had passed. I had once more turned my back on the world.

That evening Yusuf came storming into the house with yet another note he had unearthed. He would not tell me what was written on it, but his eyes were hard, his face creased with anger, and I could see that something inside him had finally been upended. "Where is the magazine? I will show it to them, and they will see how harmless it is. Then all this madness will be over."

Two minutes later, he was gone.

By the time he returned, I had already put the girls to sleep. Yusuf's voice was hoarse, but its tone of quiet confidence had been restored, and I listened as he told me his story. "They were more reasonable than I thought they would be. True, they did not like our decision, but I persuaded them that it was mine to make. Now they merely seem worried that more Americans will begin to track us down. 'The Americans have more glamorous entertainments to occupy them than my family' is what I said. In any case, we will not be receiving any more notes, I think."

And just as he had promised, the notes promptly stopped appearing.

We were given eight or nine days of ordinary household tranquillity, with the girls dashing from room to room and the scent of vegetable pilau spreading out from the kitchen, before a knock came at our door. From my chair, I could hear someone speaking to Yusuf with that strange halting conviction peculiar to Westerners and amateur politicians. "A fellow in the city told us we could find this woman here. We've come to say hello to her."

I peeked through the curtains to see two men with the close-cropped hair and spotless clothes of off-duty American soldiers. They were brandishing a copy of the magazine.

It took Yusuf several minutes to explain to them why he could not allow them to meet with me. *I-understand-sir-but-this*, they kept interrupting him, and *I-understand-sir-but-that*.

Finally Yusuf said, "This is my home. We are not a marketplace. We are not a museum. We are a family, and we wish to be left alone. I must ask you to go away now."

The Americans did not seem happy to leave. As their boots found the trail to the city, I heard one of them say to the other, "That Abdul better have our money for us, that's all I can tell you. As far as I'm concerned, a deal is a deal, and he broke it."

Afterward, Yusuf came inside and lowered himself like a tired old man onto the sofa. He sat for a long time with his brow resting on the table. Then he lifted his head to me and said, "Kashar was right. This will be only the beginning. I think we are going to have to move."

I remember watching as our daughters chased one another around the yard, saying good-bye to the hopper and the honeysuckle vines, to the dip in the earth where the puddle always formed, to the softened black stump where the walnut tree used to stand. We had hired a donkey and cart, and now we were leaving, traveling down the same road that had carried me away when I was fleeing the planes with my grandmother, that had carried me home again with a daughter in my belly and a husband on my arm.

Every road approaches, as the parchments say, and every road departs. We found our way to this small village in the cleft of the mountains, where the firs bomb our house with their long, dense cones and the pond is frozen for six months out of every year. We told no one where we were going, and so far our home has remained untouched by celebrity.

I enjoy watching Yusuf head out in the morning with his ax and his bucket to break through the ice and fetch back our water. There is a window in my room, and now and then, when the girls are playing and no one else is around, I like to stand at the glass and look outside. The sky is so sheer a blue here that I have seen stars burning through it in the middle of the day. It is a wonderful thing to behold.

I have had much time to think about my life, and I have come to believe that on the day the American pierced the air with his camera and the light came pouring through from the other side, the vision I had was no illusion. At that moment, God turned His gaze upon me, and I was captured by it. Some part of me was forever removed from the privacy of all things.

Just last night, I took the magazine out of its drawer to look at the photo on the cover, the one that made me famous so long ago. Yusuf spotted me holding it before my face like a mirror. He bent over behind me and placed his chin on my shoulder. "You are as important to me today as you were eighteen years ago, do you realize that?" he whispered.

"Yes," I asked, "but am I as beautiful?"

He did not say anything.

After a while, he kissed my cheek and walked away. He knew as well as I do that the girl I used to be is no longer anywhere to be found. She remains only in my eyes, the same color then as they are today, as bare and as green and as deep as the sea.

ANDREA IS CHANGING HER NAME

From the very beginning Andrea saw the goodness of the world as something delicate and unpredictable, a slender green grasshopper that would tighten its legs and flick away from her the moment she brought herself to its attention. Her father spent his evenings carving blocks of wood into hunting decoys. Her mother lay in the bathtub listening to the American Top 40. Andrea sat on the couch watching TV until the sun turned the screen into a square of blazing white foil, then went to her bedroom to play with her horses. Sometimes it rained while she was asleep, and in the morning, before anyone else was awake, she would go outside to inspect the big puddle by the mailbox. She could see a picture of her face in the water, trembling and breaking apart at the edges, but it disappeared as soon as she touched it with her fingers.

When she was ten years old, she returned home from school one day to find a moving van parked at a tilt on the street, its rotund rear tire flattening the grass above the curb. Her father was staggering across the yard with a Civil War chest in his arms, her mother waiting on the porch to take her inside. It came as no surprise to Andrea how brittle her family was, how tenuously made. For years it had seemed her parents were playing a game of make-believe, a game that had only one rule: they would turn away from each other bit by bit while pretending everything was the same. Their divorce was simply the final step in the game.

Andrea stayed with her mother, while her father moved to Colorado. In fifth grade she began to dream she was standing in a field of sunflowers that reached only as high as her knees, which meant she was in love with a boy she had not yet met. In sixth grade she won her school's spelling bee; her first period arrived while she was sounding out the word *quotidian*. It felt as if a tiny egg had cracked open between her legs. She knew what was going on.

She met her best friend, Rania, in junior high. They sat in the corner of Mr. Bailey's homeroom making friendship bracelets from embroidery thread, knotting them on diagonals so the colors would switch positions: green for the boys they liked, gold for the wishes they made, maroon for the secrets they kept. They spoke every night on the telephone, often for an hour or more. On weekends Rania would spend the night with Andrea, and they would stay up late eating pizza and watching MTV, or braiding each other's hair, or making a list of the ten people they would save in the event of a nuclear holocaust. Alone, Andrea liked to lie on the carpet and read: Sylvia Plath and Anne Sexton, Kurt Vonnegut and Henry David Thoreau. She began keeping a journal. She traced the lines on her palm with the tip of her finger. She bought a poster of the Beatles and tacked it to the wall above her bed. On days when she was feeling strong her favorite was John, and on days when she was feeling weak her favorite was George, perhaps because there was a vulnerability to John that she was afraid of indulging without an armor of her own vitality around her.

She turned fourteen the same year her mother remarried. Her new husband was a smooth-tempered, sardonic man named Jon, who brought to the house a strangely wily intimacy that slowly worked to soften Andrea's mother. One Saturday she sat Andrea down at the vanity and showed her how to apply her makeup like a grown woman—a little blush beneath the cheekbones, two contoured bows of lipstick. It was a lesson Andrea followed diligently until she decided that makeup was all so much folly and she no longer needed to wear it. In the summer of 1989, she learned she had been accepted into the arts magnet high school with a concentration in theater. On the first day of class, as she walked into the acting room, a feeling of nervous happiness overtook her; she had fallen upon a conclave of eccentrics. There was the boy with the Watchmen button on his beret, and the girl with the silent film makeup, a flawless white geisha mask of it, and in the desk by the filing cabinets there was me, the skinny boy with the crowded smile and the flyaway hair.

At the back end of the high school, between the library and the cafeteria, lay a pair of carpeted open bunkers called the Pits. Each day at lunch a ring of students would gather in one of the Pits to pray while other students, jocks and cutups mostly, would make a running start and leap over them. Andrea sat in the other Pit with Rania and Carla and a boy known to everyone as Turtle because of the shape of his features and the slow glances he cocked. Sometimes Andrea would let her mind wander, holding little interior conversations with herself during which she pretended that someone had asked her opinion of the goings-on in the other Pit. Even in her own imagination she found herself fumbling desperately for an answer. There was a self-congratulatory exhibitionism to the leapers that exasperated her—but then, when she thought about it, couldn't she see the exact same quality in the prayers?

Finally someone did ask her. She was finishing off the corner bite of a tomato-and-Swiss sandwich when I sat down next to her and said, "So what do you think—would you rather be one of the people praying or one of the people jumping?" It was the first time she could remember me speaking to her outside of class. I was wearing the same thing I wore every day: blue jeans, high-top sneakers, and a button-up shirt with the sleeves rolled to the elbows, a uniform she supposed I had adopted so that I could get away with thinking as little as possible about how my body was presenting itself to the world.

Andrea pointed to the boy with padded headphones over his ears, running through a Lionel Richie song, singing it vigorously, majestically, as if no one were there to hear him. "I would rather be him," she said.

She was not trying to be amusing, only honest, but her response must have been a clever one, because I smiled and said, "Good answer."

Then, just like that, I got up and walked away, rattling a ballpoint pen in my fingers. The intercom gave its five-minute warning. She did not think about me for long.

At the end of the day, Andrea always followed the crowd outside to the parking lot, where her bus was waiting in a long file of other buses, their outlines shuddering slightly as their engines turned over. Sometimes, when the light was clear, she would gaze out at the river as she rode across the bridge—at a bundle of sticks fanning open in the current, trailing streamers of brown foam behind them, or at a motorboat carving a white line in the green water. It was beautiful, but the beauty was always the same. She couldn't wait to turn sixteen. One night she was at her desk finishing her geometry homework when her eye was struck by the mound of stuffed animals in the corner. Her bedroom had become a sort of museum of her childhood: too much of her past there and not enough of her present. She began to sift through her belongings, boxing the old ones away. Her dollhouse, her Judy Blume books, her porcupine pencil holder—one by one she said good-bye to them. For a few days, looking at the sparseness of her bedroom, she felt more capable than she had ever felt in her life, stronger and closer to the center of her own experience. She gloried in the feeling, though she knew it would not last.

More and more she was immersing herself in the life of the high school. She joined the French Club and the Drama Club and the environmental club, SAFE, Student Activists for Earth. She started an Odyssey of the Mind team with Robin Crews and Cindy Jenson, assembling a performance based on the seven wonders of the ancient world. She played a street urchin in *Oliver!* and became a peer counselor. She was getting used to being in the school after hours. There was a sense of hibernation about the building once the other students had left, an atmosphere of stillness and secrecy that made it easy for her to imagine that she was watching it as it slept. She liked to think of herself as a hidden boarder there, creeping out into the hallways only after the sun had fallen.

For years she had spoken to her father only on major holidays, but shortly after the new year, he began calling her every Sunday. He had turned a new page in his life, he said, and he wanted to make things right with her. He suggested that she spend the summer with him in Colorado. "Just think it over. There's a mall less than a block from my house." He finished with an enticing little rise in his voice: "It has a Baskin-Robbins." To his mind she was still the five-year-old girl who liked nothing better than a scoop of bubble gum ice cream, who would bruise her lips eating with the pink plastic spoon, who would smile like a ghoul whenever he let her steal the cherry from his sundae. He really didn't know her at all anymore.

That summer, in Colorado, she saw her father every morning before he left for work and every evening after he got home, but because he worked in an office building on the other side of the city, she was left to fill the long sunlit middles of her days on her own. One afternoon she walked to the shopping mall to see a showing of *Pretty Woman*. The mall seemed bare and pitiless to her, with tinny synthesizer music coming from the speakers and pennies blackening on the bottom of the fountain; the movie theater smelled like mothballs and stale tobacco. She did not go back. Later that week she was walking to the grocery store when she discovered a vacant elementary school some local kids had refashioned into a skate park. That first day, she simply stood on the periphery of the lawn, watching as they rode their skateboards down the staircase railings and hopped like performing fleas over the chains hanging across the end of the driveway. The next day, though, when she returned, one of the skaters asked her if she wanted to make a drink run with them to the 7-Eleven.

"One condition—you stop staring at us and you tell us your name."

"I'm Andrea," she said, and then somebody started singing "Candy Girl," and in less than a minute she had become Andi Girl.

The boy who had invited her to the 7-Eleven was named Justin. He was the quiet skater, just as George was the quiet Beatle, and only later did she realize how much courage it must have taken for him to speak to her. No one had ever really thought of Andrea as funny before, but Justin did. She would drop a joke into the conversation, and he would screw his eyes shut and grin, producing a slow-growing laugh out of the privacy of his consciousness, the kind of laugh that seemed to have a bell ringing somewhere inside it. He began coming by the house to pick her up after her father had left for work. He gave her a copy of his favorite novel, Ray Bradbury's *The Illustrated Man*. He took her to the slope behind the Dairy Queen so that he could teach her how to skate, but the best she could manage was to sit flat on the board as it rolled gently to the bottom of the hill.

She had known him almost a month before he kissed her. It was her first kiss, and she was prepared to shrug it off, but couldn't: she felt the entire gravity of her body changing as the two of them experimented with their lips, letting them go firm and then soft, moist and then dry, closed and then open. "Wow," she said, and he began to laugh.

She was having dinner with her father the night Justin attempted to skate the wall behind the shopping mall. He wasn't wearing a helmet—he never did—and no one could say why he fell backward onto the asphalt. He lay there in a loose pile of clothing as the other skaters tried to prod him awake using their shoes and the hard tips of their fingers. Someone flagged a motorist down and convinced him to call for an ambulance. The technician who examined Justin found that he had fractured the back of his skull, chipping the point where its pieces joined together in an inverted Y and sending a splinter of bone into his brain. And while all this was going on, Andrea was dining in a restaurant where the candles on the tables wore hoods of red glass and the waiters carried satin cloths over their arms.

For the rest of the summer she spent part of every day at the hospital. How simple it was to imagine that Justin had only fallen asleep on his back. His chest rose and fell with the compressions of the respirator. Every so often one of his eyelids would twitch. One day Andrea found a hair as long as a cherry stem growing from a pore on his neck. He was not yet shaving, which was why the hair had gone unnoticed for so long, she supposed, and she took it between her fingernails and tried to smooth the kink out of it. The next morning she returned with a pair of tweezers to pull it out. She had lain awake for hours the night before, distressed by the thought that someone else might pluck it before she had the chance. She experienced an odd rush of relief when she saw that it was still there.

Something was making Justin shrink farther and farther into the distance, and she did not know what it was. First his friends quit visiting him, and then his aunts and uncles, teachers and cousins, coaches and grandparents. But not Andrea—she refused to allow him to sink into the bottomless world of her memories. Every afternoon she sat with his parents in the hospital room. "You've been such a good friend to Justin," they told her. "You truly have, dear. He's very, very lucky to have you."

At the end of August, a few days before her junior year began, Andrea flew back home. Despite all her efforts to wrest her bedroom into the present, the space seemed strangely alien to her now, and it took the better part of a week for the sensation that she was camping out in some half-forgotten region of her childhood to pass.

When you have suffered enough damage, you have a choice: you can seal off all the cracks around yourself, putting up a thick casing of diffidence and reserve, or you can let all your protections fall and leave yourself open to every touch, every collision. Andrea—and she was Andrea again now, not Andi Girl—followed the second road. She began experiencing her life with a clarity and intensity she hadn't known before. It wasn't a matter of choice: the smallest nudge from any direction, it seemed, and she would find herself laughing or crying. A song on the radio, a television commercial, a comment made by someone at school—that was all it took. Everything around her appeared to be shining from someplace just under the skin, as if no T-shirt or flagpole or blade of grass was anything more than a pair of hands cupped around a lightbulb, and at night, when she went to bed, she always fell asleep right away, exhausted by the day's continuous play of shapes and colors.

Had anyone detected the change in her? she wondered. One day, her chemistry teacher, Mr. Fuller, asked her to stay after class so that he could find out why she kept excusing herself to go to the restroom. And there was the time in theater history when I passed her a note that read, *Are you all right? You've got this look on your face,* and then a second note that read, *Not that you don't usually have a look on your face. It would be impossible to have a face without having some sort of look on it.* But other than that, no one seemed to have noticed the difference. Sometimes she imagined it was only her spirit drifting past the rows of silver lockers, a tangled wind that no one was ever quite able to see. She looked forward to seventh period, her acting class, when she could take all the pain and delight and confusion she felt and put them openly on display, as if her whole life were just some sort of performance.

Her mother gave her a car for her birthday, an '87 Honda Civic, and she began driving herself home in the afternoon. She was asked to join the Key Club and the Honor Society, which she did, as well as the Y-Teens, which she didn't. She took a small role in Thornton Wilder's *The Matchmaker.* She signed up for a five-session PSAT prep course. In November, when Justin's parents took him off the ventilator, Andrea flew back to Colorado for the funeral. She missed two days of school, telling no one where she had gone except for Rania, her parents, and, months later, me. She was reluctant to need anything too much, or to express her need too publicly. Everything good in the world—everything she loved—seemed to be straining against the tightness of its own beauty. A single ounce of pressure, she thought, and it would all burst open from the inside, vanishing forever.

Andrea had stopped writing poetry when she was fourteen, shortly after her Sylvia Plath phase, but she decided the time had come to give it another try. She bought herself a journal bound in burnt orange velvet. In class, whenever she was given a few minutes to let her mind wander, she ran her fingers over the nap, smoothing all the fibers carefully in one direction and then carefully back in the other. Sometimes, without thinking, she would begin drawing a word in the velvet—*fireplace* or *tangent, avenue* or *parsimonious,* any random word that happened to come drifting through the air. After a while she would notice the pattern she was making, brush the velvet clear, and slip the journal back into her shoulder bag. If it was January, the trees would be bare outside the window. If it was March, the first few oaks would be leafing out. She loved the feeling of peaceful melancholy that overtook her as she watched the blackbirds sailing over the branches and the gray clouds massing behind them. The air from the heater blew past her shoulders, and the sound of a distant car horn came over the hill, and I don't think she had any idea what people saw when they looked at her.

Andrea with her hair held back in a simple black band.

Andrea in her loose cotton shirt with the IMAGINE button over the chest.

Once in a while, she would perceive someone's stare, and her face would shift into a reflexive little expression of surprise. "I'm sorry, did you ask me a question?" she would say. "My mind was—you know—" and she would make a sound like a firework whistling into the sky. There is no form to this story because it is true, or at least as close to true as I have been able to make it.

One Friday, the school turned everybody loose at noon so the teachers could attend a training session. Chris Bertram and I were lingering on the patio, trying to decide what to do with ourselves, when Andrea came out the front door with Deborah Holloway, shielding her eyes with a notebook. We convinced them to join us, and together we set off for the park at the foot of the mountain, where the gutters of the pavilion were stuffed with pine needles and the water from the drinking fountain tasted like iron pipe. Andrea had never spent any time with me away from school before. She was struck by how little difference there was between the way I behaved in the classroom and the way I behaved on the playground, as if a desk and a swing were all the same to me, the one no less frivolous than the other. She was wearing a silver ring with a band that was fashioned into a snake, and I kept taking it off her finger and singing a song: "I'm Sammy the Snake / And I have to confess / That I look and I sound / Like the letter *s*."

Over the next few months she began to see more and more of me. We went to a Fishwagon concert by the river. We performed a scene from *The Crucible* at a drama tournament. For no reason at all, we bought an old surfboard at a garage sale, the wood beneath the wax already crumbling to punk, and propped it against the door of Rania's house. For a while it seemed to Andrea that I had lifted her free of something she had always believed was implacable—of the endless search for company, those innumerable Fridays and Saturdays she spent driving from parking lot to parking lot hoping to recognize someone's car. One night we took a break from studying in her bedroom, and she twisted her desk lamp around to throw a hand shadow onto the wall. She linked her thumbs together and oscillated her palms. "Look at the beautiful butterfly," she said, and I transformed my hands into duck bills and started an evil marching chant: "We are *ducks*. We hate *butter*flies. We are *ducks*. We hate *butter*flies." There were moments when I could make her laugh so unselfconsciously that she felt like a child again, expanding into her past as she was moving into her future. Sometimes she thought of me as a John, other times as a Ringo.

She loaned me her journal so I could read her poetry, and I returned it to her with a note written on the velvet: *Hi, Andrea. It's me, your journal.* My favorite poem, I said, was the one that ended "I gave you my love in an acorn shell, but you left me anyway." It was a poem about Justin, though she had not yet told me about that part of her life; and when I read it out loud to her, the sound of her own sadness coming out of my voice made her eyes well up with tears. It was a Friday night in late March, and we stopped to eat at a Wendy's, where she gave me the toy car from her kids' meal: a "salad mobile" with lettuce, tomatoes, and a radish on top, which would race forward whenever I wound the spring tight. She was amused by how much I seemed to enjoy it. Afterward, we went to a showing of *L.A. Story*, and during the coming attractions, when I tried to roll it across her temple, the wheels let go with a whir, snarling her hair up in the axle. I spent the whole two hours of the movie patiently untangling it strand by strand. She could still feel the play of my fingers on her scalp, along with the soft tingle in her stomach, as I drove her home and she told me what had happened in Colorado.

She was trying to show me that things had changed between us, that I had taken up housing in that small space she reserved for the people she genuinely trusted. The next week, she invited me to dinner with her mother and Jon. She introduced me to her father when he came to town for a business conference. She feigned an argument with me over whether the pencil holders that had been popular when we were kids had been hedgehogs or porcupines—I said hedgehogs, she said porcupines.

We were rehearsing a duet scene from *The War of the Roses* the afternoon someone shattered the window of her car. "Do you think the Civic will be safe here?" she had asked as we pulled away from the high school in my Pontiac, and for the pleasure of sharing the drive home with her, I had said that I was sure it would. When we returned a couple hours later, we found a rock as heavy as a steam iron sitting on her front seat and jags of glass sticking up out of the upholstery and the carpet. Her stereo was missing, along with a box of her cassettes: The Lightning Seeds, The Sundays, Lenny Kravitz, the Jesus and Mary Chain. This was 1991, and the music she listened to—that we both listened to—announced that we were looking in on the world from its periphery, except for the Lenny Kravitz, which announced that we did not really believe in peripheries.

I drove Andrea to the gas station down the street so she could call her mother and Jon. Then I waited in my car with her for them to arrive. It was a spring evening, shortly past six o'clock, and the sun was setting over the tops of the repair bays, propelling the long shadows of the pumps onto the grass. The two of us sat there in the middle of my bench seat, Andrea wringing the tail of her shirt in her hands and gently repeating the word *motherfucker, motherfucker,* as I held her from behind. After a while, I put my lips to the nape of her neck, touching them to the spot where the fine hairs began to taper away.

This is what I should have been thinking: *Andrea is in pain.*

This is what I was thinking instead: *I am kissing the back of Andrea's neck.*

Of all my memories of her, this is the one that troubles me the most.

Andrea watched her senior year pass in a dizzying spin of standardized tests and college application essays. *Please tell us about your career goals and any plans you may have for graduate study. What quality do you like best in yourself and what do you like least? What event has most influenced your life? Explain.* I was one year older and had left for college at the end of August, enrolling at a university two states away, and she knew that she could not expect to see me until Thanksgiving or Christmas. Suddenly she had more time to spend with her other friends, particularly Rania. The two of them started talking on the phone again, going to movies, trading mix tapes. One night they even went to the craft store and bought a dozen spools of embroidery thread so they could fill a few hours making friendship bracelets, the way they used to when they were kids. Silver for the memories they shared. Blue for the years that had slipped away.

At school, Andrea was busier than ever. She was elected president of the Drama Club and secretary of Student Council. She played the Wicked Witch of the West in a production of *The Wizard of Oz*. She wrote an essay on *The Metamorphosis* for Ms. Greenway's AP English class. Her mother told her that she was thinking about putting their house on the market, but she promised to wait until Andrea had graduated and moved away. At college one day, in the yard beside the library, I came upon two acorn shells fused at the stem, and I cushioned them inside the smallest box I could find, one that had held a staple remover, then sent them off to Andrea in the mail. Three days later, the tiniest package she had ever received was waiting on the table by her front door. A mixture of joy and regret blew through her; she was aware of the feelings I had for her, aware of all the things she had neglected to say to me, aware even of the way I saw her features in the faces of women I didn't know as I walked through campus in my beaten old tennis shoes. And yet already she could sense me beginning to disappear from her life, another grasshopper preparing to tighten its legs and leap away.

During the last few months of high school, there was a feeling of such great ease in the air that it hardly seemed like school at all to her. She gave a reading of one of her poems at the launch party for the literary magazine. She dedicated an evening a week to volunteering at a soup kitchen. The neighbor's cat died of old age, and a few days later there were two Labrador puppies chasing each other around the puddle by Andrea's mailbox, one called Jarvis and the other called Willie. It was a cold night in April when she dreamed she was a little girl again, watching her father haul all his possessions into the street. Her mother was leaving with him. And so was I. And so was Justin. And so was Rania. And when she woke up she couldn't shake the feeling that it had all really taken place that way: everyone she knew driving off in a big yellow moving van, and she the one—the only one—staying behind. She had hesitated far too long. She had missed her chance, and her childhood had reached out and snared her.

There were times she believed she would never get out of it.

But she did get out of it. She went away to college and then to graduate school, to London and Boston and Washington, D.C. She rented an apartment. She found work that was meaningful to her. She thought about me every so often, wondered where I was and how I was doing, whether I still propped my glasses on my forehead when I spoke, whether I sang as much as I used to, whether I could honestly say I was happy. I was living in our hometown again and doing pretty well. I propped my glasses on my forehead so reflexively that I frequently forgot they were there. I still sang, though not as often as I once did, and I was still happy, though not as often as I once was. Sometimes, driving past restaurants that had once been other restaurants, big box stores that had once been wood lots and houses, I imagined that if I could just make the right set of turns, the city would unlock for me, and my car would carry me into the roads of fifteen years ago. From time to time, in the narrow light of a late-autumn afternoon, Andrea would find herself walking past the windows of a high school, and she would remember how it felt to be sitting behind such a window at her cramped wooden desk, looking out at the shadows of the trees stretching over the lawn. She used to be there and now she was here, and all of it, both the freedom and the constraint, had happened in the same lifetime. How was that possible?

Not long ago, I was having lunch with a teacher of ours from high school, Ms. Goss, who offered me the news that Andrea was engaged to be married. I was startled to feel all the old adoration come tumbling loose inside me, a great surge of it that made me close my mouth and set my fork down on my plate. The look Ms. Goss gave me said that she could see something like contrition on my face.

"Is she taking his name?" I asked.

She thought about the question. "I don't know. I don't think so. It doesn't sound like Andrea to change her name, does it? But then it doesn't sound like Andrea to get married, either."

"I'm not sure why I should be upset by the idea," I said. "After all, it's not as if I've been in love with Andrea all these years."

Which, of course, was just another way of saying, I've been in love with Andrea all these years.

But even that is not quite true. The truth is that I am slightly less than half in love with all the other girls I knew back then—with Jennifer and Erika, Vicki and Allison, Ara and Emily—but I am still, to this day, slightly more than half in love with Andrea.

The last time I saw her was several years ago. We met for coffee at a little restaurant on Kavanaugh, and she told me about her work, traveling to the Middle East as an advocate for democratic solutions to public policy issues. There was a confidence in her voice, a strength of purpose I had never heard from her before. She carried herself like a professional, with skillfully applied makeup and well-cut, sensible clothing. She was beautiful, and I couldn't help but admire her, but I was also saddened by how much she had changed, by the magnitude of the distance she had traveled, the terrible impenetrability of the past. In high school, Andrea wore one long braided strand of hair that trailed past her ear like an ornament from a chandelier. Once, on a spring break trip to New York, she bundled everything she needed for five days into a small canvas backpack.

"Sometimes I remember the way I used to be," she said as we sat across the table from each other, "and I'm surprised nobody ever smacked me."

I took a long sip of my coffee so that I would not have to answer her. I wanted to tell her that she ought to be more generous to the girl she used to be, if not out of respect for herself, then out of respect for me, or more specifically for the the boy I used to be, who loved that girl, after all.

A FABLE WITH SLIPS OF WHITE PAPER

SPILLING FROM THE POCKETS

Once there was a man who happened to buy God's overcoat. He was rummaging through a thrift store when he found it hanging on a rack by the fire exit, nestled between a birch-colored fisherman's sweater and a cotton blazer with a suede patch on one of the elbows. Though the sleeves were a bit too long for him and one of the buttons was cracked, the coat fit him well across the chest and shoulders, lending him a regal look that brought a pleased yet diffident smile to his face, so the man took it to the register and paid for it. He was walking home when he discovered a slip of paper in one of the pockets. An old receipt, he thought, or maybe a to-do list forgotten by the coat's previous owner. But when he took it out, he found a curious note typed across the front: *Please help me figure out what to do about Albert.*

The man wondered who had written the note, and whether, in fact, that person had figured out what to do about Albert—but not, it must be said, for very long. After he got home, he folded the slip of paper into quarters and dropped it in the ceramic dish where he kept his breath mints and his car keys.

It might never have crossed his mind again had his fingers not fallen upon two more slips of paper in the coat's pocket while he was riding the elevator up to his office the next morning. One read, *Don't let my nerves get the better of me this afternoon,* and the other, *I'm asking you with all humility to keep that boy away from my daughter.*

The man shut himself in his office and went through the coat pocket by pocket. It had five compartments altogether: two front flap pockets, each of which lay over an angled hand-warmer pocket with the fleece almost completely worn away, as well as a small inside pocket above the left breast. He rooted through them one by one until he was sure they were completely empty, uncovering seven more slips of paper. The messages typed across the front of the slips all seemed to be wishes or requests of one sort or another. *Please let my mom know I love her. I'll never touch another cigarette as long as I live if you'll just make the lump go away. Give me back the joy I used to know.*

There was a tone of quiet intimacy to the notes, a starkness, an open-hearted pleading that seemed familiar to the man from somewhere.

Prayers, he realized.

That's what they were—prayers.

But where on earth did they come from?

He was lining them up along the edge of his desk when Eiseley from technical support rapped on the door to remind him about the ten o'clock meeting. "Half an hour of coffee and spreadsheet displays," he said. "Should be relatively painless," and he winked, firing an imaginary pistol at his head. As soon as Eiseley left, the man felt the prickle of an obscure instinct and checked the pockets of his coat again. He found a slip of paper reading, *The only thing I'm asking is that you give my Cindy another few years.* Cindy was Eiseley's cat, familiar to everyone in the office from his Christmas cards and his online photo diary. A simple coincidence? Somehow he didn't think so.

For the rest of the day the man kept the coat close at hand, draping it over his arm when he was inside and wearing it buttoned to the collar when he was out. By the time he locked his office for the night, he believed he had come to understand how it worked. The coat was—or seemed to be—a repository for prayers. Not unerringly, but often enough, when the man passed somebody on the street or stepped into a crowded room, he would tuck his hands into the coat's pockets and feel the thin flexed form of a slip of paper brushing his fingers. He took a meeting with one of the interns from the marketing division and afterward discovered a note that read, *Please, oh please, keep me from embarrassing myself.* He grazed the arm of a man who was muttering obscenities, his feet planted flat on the sidewalk, and a few seconds later found a note that read, *Why do you do it? Why can't you stop torturing me?*

That afternoon, on his way out, he was standing by the bank of elevators next to the waiting room when he came upon yet another prayer: *All I want—just this once—is for somebody to tell me how pretty I look today.* He glanced around. The only person he could see was Jenna, the receptionist, who was sitting behind the front desk with her purse in her lap and her fingers covering her lips. He stepped up to her and said, "By the way, that new girl from supplies was right."

"Right about what?"

"I heard her talking about you in the break room. She was saying how pretty you look today. She was right. That's a beautiful dress you're wearing."

The brightness in her face was like the reflection of the sun in a pool of water—you could toss a stone in and watch it fracture into a thousand pieces, throwing off sparks as it gathered itself back together.

So that was one prayer, and the man could answer it, but what was he to do with all the others?

In the weeks that followed, he found thousands upon thousands more. Prayers for comfort and prayers for wealth. Prayers for love and prayers for good fortune. It seemed that at any one time half the people in the city were likely to be praying. Some of them were praying for things he could understand, even if he could not provide

them, like the waitress who wanted some graceful way to back out of
her wedding or the UPS driver who asked for a single night of
unbroken sleep, while some were praying for things he could not
even understand: *Let the voice choose lunch this time. Either Amy
Sussen or Amy Goodale. Nothing less than 30 percent.* He walked past
a ring of elementary school students playing Duck, Duck, Goose
and collected a dozen notes reading, *Pick me, pick me,* along with one
that read, *I wish you would kill Matthew Brantman.* He went to a
one-man show at the repertory theater, sitting directly next to the
stage, and afterward found a handful of notes that contained nothing but the lines the actor had spoken. He made the mistake of wearing the coat to a baseball game and had to leave at the top of the
second inning when slips of white paper began spilling from his
pockets like confetti.

Soon the man realized that he was able to detect the pressure of
an incoming prayer before it even arrived. The space around him
would take on a certain elasticity, as though thousands of tiny sinews
were being summoned up out of the emptiness and drawn tight, and
he would know, suddenly and without question, that someone was
offering his yearning up to the air. It was like the invisible resistance
he remembered feeling when he tried to bring the common poles
of two magnets together. The sensation was unmistakable. And it
seemed that the stronger the force of the prayer, the greater the distance it was able to travel. There were prayers that he received only
when he skimmed directly up against another person, but there
were others that had the power to find him even when he was walking alone through the empty soccer field in the middle of the park,
his footsteps setting little riffles of birds into motion. He wondered
whether the prayers were something he had always subconsciously
felt, he and everyone else in the world, stirring around between
their bodies like invisible eddies, but which none of them had ever
had the acuity to recognize for what they were, or whether he was

able to perceive them only because he had happened to find the overcoat in the thrift store. He just didn't know.

At first, when the man had realized what the coat could do, he had indulged in the kind of fantasies that used to fill his daydreams as a child. He would turn himself into the benevolent stranger, answering people's wishes without ever revealing himself to them. Or he would use the pockets to read people's fortunes somehow (he hadn't yet figured out the details). Or he would be the mysterious, slightly menacing figure who would take people by the shoulder, lock gazes with them, and say, "I can tell what you've been thinking." But it was not long before he gave up on those ideas.

There were so many prayers, there was so much longing in the world, and in the face of it all he began to feel helpless.

One night the man had a dream that he was walking by a hotel swimming pool, beneath a sky the same lambent blue as the water, when he recognized God spread out like a convalescent in one of the hotel's deck chairs. "You!" the man said. "What are you doing here? I have your coat. Don't you want it back?"

God set his magazine down on his lap, folding one of the corners over, and shook his head. "It's yours now. They're all yours now. I don't want the responsibility anymore."

"But don't you understand?" the man said to him. "We need you down here. How could you just abandon us?"

And God answered, "I came to understand the limitations of my character."

It was shortly after two in the morning when the man woke up. In the moonlight he could see the laundry hamper, the clay bowl, and the dozens of cardboard boxes that covered the floor of his bedroom, all of them filled with slips of white paper he could not bear to throw away.

The next day he decided to place an ad in the classified pages: "Purchased at thrift store. One overcoat, sable brown with chestnut buttons. Pockets worn. Possibly of sentimental value. Wish to return to original owner." He allowed the ad to run for a full two weeks, going so far as to pin copies of it to the bulletin boards of several nearby churches, but he did not receive an answer. Nor, it must be said, had he honestly expected to. The coat belonged to him now. It had changed him into someone he had never expected to be. He found it hard to imagine turning back to the life he used to know, a life in which he saw people everywhere he went, in which he looked into their faces and even spoke to them, but was only able to guess at what lay in their souls.

One Saturday he took a train to the city's pedestrian mall. It was a mild day, the first gleam of spring after a long and frigid winter, and though he did not really need the coat, he had grown so used to wearing it that he put it on without a second thought. The pedestrian mall was not far from the airport, and as he arrived he watched a low plane passing overhead, dipping through the lee waves above the river. A handful of notes appeared in his pockets: *Please don't let us fall. Please keep us from going down. Let this be the one that makes the pain go away.*

The shops, restaurants, and street cafés along the pavement were quiet at first, but as the afternoon took hold, more and more people arrived. The man was walking down a set of steps toward the center of the square when he discovered a prayer that read, *Let someone speak to me this time—anyone, anyone at all—or else . . .* The prayer was a powerful one, as taut as a steel cord in the air. It appeared to be coming from the woman sitting on the edge of the dry fountain, her feet raking two straight lines in the leaves. The man sat down beside her and asked, "Or else what?"

She did not seem surprised to hear him raise the question. "Or else . . ." she said quietly.

He could tell by the soreness in her voice that she was about to cry.

"Or else . . ."

He took her by the hand. "Come on. Why don't I buy you some coffee?" He led her to the coffeehouse, hanging his coat over the back of a chair and listening to her talk, and before long he had little question what the "or else" was. She seemed so disconsolate, so terribly isolated. He insisted she spend the rest of the afternoon with him. He took her to see the wooden boxes that were on display at a small art gallery and then the Victorian lamps in the front room of an antique store. A movie was playing at the bargain theater, a comedy, and he bought a pair of tickets for it, and after it was finished, the two of them settled down to dinner at a Chinese restaurant. Finally they picked up a bag of freshly roasted pecans from a pushcart down by the river. By then the sun was falling, and the woman seemed in better spirits. He made her promise to call him the next time she needed someone to talk to.

"I will," she said, tucking her chin into the collar of her shirt like a little girl. Though he wanted to believe her, he wondered as he rode the train home if he would ever hear from her again.

It was the next morning before he realized his overcoat was missing. He went to the lost-and-found counter at the train station and, when he was told that no one had turned it in, traveled back to the pedestrian mall to retrace his steps. He remembered draping the coat over his chair at the coffeehouse, but none of the baristas there had seen it. Nor had the manager of the movie theater. Nor had the owner of the art gallery. The man searched for it in every shop along the square, but without success. That evening, as he unlocked the door of his house, he knew that the coat had fallen out of his hands for good. It was already plain to him how much he was going to miss it. It had brought him little ease—that was true—but it had made his life incomparably richer, and he was not sure what he was going to do without it.

We are none of us so delicate as we think, though, and over the next few days, as a dozen new accounts came across his desk at work, the sharpness of his loss faded. He no longer experienced the compulsion to hunt through his pockets all the time. He stopped feeling as though he had made some terrible mistake. Eventually he was left with only a small ache in the back of his mind, no larger than a pebble, and a lingering sensitivity to the currents of hope and longing that flowed through the air.

And at Pang Lin's Chinese Restaurant a new sign soon appeared in the window: CUSTOM FORTUNE COOKIES MADE NIGHTLY AND ON THE PREMISES. The diners at the restaurant found the fortune cookies brittle and tasteless, but the messages inside were unlike any they had ever seen, and before long they developed a reputation for their peculiarity and their singular wisdom. Crack open one of the cookies at Pang Lin's, it was said, and you never knew what fortune you might find inside.

Please let the test be canceled.

Thy will be done, but I could really use a woman right about now.

Why would you do something like this to me? Why?

Oh make me happy.

ACKNOWLEDGMENTS

I owe thanks to my editor, Edward Kastenmeier, and his assistant, Tim O' Connell; to my agent, Jennifer Carlson; to the editors of the various magazines where these stories first appeared, most especially Carol Ann Fitzgerald, Matt Weiland, Michael Ray, David Ingle, Rachel Tecza, Sumanth Prabhaker, Dave Daley, Benjamin Rybeck and MMM Hayes; and to the John Simon Guggenheim Memorial Foundation for financial support.

THE BRIEF HISTORY OF THE DEAD

The City is inhabited by those who have departed Earth but are still remembered by the living. They will reside in this afterlife until they are completely forgotten. But the City is shrinking, and the residents clearing out. Some of the holdouts, like Luka Sims, who produces the City's only newspaper, are wondering what exactly is going on. Others, like Coleman Kinzler, believe it is the beginning of the end. Meanwhile, Laura Byrd is trapped in an Antarctic research station, her supplies are running low, her radio finds only static, and the power is failing. With little choice, Laura sets out across the ice to look for help, but time is running out. Kevin Brockmeier alternates these two story-lines to create a lyrical and haunting story about love, loss, and the power of memory.

Fiction/978-1-4000-9595-7

THINGS THAT FALL FROM THE SKY

Weaving together loss and anxiety with fantastic elements and literary sleight-of-hand, *Things That Fall from the Sky* views the nagging realities of the world through a hopeful lens. In the deftly told "These Hands," a man named Lewis recounts his time babysitting a young girl and his inconsolable sense of loss after she is wrenched away. In "Apples," a boy comes to terms with the complex world of adults, his first pangs of love, and the bizarre death of his Bible coach. "The Jesus Stories" examines a people trying to accelerate the Second Coming by telling the story of Christ in every possible way. And in the O. Henry Award winning "The Ceiling," a man's marriage begins to disintegrate after the sky starts slowly descending.

Fiction/978-0-375-72769-6

Celia is seven years old on the day she goes missing. Her father, Christopher, is giving a tour of their historic house; her mother, Janet, is at an orchestra rehearsal. Celia is outside playing. She rides her bicycle. She throws a rubber ball against the roof. She disappears. A writer of fantasy and science fiction, Christopher finds himself drawn into a grief-induced world of wishful fantasy in which Celia still exists. Plunging into his work to help him cope with her disappearance, he writes of its effects from the points of view of the people who are still haunted by her absence: Janet, the policeman who is in charge of the case, and Christopher himself—each voice contributing to the heart-wrenching picture of a town subtly, but lastingly, changed. *The Truth About Celia* is a novel of remarkable understanding—an extraordinary exploration of profound loss and inconsolable grief.

Fiction/978-0-375-72770-2

VINTAGE CONTEMPORARIES
Available at your local bookstore, or visit
ww.randomhouse.com